The Earlie King

&

The Kid In Yellow

THE EARLIE KING

&

THE KID IN YELLOW

A WAYWARD MYTH

FRAGMENTS SHORED AGAINST RUINS

DANNY DENTON

GRANTA

Granta Publications, 12 Addison Avenue, London, W11 4QR

First published by Granta Books in 2018
This paperback edition published by Granta Books in 2019

Grateful acknowledgment is made for permission to reprint (and, in keeping
with the nature of a fallen Ireland, alter and misquote) excerpts from the
following copyrighted material: Michael Hartnett's 'Death of an Irishwoman'
from *Collected Poems* (2001), by kind permission of the Estate of Michael
Hartnett and The Gallery Press; John Moriarty's 'Chorus of Europeans' from
Turtle Has Gone a Long Time (1997), by kind permission of The Lilliput Press;
lines from Louis MacNeice's and E.L. Stahl's translation of Goethe's *Faust*, by
kind permission of David Higham Associates.

A CIP catalogue record for this book is available from the British Library.

9 8 7 6 5 4 3 2 1

ISBN 978 1 78378 366 3 (paperback)
ISBN 978 1 78378 367 0 (ebook)

www.granta.com

Typeset in Adobe Caslon Pro, Adobe Garamond Pro,
Fournier MT and Warnock Pro by Lindsay Nash

Printed and bound by CPI Group (UK) Ltd, Croydon, CR0 4YY

for Jessica Rose,
& Mam & Dad

THE EARLIE KING

&

THE KID IN YELLOW

ROLL UP! ROLL UP!

to hear a tale of

RAIN and FIRE, of KID and KING!

COME ALONG WITH ME, LADIES &
GENTLEMEN, to where a body can talk *FREE!*
Let's go to the *WORD PLACE*, where [for a small fee]
you'll gain a slice of authentic *HISTORIE! ANCHORS*
AWEIGH! on a tale from yesterday. *SET SAIL!*
to a time when rain never failed! It's now time
[for the first time] to spill the beans about that whole
SHITSHOW in Ireland. Here, today, in the world's last
true *HEDGE SCHOOL*, you'll hear a tale from
the deep, told to you by the last 100% authentic
TRUE IRISHMAN! Not from 'Once Upon
a Time' Time, but from *REAL OLD IRELAND*,
the *EMERALD ISLE OF SAINTS AND SCHOLARS*,
FORTY THOUSAND SHADES OF GREEN…

And *RAIN*.
And *FIRE*.

STAND IN HERE, YE BASTARDS! Hear the truth—
THE TRUTH—about that brave land. Never mind
the books and the plays and the TeleVisio displays!

Listen to a man who was there and saw it *WITH HIS OWN EYES!* That's right! You'll hear of the *EARLIE KING* & the *KID IN YELLOW*, of *SAINT VINCENT DEPAUL*, of *THE REPORTER O' Casey* and even *MISTER VIOLENCE HIMSELF!* You'll meet a city with fire in its veins, and hosts of *GHOSTS AND LIARS* in the rain!

Lean in here *LADIES & GENTLEMEN!* Learn some culture, folks! Come along with me! Based on *TRUE DOCUMENTATION* and the testimony, given to you here today, of the *LAST EYEWITNESS.* Roll up, *ROLL UP!* Last call for a myth of *TRAGEDIE* from a *DROWNING CITY*, an eyewitness to the *MARVEL*, to the *KID IN YELLOW* and the *EARLIE KING* himself. Here it spews from the mouth of the *LAST IRISHMAN!* In we go now *TA FUKK! LET'S BEGIN!*

HERE COMES THE WORD OF WARD!

THE WORD OF THE SPARK, AND ANNIHILATION!

HEAR IT WELL!

Are you recording now? Perfecto.

Δ

Thinking people—like ye!—had theories about why it rained for so long without ever stopping. Some said that all life came from water, and that a country that drenches itself in rain for hundreds of years is maybe trying to rebirth itself. It's probably true that things went very bad on our island, and so maybe there's truth to what those people said. But for that to happen a country has to have a mind and a spirit all of its own. And maybe that's true too. Maybe all I know is my own small part in it, that I was born near the capital and raised and lived most of the years of my life before I saw a break in the Irish cloud. The time I first saw the sun with my own eyes and not on TeleVisio is a day I can no longer talk about. But I'll tell you what else I can.

So, what *you* know about that drowned world, you know from scraps of information, shreds of data; voices that vary, conflict, struggle to... recall. I've water-stained photographs here; some other snippets of audiovisio stuff. A few papers... But it's all up here. In the head. The noggin. The Digital Catastrophe took almost everything from us. But it didn't take me! Fran Ward— former officer of the law, and the last true Irishman!

Δ

I asked O' Casey at one point, much later:
'How much of your stuff is actually *true*?'

5

'Oh, it's all true,' he replied. 'I just don't know which bits are made up.'

Δ

Every culture has its myths and Ireland was no different. They say that she was won over from the Tuatha Dé Danaan by the warrior-poet Amhairgin. Sent out over nine waves, Amhairgin invoked the whole country with a poem. He was the *seawave*, and that was the start of Ireland.

Then they say that Ireland was lost to fire, to digital collapse and environmental drowning. The culprits this time were the Earlie King and the kid in yellow. They say that the kid stole the cure for the rain from the King, and that the King and his men pursued the kid across a drenched land—plain and dale, river, lake, valley and mountain. The King was the strongest man in Ireland; the kid was a hard fist of bright yellow. This is what they say. Well, they're not far wrong. You've heard different versions, of course, but I like this start the best:

MISTER VIOLENCE PREQUEL

Wears a long coat and black boots, and maybe a hat above his collar. Maybe a fedora, maybe a bowler. Or, he wears no coat and goes barefoot, and his feet are dead animals washed up and his hands are vise-grips and his blood is slick oil. He is both hairy and scaly. He is made of a complex plastic. He can't ever think straight.

For every man, woman and child exercising pain in a kitchen or a bedroom or an alley or a pub, he is on the other side of the window, watching. He is delighted! Whether it is the vigilante Vincent Depaul setting fires for the poor, or a Heavy's boot on a pickpocket's head, or a girl taken down by a slipway, he is dancing a jig in the shadows of that place!

But they don't see him; shadows are all that they see.

See him now at the window! Watching in the house the midwife and the girl and the mother. Hear the screaming! Is the screaming that brings him into the room, grinning with glee. Big yellow horse's teeth in that grin. Two lamps are lit, and the single bed of that girl's childhood is ruined by sweat and blood and mucus and muck. The mother stands back, her hand on her mouth. The girl screams, as if the other child, the child within her, is eating her from the inside out. The midwife, a gangly string of misery, stoops to her work, knowing that she too is helpless. Then Mister Violence decides he has seen enough, and takes over.

/Will bring in that child!/ he laughs, and his laughter is sirens wailing.

He removes his hat to reveal his neon skull. Then he *is* the

7

midwife, and he bends to the work, ripping out the child from within, tearing skin with surgical fingers, blood flowing as life drains from one and fills the other.

Mister Violence holds the baby aloft for the King, who arrives dumbly, thinking it is over.

/One for now/ Mister Violence laughs, /and one for later!/

Life goes out of the thing on the bed.

/*Coo! Coo!*/ Mister Violence tickles the babba with pointy nails. /That was fun!/

The midwife is exhausted, and sorrowful, and tends to the lost cause.

The mother is silent.

The King stands with his hands on his hips, surveying a scene in which he had two girls, and realises now that there is only one again.

The babba cries aloud and reaches out.

Mister Violence tips his hat and goes back out the bend in the window.

BIT CALLED

UNREAL CITY INTRO

[O' CASEY'S PREFACE]

Rain is the constant moment. It perpetuates the city streets, the alleyways, the gutters, the canals. Streaming down windows, the hiss of the few cars, the steam. Beads of rain like messages, like words from ghosts that we just couldn't understand. Sheets of rain. Systems of rain.

A sound comes out of the night cloud, an endless patter, a spectrum of single notes that are finite each but somehow infinite altogether. Pattering, slapping, pounding, tapping, hissing, hammering, teeming, gushing, spitting, thrashing, thundering... In plastic skins, the people hold themselves tight. The dampness seeps into the bones of each citizen, into everything. The echo of water covers everything, lulls every thing.

And then rainshadows, under cloudlight. The sound of engine. Mechanical breath, and under that low voices. Yellow light, bright. A man in a heavy trenchcoat. His head iceberged the folds of an upheld newssheet: the headline said that Vincent Depaul had struck again. This time, the vigilante—the man with fire in his fingers—had lit up a bank's server facility in the Financial District. Burned it to the ground.

In the windows of the carriage there were reflections: people's ghosts at a slanted angle. He watched his reflection: was he the ghost or the passenger? He, the reporter who was paid a pittance to perpetuate these stories to these very passengers. Or were they ghosts?

A cough. Elsewhere, a sneeze. Someone fell asleep and their device dropped out of their hands to the floor. It was a journey of sadness and boredom. Time melted into enginesound.

And then, sometimes, these nervous hours did not wait for their cue, but like skittish horses they bolted, and it was suddenly seven o'clock. It was half past seven. And yet it seemed like the reporter had not turned a page of his newssheet. The sleeping stranger only just now stirred to pick her device from the trembling carriage floor. The expressions of the ghosts in the window had not changed.

The dingy darkness of the marshlands and lakes was replaced by a moving picture of dim back yards, a labyrinth of awnings and tarpaulins heavy with water. And high-rises too, and dark shimmering streets and murky canals.

And beneath those streets and canals, oily sewers and cracked pipes quivered. Felt from the city above the flicker of Vincent Depaul's fingers. Imagined the lick of the flame. These were sewers and pipes that wept into each other—wept the gunk and the grime and the petroleum and the gas and every colour of shit as far as the Docklands and on out to sea.

At first the reporter could keep up with the details: 25HR, canalside, racetrack, car park, estate. Like foreign languages partly known, he could almost understand their rhythms. But the city grew. Soon the window couldn't contain it. As the city sprawled he lost his grip on its meaning. The foreign conversation he tried to piece together had become a kind of rambling. Or, it was every conversation behind every yellow window tangled up into one scrapheap of words. The city was the mind of a mad raving lunatic. The city was a scream. A sob of depthless confusion. Could he pull the kid's story from the chaos?

By the time he slipped off the train in the belly of the station— which itself was in the belly of the city, which itself was a place of three million bellies, full of concrete and glass and oil and gas, of tile, tarp, petrol and tar, forever digesting, forever starving— he was lost in the words. The city intercom spoke the words. The newssheets blared the words. *Unreal City.*

He slouched along the river with his face in his hands. The hourly bell tolled. He remembered the story of Mister Violence, who had no face. If you thought of all the bad things that happened to all people in all cities, all that rage and frustration and sadness added up was the mind of Mister Violence, he who looked like a man and walked like a man, and he who wanted nothing but the end of the city in a big smoking heap of rubble. He who wanted nothing but fire. And yet the city back then was all puddles and rain and warm drunken winds and smoke and rotted wood and crumbling brick, and it was the stale breath of three million souls, and yet Mister Violence's work was almost done.

And the reporter walked on into it. He was the man who told the story.

And he was Mister Violence. They all were.

BIT CALLED
WHISPERINGS / GODAWFUL

O' Casey was his name. Rosy cheeks and hunched bird-wing shoulders above his pot belly, and thin, scraggly beard, younger than the beard suggested, drunk on vino tinto.

/Ta fukk/ he mumbled beneath the folksinger's song. /Where is that kid and what has he been up to?/

Who knows how this man had spent his life so far, what cruel bouts he had endured under the shimmering rain of this fallen city, propelling himself forward on short, powerful legs, feet that had fallen upon ten thousand pavements and gangways, that kicked out, thrust onwards … he who had to this point been years following the trivial stories—the seagull thieves, the inland ark cults.

/Immaculate conception ME FUKKEN HOLE!/ he cursed aloud. /The grape's the reason for it I bet!/

The tidy waiter lifted his head above the parapet of the café punters and said, /Sure it's only raining…/ and swept away a sugar packet into the many folds of his apron. The tidy waiter was addicted to sugar.

Beyond the beaded windows a crowd swirled in ideogrammatic formulations, businessmen and businesswomen—the city's last—moving all hours of the compass, purling in eddies, shoals of souls in the malleable plastic shrouds they called 'skins', directing the low murmur of their speech into the microphones of their devices; ten thousand whispering souls in shrouds. He liked it here in the Financial District, away from the decay and tumult of the Centre. In the Centre, across the pubs and cafés and marketplaces, the rain was a fog, and the speech of the people was

17

sewage in his ears. It was, of course, his own speech—the speech of his youth—and it was, of course, the people that he loved. But nonetheless…

/Enough!/ he bawled. /Enough with your song! Is meaningless! Is godawful!/

The folksinger reined in his accordion and, pulling the box to one side, called out from his corner stool: /Want to come up here and do better, O' Casey? Keep your fukken gills shut!/

/Better?/ The reporter pulled frantically at the small bucket of sugar packets and threw their contents towards the folksinger. /Better? The one-armed deaf childer of the Croke Park Flats could do better!/

/Enough, O' Casey/ the tidy waiter counselled, retrieving sugar packets from the stained tiles. /You make our lives hard enough already/

/Ah, ta fukk/ the reporter gasped, covering his forehead with a rough palm and burying himself in the bend of his elbow. /You do not know the work I carry out for this city. *Godawfulgodawfulgodawful*…Where do you find these broken-home troubadours who cannot muster an original line? I'd rather be with the squawkers, listening to kumbee/

/You know where to find them/ the tidy waiter said, slipping away again into the dim haze of the room, and the accordion music was a rough sea across which the reporter rocked whether he liked it or not.

/Don't care for the music/ he announced finally, placing his coins on the table with great care. /Came for the chicas/

Δ

No city like it: water filling every nook and cranny; citizens dipping into every street-corner bin. Armless children, legless children, eyeless children: generations deformed by every kind of badness in the water and air. The flashing blue and white and red lights of the Heavy Gang motors passing periodically the window of his drizzled vision and the countless stories he kept shoring up against his own life, and the calls of street vendors came to him through the steady hiss of the rain, and the distant rambling of the city's great intercom, and the cacophony of droplets on the skins of the citizens of that drowning city, in all its squalor and petty efforts. Blurred vision and pain and sweat falling in waves: this was the city in the days in which the reporter crossed it, stopping on a bridge to be sick in the oily Liffee, to say, /How?/

To say, /What he do? Why they so quiet? How can I best do my work? How will I learn the story of this kid?/

He keyed the door next to the back entrance to the Pup& Pendant, where he dared not drink, and hands and feet he ascended from the depths of the dark doorway to the top of the stairs, bawling at the mouldwet walls, stories of the past bobbing across his mind, stories of crashed rivertrucks at the Liffee Barrier, of thirty thousand animals drowndead in a Connacht island storm, of a slug that could be trained, of a statue in Dingel that promised an end to the rain, of the punishing revenge fires of the vigilante Depaul. These were the stories that earned him his glass and crust—the Hub consuming the content he produced—so he had to be thankful for them really.

Dark folds and damp smell of his chamber, lit by the singular bulb above. He sat over the ledger, held upon the piece of reclaimed car bonnet that he used as a knee-desk. He reviewed some pages: when would he add the boy to the ledger?

He sighed as he pulled the ledger back onto the groaning bed with him and let the bonnetdesk clatter to the floor. Here was his most important story when he could find someone brave enough to publish it. If anybody knew he was writing it—especially those in the pub below—he would be killed himself. But it was his secret document, his legacy. Pulling the pages up to his face, he saw each of the names as baby names.

And then he rose, no clue of the hour.

Through the warped wooden floorboards of his chamber, which contained only a groaning bed, a single flimsy chest of drawers for his clothes and papers, and a beigestained and cobwebbed washbasin, O' Casey undertook the habitual and deliberate act of listening.

There behind the pedestal of the washbasin he had one evening discovered a hole the size of a wine bottle's base. Up through the hole came the click and muted thud of a billiards game. It was here, he had discovered over time, that the Earlie Boys played and planned and boasted of their feats. It was here that he had first discovered a whole anthology of death, and began to count, and record.

Over months and then years he listened and took notes:

/I threw it over him/ the one called Crooner Bart, or the Bard, once said. /Bopped the empty glass off his noggin, held his head back by the hair and gutted him like a mackerel...

/Told him I'd throw it over him and all! He pulled the stout straight and I said to him, I seen you pull that straight and if you put it up here in front of me I'll throw the fukken thing over you. I just serves the drink, the cunt says. So he puts it up on the counter in front of me and I throw the fukken thing over his head/

/And you stiffened him, Barty boy?/

They all had names like Rice, and Mike the Hat, and Holloway, and the Spanyard. Stupid Irish nicknames. They stroked Bart's goat when he started into his bulltales.

/Did/ Bart would say. /And so I up and fukked off out of it. Up the road in a gusher, laughing me fukken hole off. Next thing I know am gone a mile the wrong way. Am standing on some backwater canal looking at a riverbus to Gra-fukken-hán!/

And the neat stamp of pint glasses on the counter would march along their roars and the walls and upwards to the straining ear of the reporter in his room above, using a hose from an ancient hoover to plug the hole in his floorboard and carry the sound to him where he sat against the end of the bed and listened for long hours. He heard it all with fascination etched across the shape of his bulging eyes and lips: punishment beatings, imprisonments, revenge murders, crucifixions, beheadings, rapes of men and women ... Each crime he noted down carefully for further investigation, his lexicon unique and coded.

And then at some point on these nights the Earlie King himself might come in, from training horses or meeting men.

/Get me whiskey!/ he'd cry. /Give me a beer!/

And they'd cheer him always when he came in roaring that.

Long nights the reporter listened and jotted, fantasizing about telling others, about publishing the ledger, names and stories and the most candid confessions.

THE CRIMES OF THE EARLIE BOYS EXPOSED.

Our own rogue reporter holds the key to a thousand murky crimes ...

He thought of the glory: fathers shaking his hand, tears streaming down their grey faces; mothers kissing recovered bones, holding the bones to their cheeks and caressing them.

But it could never happen. Even if an editor could be found who was bold enough, the Heavy Gang were too corrupt to allow it. It would only show them up. Yet still O' Casey kept the ledger; still he compiled it day after day. He knew of nothing else to do but to live his life for the recording of these details—to live the stories as they unfurled, one dark petal at a time. And yet his was a helpless whispering voice, disembodied from action, echoing nothing new.

BIT CALLED

FLASH & DISAPPEAR

The kid in yellow rubbed the shine of his pantalones, his legs being cold. In the afternoon of a day which he would not remember he was woken by the hourly bell. The sound of his brother shooting returned him to the world of the flat, all drip and drop and flow and splatter and bedroom gunfire and pit-terpatter. And cursing and quiet: dreadful quiet of no mother to say STOP THAT NOW and no father to say COME HERE. Dreadful quiet yes.

/Tommib/ he said. /Tommib and silence and rain and violence/

/Never even got to say goodbye/ he heard himself say. /Or yoo-hoo/

Fire, he longed for fire. And he saw the rain too, from the fire escape door as he lay on his sofa, rain falling night and day, and he imagined some dark heaven above it.

/Tommib/ he said. /Tommib and fire and tall mossy spire/

He pushed off the couch.

Skins on.

To the brother: /Am going out/

From the brother: no response.

To the brother: /Want anything?/

The brother grunted no, lost to the world of a game where he murdered scores.

From the twenty-sixth floor of the Croke Park Flats he was carried down. Words were graffiti-written up and down the broken mirrors. WHAT YOU TINKIN, he read. The King's Eye, he saw. And his message to T. And the promise of Vinny Depaul to burn the oppressors of the poor. And the slogans of the politicians, and all the other words people lashed out with.

It was a glittery drizzle that day, rain sparkling, sticking to the buildings and the boats. From the entrance to the flats he took the network of alleyways, the alleys being narrow and waterlogged and lined often enough with people nearly dying from Fadinhead. That day though they were quiet. He saw only two boys in close against the fence, holding each other. They were without skins so that the rain ran down their shaven heads and soaked their underclothes. He gave them a wide berth, but they were shivering and crying out their last and didn't even notice him.

At the end of the alleys was the canal, and the stables where he kept Honest John. At the stables there was only the old buck, with the long grey ponytail and the moustache. They'd seen each other most days for two years without ever knowing each other's names.

/Help thee, lad?/ the old buck asked as he swept water towards the perimeter drain.

/Collecting John is all/ the kid said.

The buck followed the work of his brush. /Sound/

A lovely calm animal, Honest John showed no pleasure at seeing the kid. The pony watched the horizon instead, with eternal patience, dull lids drooping over chestnut eyes, tail flicking at chubby flanks.

They left the yard together side by side, connected to each other by a length of cable that the kid held. He never got up on the pony, he didn't think that was right. The way he saw it, if horses and ponies were meant to be ridden they'd have been born with saddles on their backs. Of course people mocked him for that, but, yes, he walked Honest John like a dog of old, and had found that him and John walked at the same pace, and were interested in stopping to look at the same flowers and the same canal vessels.

Pony and kid had each other two years. The kid had bought the animal with money made from running for the Earlie King. In the pub too they gave him tithes for doing their bets. They slipped him grade if he spiked women's drinks for them. Two years, but when you see someone every day for two years it does not feel like you have known them only two years. It feels like whole lifetimes you've spent together.

The canal beyond the stables led to the river, and they walked in that direction.

/See, the world is full of other yous/ the kid was telling John. /Is full of people who are just like you but somehow different. They may look different; they may sound different. They may have different favourites; they may have different mammies, or memories, or names. But something in them will be the same as in you. Something in them will reflect in you as with a mirror. You and me are like mirrors of each other, for example. And, somehow, me and the King are like mirrors of each other too/

Honest John stopped to pinch a mouthful of canalweed for himself.

As they walked the riverbank walls he plotted and spun plans but found himself down dead-end alleys with each idea. He alone was responsible. Anger grew and faded. He felt lost. He tired himself thinking about T and the babba.

/Tourists came to Dublin once. Ebb and flow and whack on the bonce!/

/*Tommib* and weft and warp and sea. Be the thing you want to be!/

The rain began to come down heavier, hurling itself against the river, but they kept on at their own pace. Rickshaw amphibians stopped on the path, ringing bells and shouting slogans, and gondoliers called destination prices from the water. The road and the river were busy, but it seemed to him like the kid and Honest John were the only ones out walking. They were fine on their own, walking.

The city intercom relayed advertisements and statistics to the unhearing people. The lashing went on and the lights came on strong. The kid began to feel the mystery of the rain. Coming along by the city buildings he wanted to get lost in them.

/You ever wonder, John, are the buildings sleeping? And are all the people going around in them the buildings' dreams of people?/

He wanted to be inside one of those buildings, inside one of those dreams. He wanted to be just a normal office worker in a shirt and tie, walking corridors and chatting nice to people under bright lights. To be older. A grown-up. A father, with T his wife. To see everything in one straight line. But the way it all happened it was like he was treading water in the night, in the windy rainy sea, and he was drunk, and he didn't know which way was land and which hole piss came out of. Panic and sadness grew and faded, grew and faded. Anger flashed and disappeared. What could he do? He could not do what she had asked.

Traffic lights, shining cobblestones, the whale song of drones and overpasses. Yellow lines, leaking sewers. Fuming vents. Into the city building streets walked the kid and Honest John, the two of them streaming. The city was a steaming mess of steel and glass. Yellowblack. The TeleVisio said that Vikings came down that river once and built a town of wood on its banks, and the sun shone through the rain and blonded their hair for them, and if you dug down far enough into the river now, through the oil slicks and petroleum clouds, through the mutie fishbones and old boats and trolleys and tyres, you would find the wood of that city they built, even now. He wanted so badly to understand the world, but all he had was confusion and numbness and boredom and anger. He felt nothing good could come of his life. The Earlie King. Honest John. T and the babba. Crooner Bart. Brick. Perspex. Fountains in the rain. His brother on the computer, shooting. The wet walls of the flat. The leaking, creaking dockyards. He tried to piece it all together like a story but he was still lost. On a deserted pavement he picked a chunk of concrete from the ground and hurled it through a building window, and the banshee wail of the alarm chased them down the road, Honest John trotting along with him, with the same look of eternal patience in his chestnut eyes.

BIT CALLED

FIST OF BRIGHT YELLOW

It was at the Croke Park Flats that the reporter had first truly seen the kid in yellow. He was on his way to see a woman about her son, some Brave who had insulted Jeanette Ma-lee on the way out of the g-ball arena after a Stars game. The Brave had said that Jeanette needn't bring tyre tubes around with her because the water wasn't rising that fast, and Jeanette's fellow, not being a Brave or an Earlie Boy or a member of any other of the city's gangs, being only a shopkeep on Bailey Quay, did not feel up to defending Jeanette's honour. And so instead she told her mother over tea when she got home, knowing full well that her mother would tell her only brother, who was Francis, who was an Earlie Boy four years at this stage. Francis received the name of the Brave with a vacant glare in his eyes, through which glare any knowledgeable man of that time could read the future of the Brave named Jamie Corlan. There was the formality of Permissions, which went through Leg or Crooner Bart to the King and back to Francis over the length of a cold, spraying evening. And this sequence of conversations on devices led to the conversation that the reporter would have as soon as this middle-aged mother—Mrs Corlan, husband disappeared from the factories himself—answered her door, wiping her hands on her pinafore.

On seeing the reporter she knew. They always knew. His long trenchcoat and crooked gaze, his drooping left eyelid: the residents of the Flats knew that whomever the drooping eye of O' Casey fell upon, death had been to visit.

This mother did not burst the dam of her tears; she did not crumble or whimper or say NO from a O-shaped mouth.

/Come in then/ she said.

He followed her and removed his trenchcoat by the drains. There was a clean metal smell about the place. He noticed the skins of the young Brave hanging there too, the colours of the Stars. Of course this young lad would not have been innocent either: his knuckles had met with flesh and bone too.

/Have no drink/ the mother sighed, sitting on a stiff dry couch and beckoning him to take the wooden chair at its portside.

/Is plenty in the city for those that want it/ he said, bolting himself upright in the seat.

/Will you take tea?/

/Won't, thank you/ He lied: /Am meeting a comrade for a jar soon enough/

She nodded, understanding that a particular procedure was underway, and as with nearly all the other mothers, she looked at the floor when she spoke. What floor in the world could explain the death of your own child?

Her hands, he noticed, were the hands of a hardworking man: large, swollen with the effort of days, trembling so slightly as they passed over her tight bun of grey hair.

/Dead then?/ she said finally.

/Am sorry/ he said.

/Okay. Okay/

/Do you want to know the details?/

She shook her head at the wooden boards. /Dead is dead/

/Sorry/ he said, finding a spot for his own gaze out the window. /Only sometimes they want to know/

/They/

/Am sorry, Missus Corlan/ he said again. So many apologies he had made to strangers.

There was a period of time he waited. Eleven long breaths. If they elapsed without words, he made his excuses. He felt it was a courtesy to give eleven, but for him also it structured moments of agonising mystery.

On the ninth breath her questions came.

/Day or night?/

/Pardon?/

/Was he killed in day or night? Light or dark?/

/The daytime. Morning I believe. He did not turn up for work at least/

/Should I look for the body?/

She scraped that floor with her eyes, whether for memory or remains he didn't know or feel like guessing.

/Am afraid it won't be found/

One ... two ... three ... four ... five ... six ... seven ...

/Grand so. Thanks for coming/

He stood too quickly. /No. Not at all. Am sorry, I am/

/I knew this time would come, I think. We outlive our children now.../

His boots knocked sharply at the floor, filling the room with a kind of ticking. He took his trenchcoat by the door but would wait until he was alone again outside to return it to his hunched shoulders.

/Why?/ she asked with a hand on the white frame. /What happened?/

/An insult to a family member/

/An insult/ she echoed blankly. /What he say?/

/Said someone was fat. The *wrong* someone/

/Fat.../

And she closed the door.

In a flap and an awkward twist he had his trenchcoat on and the collar pulled up and away along the walkway he brought himself, squeezing at his back that ached. Spagbol moss and wretched mare's tail grew from every crevice of the walls alongside him, and the walkway awning above him, so that the whole place seemed furry. My back, he thought, I must do something about my cursed back.

And it was on the walkway that he saw a hunched fist of bright yellow leaning into a low part of the wall between two boarded-up flats. He heard even through the unsheltered rain the hiss of that fist's spray.

/Illegal!/ he cried, eager to be cheered up. /Illegal graffiti! I'll be informing the Heavy Gang presently!/

The hunched yellow fist unfurled, stood, revealing from within its clench a boy. Skinny face, cowlicked forehead, freckles spread across cheeks, blue eyes wide, alert, like the rare sparrow's.

/Am only joking/ the reporter scolded, still fifteen feet away, feeling suddenly threatened by the rigid yellow thing.

But the boy only turned and trotted to the corner and disappeared up a skyway, as if in flight, a yellow blur against the green and grey of the streaming walls.

Why the kid would have been frightened of him, the reporter had no idea. In passing, he crouched—wincing, grimacing, squeezed-out guttural groans!—to see the work of the lad on the wall: an angular yellow loveheart with the letter T at its centre.

/Behold now the horny youth/ he concluded, wheezing again as he stood.

The glitter drizzle over the city was bringing down with it the threat of night and he hastened then from the Croke Park Flats. He did not like to be there too close to darkness, and of course he had also begun to think about a drink.

And all through his first bottle of vino at the Tortoni the image of the fleeting yellow lad had recurred to him, as if out of some earlie-morning dream. Nothing about a teenager spraying on a wall was strange, whether tag, sign, bomb or political slogan; the Croke Park Flats were a slum on rungs and covered in graffiti already. But love? Most of the markings of the unwashed were violent—the Braves with their war cries, or the eye of the Earlie King watching from every wall. Few confessed love. And if confess love, why only a letter? How could T possibly know who she was? And that boy was familiar, but from where? More questions than answers, and this usually meant a story.

Across dark tides of wine these questions stayed with the reporter, and so much later on he thought of these blurry hunches as proof that sometimes the story was seeking *him* out, and it was not the other way around.

Δ

And it was in the corner of the Tortoni that he finally found the three Spanish ladies, and dropping a fresh bottle down on the table in front of them was his way of joining them, feeling as he lowered himself into a seat the hard, spasmed fist of muscle in his back. They were large, dour ladies, with strong lipstick applied around the general circumference of their mouths. They wore pinafores over their cardigans and long skirts.

/Buenas noches, viejitas/ he said.

The one with the harelip nodded to him. She liked him; the other two did not.

The four of them stared out into the café, a panel of judges. Minutes passed in silence, as was usual, before the ladies began to share local news and observation again, in sparse intervals of Castellano; he understood in patches and tried to pitch in now and then in broken fragments of the language. The land and language already infused with displaced Spaniards, these ladies had come in with the last Spanish trawler fleets. Presumably their husbands had drowned in the time of Wild Atlantic Storms, and thereafter they had stayed on, whether by choice or not he didn't know. He insisted on filling their glasses as they emptied them, and he enjoyed their sullen company and the snatches of conversation he understood; there was little these ladies did not know about the happenings of the Flats or the Docklands.

Over the course of the bottle an easy, relaxed rhythm developed, so that each sup felt sacred, became a prayer. On the TeleVisio in a high corner, a show set in some bright, hot country played out; the storyline was unimportant and unfollowed, the acting terrible; yet the imaginations of the punters were nourished by the light. The Spanish ladies watched with arms folded over their bellies, mouths working on invisible morsels, while, out of habit alone, the reporter smoothed the creases in his filthy trousers.

/I saw a chico/ he said at last to the one with the harelip, /on the fifth floor of the flats. Hace un tag con 'T' en el ... in a kind of angular heart... Bright yellow skins he had... amarillo... Intiendes? A T in a heart?/

/Si, si/ she nodded, eyes bathed in the bright flickering scenes of the TeleVisio.

/Le sabes?/ the reporter asked. /Do you know him?/

/Si, no/

He raised his glass and relished the draw from mouth to throat. /Might he be the one who is banished from the Earlie Boys? Have only vague whisperings, overheard... Know ye anything?/

The strum of music started and stopped. There was the sound of cars from the glistening street and cups landing on tables and laughter. The bottle felt too light when he tested it.

/Conozco el chico/ the middle Spaniard said to the harelipped one. /Con los skins amarillos... Él es loco. Es muy interesante/

That middle Spaniard told the story without passion or interest, as if it were a series of instructions for a simple task: she did not know whether the kid's own mother had disappeared or died, but he'd been running errands for the Earlie Boys since she'd gone.

/Ah!/ the reporter interrupted, pulling at the thin beard of his chin as he pulled too at the memory. /Now I see the light!/

He was a runner. The reporter had seen him on his cycle, waiting on street corners, leaving or arriving at pubs, one of a network of young lads who passed messages and packages between the Earlie Boys so that there was no paper trail or feedback on devices. Many of these children came from the Flats; most of them cycled the walkways the days and nights long. The reporter tapped urgently at the waiter's hip as he passed.

/Another bottle, chief/ he said, indicating the wine as if the waiter might not understand. Turning a pale meaty cheek the waiter nodded and left. The middle Spaniard was now on another road of the story, talking about a pregnancy that, if he understood, had lasted twelve months.

/Que raro/ the harelipped Spaniard said, as the other two nodded and gasped gentle noises of understanding.

/Momento/ he said. /Quien es embarazado? Who was pregnant?/

The middle Spaniard's impatience was not softened by the presence of the waiter filling their glasses. She said, /La hija del Rey/

/The King?/

/The *daughter* of the King/

Many-coloured light diffused through the windows of the Tortoni and hit the tables and glasses in long, weak bars. There was for the reporter that sudden, pure bolt of realisation, the world's occasional power to be, in a moment, utterly strange. How had he not already heard this? It did not make sense!

/Es como ellos dicen/ the harelipped Spaniard stressed, attempting now to soften the blow of the words that had been spoken. For even in cafés the people feared him—the King—and watched out for listeners and regretted as soon as they spoke words that might cause them trouble.

/Es como ellos dicen/ the middle Spaniard confirmed, simply another reporter.

/Wait/ O' Casey said. /I want to make sure I understand. This boy—in yellow—he is the father of the child of the daughter of the King?/

/Es como ellos dicen/

/Is what they say/

He fell back into his seat. This boy he had seen could not have been more than twelve, thirteen, fourteen. The King was rumoured to have children, but no one knew for sure. For all the violent boasts O' Casey had heard through the floors of his chamber the Earlie Boys never spoke of the King's family. They too were afraid, and mayhap that was why he hadn't heard the story, only vague references to a runner's banishment.

/That's why he's cast out/ he said. It was as if he had stumbled upon the existence of a whole new shape or species, something that filled the world with wonder again. /But what about the girl?/

He did not understand the words she spoke next as the words

they were, but from the whole he got the sad gist. The Spaniard's story was attributed to a drunken midwife who claimed to have delivered the child and seen the girl speak her last words.

When he was a boy, O' Casey's father had told him that the conception of a child was a moment of pure light. It was not so.

/Raro/ he said. He no longer tasted the wine he drank.

/The boy should be muerte if it is true/ he pointed out to them. /He should be dead/

They accepted that with outward gazes towards the TeleVisio. It became clear that they did not want to talk about it any longer. Gossip was like that: a puff of smoke to the story's fire.

But the boy *should* have been dead, an entry in his ledger, and probably the youngest at that. But he was not dead. Why?

Later, as he drank in another place, in the company of a group of sailors—hairy, slimywet apparitions, yelling at each other to heave aweigh, singing, falling forwards onto him at the table where he had decided to rest his head on crossed forearms, where he heard above him glass clinking and bawling and stamping and clapping like some kind of demented jazz in the kaleidoscope of the light—he thought of the kid, a fist of yellow, a blur in the rainworld. The city outside was a kind of theme park of faded illusions, a creaking thing, and the boy out there might not be an illusion or an overheard ghost, but a real thing, with love in his heart. Was this 'T' the girl or the child? The drunken vision loomed: the yellow skins of the boy, skinny face, cowlicked forehead, freckles spread across cheeks, blue eyes distracted, wide, like the rare sparrow's … If not already dead, this boy would die at the hands of the King. No doubt. Would be the youngest on the ledger. Up in that slum on rungs they'd find him—spraying messages to T mayhap—and they'd haul him away. They'd get him in a boot or a riverbag and they'd take him to one of the yards they used—above ground or below—where, surrounded perhaps by defunct, crash-landed satellites, he would be executed, and join all the other ghosts of that city. He'd have his head cut off, or mayhap worse. Mayhap, he would be undone by the man himself.

And the reporter would find out about it, somehow, and he would make the trip to the Flats to inform the relatives, who would care or not care, depending, and in those moments—after he closed the door behind him and placed his hat upon his head and pulled the trenchcoat around him—he would think that really none of it mattered a single bit, that these were all just passing beads of water, lost in rain, and that a whole life could be reduced to a moment's downpour, noticed by no one, and reduced entirely then, disappeared into nothing in one maddening view of the sea, that which drowned all words, and he'd need a drink then, and yet here he was, drinking, and the sailors all roaring around him, /Water, water! Get your duds in order! Heave aweigh, me jollies, *heave aweigh!/*

BIT CALLED

DROWNING CITY

How T died was less important to the kid than why. She died because of him. Mister Violence stood in the window and watched with glee. He patted the kid on the back of his yellow skins and said, *Hurray!* Because of what he did to her. If he could have one thing in the world it would be for her to be back and him gone. No babba, never meeting. Just T in her own life as normal and him never existing. Him drowndead or burned by the vigilante or some such.

He would ask God—whoever: /Why did you punish me like this? Why did you take her? For what she done? She done nothing/

But no God replied.

Instead of God there was only the disembodied voice of the city intercom, supposedly offering advice and instruction and news, advertising products and services, telling people to keep safe, warning against ill-citizenship, giving traffic updates and precipitation measurements...but even that voice was fuzzy, incoherent, garbled, rambling, frantic, unseeing, imprisoned in its own confusion and altogether ignored.

So instead the kid put her into a room in his mind, and in his raindreamings he visited her in that room—the vision of a clean, dry place, bright, with pale blue walls, where white clouds moved about, and old books turned yellow from dryness on a clean wooden shelf—and from that room took her out to the merries, where he won her prizes and they queued for the teacups. Took her for walks in the Financial District. All these things they'd done in the months of courtship, he did with her again in his mind. Huddled in a corner of a walkway, spraying her memory onto the wall, with drones whirring on overhead journeys and the ghosts of footsteps tracing up and down the walkways of the Flats, he would be taking her from the room and paying her entrance fee for the merries out of their own money that he earned from honest work as a pony man. To the amusements and dances she was always first, skipping ahead, turning to drag him on in wild gestures of excitement, and what was exciting to him was not the merries, where once he had smirched and fought and snarled, where he had seen Crooner Bart and the others flogging women into the darkness of their own nightmares. What was exciting to him was her. T. The life in her. The bounce in her step and her hair. He would do stupid things for her: he'd try to dance in steps; he'd sit on bobbing horses and pretend to love it, the big grin pasted on his face because of her, not because of anything else.

But that music faded, the swirling many-coloured lights would dim, and he would return to the dereliction and the graffiti of the city. Like all the youths of that city, he had nowhere to go but into his own fantasies, and he was tormented by the growing and fading of the strongest emotions. And when he returned to reality there was the eye of the King, daubed on every wall—as a runner he had sprayed many of them himself—to remind every wary citizen that *he* was always watching. And it seemed to the kid when he saw that eye as if even then—even as he squatted in the walkway spraying his own sign for T—that the King knew about the promise to her and knew what he was thinking and was almost egging him on to it. Was saying to him, *Come back into my true gaze so that I can finish you.* And mayhap that would be best. Mayhap it would be best to go that road to the King in honour of the promise and to die at his hand and to join T in that room of hers. But that was not the promise. To *give* life was the promise.

Δ

He knew her first from running money and pharm and messages between the Earlie King and his Earlie Boys. He'd get a

44

message on the device—he'd be told: /Go to the corner of Lacy & Sirens and meet a tall gent with a goatee face. He might be wearing cowboy boots also. He will ask you how much your bike is worth. The answer is six thousand sponds/ It was always like that: strangers on street corners. If you were a good enough runner, you eventually became an Earlie Boy. And he was a good runner. He was the King's closest runner. And it was there at one of the King's houses that he saw her first, in a back garden, where the smell of horse dung spread over the dampheavy shades of the tall green grass. And T there watching him from the cinder path, with only a cotton hoodie and the shelter of a yew tree. Pale forehead. Cheeks like teardrops. Dark eyes.

/You work for my da?/ she said.

/I do/ he said.

/They call you the Kid Yellow?/

/They do/ He put on wisdom: years in his voice, like Sweeney's. /The very buachaill/

/You can call me T/

/Yes, T/

And she went back to her reader.

He stood there like a gorse flower in the green, trying to think of something to say.

/What are you reading?/ eventually came. /I know some poems. Here: Nature is a temple whose living pillars sometimes give forth a Babel of words/

She looked at him a good long second. He couldn't read the look.

/What's your comm-code?/

He called it out and she put it in her device. Then the King came out the back door looking about him, steam rising from the wet head into the misting.

/'Asy, runner/ he said. /Don't be distracted by women/

For days after that first meeting, he willed his device to go off. But when it did it was never her. It would be more work from Bart, or the King, messages to be delivered or collected, or his old pal Clem off his game and having mad thoughts to be discussed. He went through the HubbleBank on the TeleVisio and tried to find some record of her con'flux, but there was nothing of course. You couldn't do much with a name like T. And that picture of her, a pale apparition in the garden, remained imprinted on his vision.

/Would wonder about girls, wouldn't you?/ he'd say to Honest John on their walks.

/*Tommib* and girls and tits and curls/

Δ

Six vast leaking blocks, the Croke Park Flats were the oldest accommodations in the slums north of the city. The lower-ground floor had been all shops in the old days but that was under four feet of water now. And the underground car park was completely submerged. They said there were bodies floating around down there. But the roof leaked also, and it came down through the top floors, and sure enough their place had as many drips as any other place on the twenty-sixth floor. Buckets the kid had under them, and some nights he was up at four or five in the morning emptying the buckets. One such night, as he watched TeleVisio and waited out those brimming buckets so that he could chuck their water out the window, came a message from a private comm-code:

/Petey Boy Pan/

He rolled his sleeves up. /Who's this now?/

/Wendy!/

/Know no Wendy/

/T, you clown. They say you know all the stories and poems by heart. Not know Petey Boy Pan?/

And he did know some. Petey was the flying boy who never grew up.

And he wrote to tell her this.

And right then the kid ran out of credits.

He lay there into the wet and dark of the flat worrying that she'd think he was worse than a clown for not replying. There

46

was nothing else for it: he turned off the TeleVisio and left for the 25HR.

Along by the Liffee Barrier it was all docklands. Empty since the bust times, sad and spooky were those industrial places. Immense warehouses once filled with food were now filled with servers, and underground bunkers there were full of petrol and oil and other stuff. Small factories also, slumped all along, and old mills and grain dispensers, storage facilities and warped wooden hoardings and aluminium fencing. He had often imagined huge trucks pulling up and leaving in scores, all roaring in and hauling out. Often he heard in his mind the shouts of hooded men but he never could make out what they'd be saying. Further down were tarmac yards, in fierce decline now, all rusty machines and cracked ground and flooding. Everything leaked into everything else. The train tracks would've brought old engines that came in empty and left full of tarmac or hardcore or sand, but now they too were buckled and rusty and seen only by the pharmheads and bums that found themselves down there at the end of their tethers. And him. Sometimes he'd cycle all the way down there just to sit and imagine the spotlights moving as cranes swung round and trains shifted on the elevated tracks of the Ardaithes without ever getting tired, the whole night grinding away into the dawn. He liked thinking about all that activity. He liked being in the abandoned place and imagining it not abandoned. That the place was haunted by drenched old memories was another thought he often had.

And on the dark water clippers and rivertrucks would go back and forth between the pods of the Liffee Barrier. High silver pods they were, lit up at night, great big helmets of things on mossy concrete beds, pointing straight up into the gloom, always wet, always shimmering with red crosses or green arrows flashing in the darkness. The water roared against those mossy slabs and those shiny helmets and he would bench himself at water's edge and smoke some herbal and listen for hours. For the sound of water was a serious sound, no matter whether it was pattering on the hood or being split by the ships heaving against the banks.

It meant so much to him—that sound, that abandonment, that mystery—without meaning anything at all.

/*Tommib!*/ was all he could say to explain those feelings.

On the night T first messaged him though he didn't stop to ponder—he cycled right through all that loneliness and haunting and those sheets of rain to the 25HR, through industrial lanes and across the broken and flooded yards to the part of the port that did still operate, and the garage that never slept, where you'd always find a man or two in the shelter of the forecourt with their hoods down, sipping coffee and smoking and mayhap having a quiet chat about the sea or the sky or both.

/Quiet out tonight/

/Sure she's only misting/

/Calm before the storm, ladies/

/Oh aye?/

/Warm front/

/Up from below?/

/Is right/

/Is always either up from below or down from above/

/Is about fukken right/

/She'll be pounding by noon/

/For what it's worth/

/Are you due out?/

/Arra, my days out beyond are done. Have enough trouble wading out here now/

/Think it's getting worse or better?/

/Worse. Much worse. The days you could sense the sun behind it are gone/

/Long gone is right... And yet sometimes I wonder/

/Wonderings are what caused this/

/But yet there are days .../

/You wish/

/Am only saying/

/And is only raining/

/And is only raining/

/20 K-TOP, moc/ the kid said to the old padre behind the plate glass. Thumb pressed to man's device, credits got. Next problem was what note to send her. He went back through the three messages, read them over.

/Petey Boy Pan/

/Who's this now?/

/Wendy!/

/Know no Wendy/

/T, you clown. They say you know all the stories and poems by heart. Not know Petey Boy Pan?/

/And is only raining/ he eventually typed.

He cycled back slowly, hissing through a misting that got dirtier as the morning drew out. He kept thinking of better things he could have said. Quotes and the like.

When he got home the buckets were full and dripping. He took off his yellow skins and hung them over the hall drain. Emptied the buckets. Threw himself up on the couch, banged on the TeleVisio. He slept in the front room of the flat at that time and the brother slept in the bedroom. The kid watched local news then—stories about the endless stupid things happening around the country—and then a shopping show, a man selling babba skins that would keep the babba dry but was also kind to their flesh and less likely to suffocate them. He closed his eyes from time to time to picture T in her garden, and somehow she was in sunshine. He fell asleep like that, and no message came back from her that night or the next morning.

Δ

Sometimes the flat became so wet that he did not have the energy to sort it out and did not have the comfort to sleep. Instead, he might wander like a ghost the walkways of the flats, shooting at slugs and rats with a BB. It was too earlie or too late to go for Honest John, so if there were lights on he might call to other flats, Clem's mayhap. On such a night, weeks after he first met T, he wrote a line from his device to hers:

/She flies so free, who flies above the sun, who walks on clouds and laughs with the blossoms of a million bright springtimes/

She hadn't replied to anything yet.

He wrote: /Left school at ten but am a grand rememberer of lines. A runner, yes, but have culture in these veins! A runner and a rememberer/

Sometimes, before, the Earlie Boys used drag him up onto the table in the Pup&Pendant and have him spin a yarn or recite something mysterious and full of wonder. But the truth that he didn't tell T or anyone was that he never understood the things he said. They were just words called up from memory.

Later again, he added this next line to that first one of his poem for T:

/She flies so free, dancing eights and waiting for me?/

And yet no reply. No conversation.

And then one evening they glimpsed each other through the back door of the King's house, as the kid in yellow waited in the cast light of the greenhouse and the girl's face loomed in a dark window, and they both smiled, and he knew. That was the start. A conversation between their eyes.

Memories. That was one he held dear, now, with her gone and with a promise to be kept. In a wild teeming he cycled to the Jolly Bridge, an establishment on the second floor of a low office building that seemed to cower under that teeming. He hid his cycle behind an old skip that was filled with water and watched for a while pale tadpoles moving in the dark of it. Then he climbed the fire escape stairs, the only way in at this hour of the night.

Inside, fluorescent light in strips along the ceiling of the hall.

Sweeney sat at the bar, as always, an old cap on his head shielding him from the light. Tonight he was the only one. He had a lighter in his fist, and he was saying to the flame, /You are so fukken beautiful/

They said about him that he sold his soul in order to live long enough to see the country drown at last and the new country born. They said he was of mystical roots—of land and dreamings—but

50

he drank all the time and really nobody took much notice of him except the kid.

/Ah, young mockeen/ he said, tipping his cap to the kid. /How are you, me auld shipmate?/

A hench dunce they called Rotter came to the bar from out back.

/You'll not be served here/ Rotter put two fat hands on the taps and leaned over them. He grinned and the kid saw his brown teeth. /Too young/

The kid said nothing but stood there, a few stools away from Sweeney. There was more to it than that, he knew.

/Ah, come on/ Sweeney said. /Give him a bottle, moc. If not here he'll get it elsewhere ... And we could do with the company/

Rotter grinned like an idiot, the drool on his cheek a first sign of the Fadinhead rising.

/Come on ta fukk/ Sweeney said, impatient now. /I'm buying/

/Is yours to look after then/

Rotter took great effort to bend and pull a bottle of UpYaBoyo from the bright fridge below. His neck was all volcanic spots.

/Anything other than UpYaBoyo?/ the kid asked.

/Fukk you/ Rotter tapped the bottle on the counter. /Will bust your noggin with it/

/Take it/ Sweeney said to the kid. /Beggars be not choosers/

/And sure it's only raining/ the kid said in a wise Sweeney voice.

They sat in silence a while, before Rotter disappeared out the back, the Fadinhead rising, taking hold.

Sweeney sighed. /He'll be kicked out in a week, if he's not dead first/

The fluorescent light burst out of Sweeney's forehead whenever he removed his cap to scratch at his bare skull, and to stare into space with a look of dignity. The kind of look that you practise. Still, Sweeney wasn't without a dose of wisdom in the earlie hours.

/I've used the F myself/ he admitted. /For a week or so. More than enough/

The kid knew. You took it first and there was the slow sadness, pure sadness, and even a good thing. You bawled and it felt good to bawl. With your bawling you felt like you were fixing every wrong thing you'd ever done. And after that it was calm bliss. The world was beautiful no matter what was in it, and that same world couldn't touch you because you were to be set free. You faced your last hours with an unreal spirit, because you knew you were going to heaven. To join mother and father and T. You knew with absolute certainty that this life was only a preparation, a test you had passed, and the next life was eternal reward. The mystery would be solved at last.

That vibe lasted hours, depending on the quality of the F, and then suddenly some gesture in the world occurred and you knew the end had come. A gull might suddenly pass across the raindrift on its way to sea. A hand might be lifted in greeting, mayhap not even to you. And when this gesture came—whatever it was—you realised that the end was here, that it was coming fast. Was over now, everything. This ten minutes was where you'd die, with that intercom voice rambling over you the whole time.

Your heart started pounding, your breath sped up. You rattled. The world started to close its jaws around you, and like every other animal on the planet you looked for a quiet place to go. You settled into some dark alleyway corner, behind a skip mayhap, out of the rain, where rubble lay scattered. You closed your eyes to sleep. Then the fear was sudden and hard. This was really happening: you *were* going to die, and death was the loneliest place. That was when you realised that there was no God. There was no other place. No mother or father waiting. No T. All of that was an illusion. You were going to disappear, into nothingness. The worst things you'd done in life were the things that they'd remember you for. You were scum, a stain on the land. Your own mother hated the sight of you. Your body would rot in the dark and the cold rubble and not one person would care. You were alone and you were going to die, and the adventure was over. Rats would eat out of your cold body and you could not protect it. You felt them doing it. Tiny sharp bites. Slugs passed over your open mouth, suffocating even your dying breaths. Your heart started to fail. You lost the feeling and the movement in your limbs. You collapsed into your fate. You emptied your bladder and arse into your skins. The world lost its focus. The heart stopped, the mind set adrift.

And then you awoke, after a few hours' sleep. You felt perfect, right as rain. The highs and lows depended on the quality of the F.

/Have seen my city crumble under the weight of Fadinhead/ Sweeney was saying. /F'heads squatted in every alleyway, fellas like yourself dead at thirteen. And not the rich of course. The poor. Always the poor/

Sweeney took out a coin and told the kid to put something on the jukebox.

/Not junk now/ he warned.

The kid went and straight away picked the old folk lady.

/ *The city's din can't hide your sin*/ she sang, all slow and sad.

Δ

Hey! Is me, T. Your Wendy.

Thought had lost you!

No! Never! He just found the device I had. Don't think he saw the messages though.

Thank god.

Δ

/Forgot you like the old stuff/ Sweeney wansmiled. /Good lad/

But the song turned the kid all slow and sad.

/Were you working?/ he asked Sweeney.

/I was/

/Fish farming?/

/Minding my fish/ Sweeney stroked his dome once more. /Yes and you? No more running?/

/None more/

53

The memory flashed: meeting Crooner Bart in the Pup&
Pendant, and the Crooner bought him a vodka lemonade. He
was eleven then but it was not his first drink. The Crooner said
he'd been doing well and that they were going to give him more
important work. He was going to work with the King now. The
Crooner warned him not to fukk up this chance.

And then he was part of this world. Of these men who were
recognisable, in their outrageous Kandinskee shirts, and their
waistcoats, singing shanties and drinking and terrorising people.
Terrible things were done in the haze of those bottles. And later it
was Bart, the same man who had brought him in, who turned on
him first when the news broke that T was having his child.

/Tell me about the salmon again, Sweeney/ the kid said.

Sweeney drank from his pint. A tiny tired finger stuck out
from the hand that drank, but he drank like he didn't enjoy it
much. He crossed his legs and the kid cocked his ear.

/Well, once upon a time the salmon lived along the coast of the
North Atlantic and in the Pacific Ocean. Before it was all one big
acidic mess. Before it was a shithole toilet for the factories. And
the salmon were born in freshwater and yet each one migrated
and went to saltwater, to the sea. That's no small journey, moc.
And this next bit is the real good bit. To keep the candle lit, to
have babbies, they went back to freshwater, and back in fact to the
very spot where they themselves were born. Old factory memory
is what it was called. That brought them to the very spot/

The kid would have loved to have had old factory memory. To
have known the truth about where he was born, to find by instinct
the very spot where he breathed first, to bring T and the babba
there.

/...salmon spent mayhap five years in the salt ocean, figuring
themselves out mayhap. And when they came back freshwater way
they made unreal journeys. Travelled hundreds of miles upstream
to get back to that place of birth. It wasn't all one swamp then,
like it is now. They had to avoid storms, fishermen, bears, the
dams of the beavers. These were animals that existed!/

/You ever feel sorry for the fish?/ the kid asked.

/Do I fukk feel sorry for them/ Sweeney shook his head. /I have me own problems/

Sweeney and the kid served themselves those last couple of hours because Rotter didn't think there was any point in doing anything any more. He was out on the balcony in his shirt, getting soaked to the bone, gaping out into the whispering rain. Inside, they talked about fish, and Sweeney cursed lamination, and eventually the kid asked Sweeney about the babba.

/Knew you'd ask sooner-later/ Sweeney said.

The kid in yellow, leaning forward, head hanging over the counter, just waited for the answer. People gave more when you let them speak.

/You're only a boy yourself/ Sweeney sighed.

He rapped his bottle of HappyDaze on the counter. His eyes searched the room. /What in the fukk happened this place?/

/Dunno/ the kid said.

/Gone to fukk/ he said.

The kid sat there and twisted the beer bottle around on the counter. /Just want to know if she's okay/

/Who?/

/My little girl/

Sweeney wiped his nose. /She's grand, from what I overhear/

/Where is she, Sweeney?/

/She's up in the house with her granny and granddaddy, two fukken nobles, where she should be. You're only a child yourself/

/The Earlie King/ the kid said.

/That's right. Well you know about it/

/She's not his/

/And what can you do about it? She's his granddaughter/

And the kid downed his bottle of UpYaBoyo and went for the t'ila then, and neither Sweeney nor Rotter was in the condition to stop him.

Δ

Earlie in the morning he staggered out of the Jolly Bridge onto the fire escape, his yellow skins shinybright in the gloom. He made a job of trying to hold on to the beer bottle and the slippery rail at the same time. Sweeney he'd left inside, asleep on the floor by the bar, muttering in his sleep about slugs and fires. Rotter lay at that moment on the fire escape, looking up into the light, and he was pleading with the light, /Not now. Not now! Am sorry. Am sorry!/

/*Tommib, Tommib*/ the kid chuckled, and then he whispered to Rotter:

/To enter the ring with the storm, to grapple and clinch, to enter the jaws of the shipwreck and never flinch. Over me comes a mist, the moon muffles her light. The lamp goes dark. The air goes damp. Red beams flash!/

And leaving Rotter behind him he cursed, because his hood was down and the water had gotten in. The golden rule was to never let the water in.

/You *never* let the water in/ he scolded. /*Tommib, Tommib, Tommib*. Yurt!/

Then he slipped the last few steps and landed on his elbows. The bottle smashed loudly by his ear and he yelped with fright and rolled laughing onto his back.

Δ

Rain out of a purple sky soaked his face and pattered in his eyes. How much time had passed? Rain pattered loud on his hood that was flat by his head. The yellow offices of the high-rise buildings swirled.

/*YURT!*/

The kid was alive!

/*Tommib* to the city I love the most! *Tommib* and up and abandon your post!/

He leapt to his knees in one movement, staggered, whipped his hood up. Water ran down his shoulders and back. Brown liquid streaked the yellow skins; he rubbed grit from his hands and

56

sleeves. Falling forward, he was against the wall then and singing, /*I am a girl's fist raised, I am the joyous sounds of industry!/*, sinking to his knees and pulling his hood tight and the whole city whirling around him like in a storm, and rain all through his world. /*I am the ghost of a fish, I am boat lights in the rain!/*

Under the beam of a tall streetlight blood on his hand. Purple morning light on the blood, blood that was fire spreading. No mercy, it said. It was like an animal in the night seeking food. There was a thing he needed, the kid. What was the thing? He used the wall to help him gain his feet and he pissed behind the skip before fetching up his bike. What was the thing?

Bit from

WORD OF WARD—

You know I remember O' Casey—the reporter that is— vividly. Can still see this squat, red-faced fellow with a scraggly blond beard and a grand belly. Narrow shoulders though: drinking made him fat, not nature. Hair on top, a fair bit of it, but thinning, you know? The man looked older than he was; he walked with purpose always. He told me about that once. In a café, too much wine as usual, not long after the end of the trouble. We knew each other then; we were not friends and would never be, but after trials like these there is an obligation between two people who find themselves on the same side. The obligation is to meet, to drink, to talk about it, to go your separate ways, and leave it behind you in the empty glasses you've shared. Well, the reporter drank more than I, and he told me more than I told him, and he told me that he'd wandered through life, until he found the story.

The story—the deaths—were him finding his purpose I suppose, telling the one story he *had* to tell, and made him what he was, some kind of grim reaper, or boatman on the jetty of the Styx, seeing the murdered across safely, telling them he'd pass word to their loved ones. And apart from his drinker's nose, and cheeks like an infection, he was pale as the grim reaper too. Pallid.

What brought us together was the boy, and mayhap more so than that the Earlie Boys, for they were the cause of everything here. You see the country then was oxter deep in black market activity. The Earlie Boys moved pharm, dolls, organs, clones—you name it—to port and to starboard. They washed money to port and to starboard. Stuff arrived into our dockyards and onto our jetties from all over world, and was held or moved and then shipped on to somewhere else in the world. And us guards—*the Heavy Gang*—were understaffed, under-gunned, under-everythinged. But maybe that's an excuse.

Let me tell you about our country. When people accepted that it would never stop raining, we weren't long losing farming. People just walked away, and one of our biggest industries disappeared almost overnight. They were tired of floods, you see. Of not being helped. And the same thing happened with fishing when the seas around us became too acidic and what was left of the catch turned hard and mutie. Once automation became the industry standard our last hope of a stable economy was gone. And the whole thing crescendoed. I remember my father telling me all this, and mayhap his father told him, or lived it, I don't remember. All these stories are ghost stories now.

Other economies crashed, other recessions took hold. What we had left, no country wanted or could afford. Only pharmaceuticals survived here, so that those who had farmed and fished began to haunt the conveyor belts of the pharm factories. Then, like a bad joke, or a tragedy, the New Labour Laws were written, and these factories became unregulated hellholes. Old culchies and teenage jacks alike wandered into industrial estates looking for a start and were never seen again. Things got very bad. That was when vigilantes like Saint Vincent Depaul started to burn things up.

The people moaned of corrupt governments, the badness in religion, of the environment, of dark magic. Hippies began to speak of an old god named Manannán Mac Lir coming back. There were many theories around this time. I remember even that people worshipped a defunct satellite. They begged it to cure their sick children. But everyone was too … distracted … too addled by different entertainments … too duped by government messages … to do anything about anything. Eventually they stopped talking and praying and those who could afford it left for healthier places.

The cities festered; the suburbs drowned. And the countryside changed forever—no longer farmland but marsh, swamp, fen, fish farm, labs and compounds on concrete stands in the mangroves. The first Irish pink dolphins were discovered in the Boyle, the first green dolphins in the Lee. These were scientific triumphs until it was discovered that the animals were deaf, tormented animals. Ireland became a cesspool for deranged life.

Then, I suppose, we stumbled across a business plan—an *economy*—that worked: sell what people won't admit they want. Fadinhead. Herbal. A tasty plastic dish. A kidney. A perfect genetic specimen. We became the crooked nation. And who administered this market? Not the Heavies, not the government. Crooks. Criminal gangs. And out of a garden full with weeds like that grew a great bramble. Roots mysteriously deep. This was something untameable. This was the Earlie King.

You may look at his life in different ways. You may look at his life as a life of crime, or a life of violence. But there are many other lives in him as well. That of a father. That of a husband. A child grown up. A boss. A trader. That of a noble life—they called him King after all. That of a god, for I don't know when he was born, or where. His origins were a mystery.

We knew only that he showed up at a city fayre one time trading ponies. A tall young buck with a belly and a beard down to his belt. A hill accent they said, though no one person could tie it to a particular network of hills. But, as the legend goes, on the last day of the festival an older local trader insulted the young stranger's ponies in passing, and the stranger did not take the insult well. He stood out in front of the local, a man with a reputation for toughness, and the young stranger told the local he would see him about the insult in the main square in ten minutes.

The local trader laughed. His people and all the people around laughed. The tall stranger did not laugh. He closed up his pitch and set about the task.

Now, people argue about the next part. Everyone agrees about the cobblestone square in Smi'field, there just up from the Liffee, but some say that it was lashing the whole time; others again that the whole thing happened in a boring drizzle, heavy and sweltering. But others again say that there fell a thin rain until the stranger delivered the beating, and that as the beating got worse it began to pour, as if the rain fell in line with the stranger's brutality. So the story goes that this long-bearded young buck who nobody knew came down to the square without his skins and without a second. He was bare-chested, in short pants, and the whole time he pointed at the trader who had insulted his stock. The local handed his gear to his second, another big man. The local was bare-chested now too, with pantalones and boots on, and either twenty people or two hundred were watching this, depending on who tells the story and who had which version handed down to them.

The stranger called the local trader to the middle of the square and the trader called out that he was going to teach this pony-fukker a lesson. That was the last thing he said. The stranger took one stiff punch from the local. Older men I've met in pubs shiver at the memory they claim. The local was out cold in thirty seconds but the stranger did not stop beating him. And nobody stepped in to stop him either. He stamped on the head of the local until it was squashed in. That was what he did.

And then the awful thing, the thing that sat worst with people. He tore the slicks and boots off the dead trader and tore his jocks off too, so that under the rain in the middle of the square they found themselves looking at a fat, naked broken body, near headless. The stranger spat on the meat of the dead man, threw the slicks and boots aside and left the square without another word.

The dead trader's second and a few others came to the body and covered it with the dead man's skins. The crowd moved off different ways, full of words and yet utterly speechless, as you can imagine. Later, when the Heavies asked questions, everybody said they hadn't seen anything. That was the way of things then, and after, and now.

The young, bearded stranger—well—he returned to his stall, and continued to trade. Nobody else insulted him.

The next year he returned, again with ponies. This year the beard was longer; he was bigger again. The family of the murdered local were out for revenge. The fayre was not a day old when the stranger met the brother of the dead man in the square and felled him too. This time he didn't kill. This time he dragged the brother's heaving body to the corner of the crowd where his people waited. Only honour kept them from all pouncing on the stranger at once. He dragged the body by the arms and told his people to bring their best man to the square on the last day of the fayre. He told them bring the city's best man, he didn't care.

Over the week of festivities and fights and animal-trading people sidled up to this stranger at his stall. They pretended to be interested in the animals but soon came to asking him about the incidents in the square, about himself. He gave nothing away, and some decided that they liked him and most decided that they feared him. Either way, they gave him information. You see, this is what I often found, that information flows the way of power. They said this after, that it made him the chieftain he was, his way of giving nothing out but yet people wanting to tell him everything. They told him who he was to fight, the weaknesses of that man. They found themselves paying for animals they did not want.

It happened at an unflooded car park beneath a derelict highrise. In out of the rain the ceilings of the car park still dripped big juicy algae droplets. The man that stepped in front of the stranger was MacDowd, and in fighting terms he was the king of the province. Yes, it was a time when there was such a thing. He wasn't so tall but he had never been beaten.

So MacDowd stepped in front of the stranger... I met a man once at a g-ball match. He said he'd been there. Was only a boy at the time. It was a true and fair fight as he saw it. It went on for more than half an hour but it was at no point even he said. It was one man slowly breaking down the other. The stranger of no name coming on and demolishing his opponent, piece by piece. Mayhap twenty minutes, mayhap half an hour—it was hard to watch they said. MacDowd was a hero around the place, a decent butcher, much more popular than that first dead trader.

Poor MacDowd. My g-ball friend said he heard bones crack.

When MacDowd did not get up, the stranger knelt over him, beard falling to the other's chest. He lifted him up like a sleeping baby. He said:

'Is that it now? Is there anyone else wants to fight?'

No one answered, and so he carried MacDowd to his second, a tall, sad man, a butcher too, and the stranger gave MacDowd over and said to the second, 'Your late king.'

And that—they say—was how he came to be called the Earlie King.

Then he turned back to the crowd and he gave them a big gaping smile. A big wide friendly grin.

'I think I'll stay now,' he said, and he walked from the crowd.

And his words were true. He didn't leave when the fayre ended. He took a room above a riverside pub and put what remained of his pony stock into the very stables where years later our beloved kid kept a pony himself. According to O' Casey anyway. The stranger had become the king of the province now—that was the way it worked—and this drew different types of people to him. But what is said is that while people came to the Earlie King at his hotel room with offers of business or work, of payment for protection from gangs, of family and marriage, it always felt when he decided to deal with them that *he* was taking what *he* wanted. Everything was on his own terms. You wonder whether it was all intentional, from that first insult from that first trader. Whether everything that happened, happened by the sheer dint of his will. This is what a god does. Or a daemon.

There were rumours, later, of a young wife, a thin quiet woman with dark bushy hair and black eyes, so quiet that those who claimed to have met her were convinced that she did not speak English. None of that was ever proven in my time with the Heavy Gang—in a world of near-omniscient surveillance, we couldn't get close enough to gather an iota of intelligence. There were too many mirrors around that man, too many stories.

He felled a man named Picardo too, a Connacht champion, and people thought of him then as the king of the whole country. After that he fought only when challenged, and he killed every man that challenged him. It was as if the price for trying to gain a title was your life, and it could only end in death. How everything else got involved—all the crooked stuff—is a long, winding rumour, and there might be time for it later, but I want to tell you about the Earlie Boys too.

You knew them by their dress—loud shirts, sometimes Hawaiian, Kandinskees they were called, with leather waistcoats—and by a tattoo of the right temple, which was four dots marking the corners of a square with one dot at the square's centre. That tattoo stood for revenge: for every Earlie Boy killed or in prison, four more would soon surround the person responsible, exacting merciless retaliation. This was supposed to put off Heavies, and crusaders like Vinny Depaul.

. .
 .
. .

There was always ten of them, Ten Peers they were called, and their brutality was total. That was the King's order. And he had his own sign, sprayed on walls all over by runners. It was simple: an oval eye and a crooked crown on top. It burned itself on the mind, always watching.

The Earlie Boys carried knives in their boots or their coats—rarely guns—and they were not afraid of the Heavy Gang either, not one bit. They hated punks, the Molly Men, who were plentiful in the city at that time but who were generally not dangerous. Still, the enemy of the Earlie Boy was the lad who had a mohican, or who dyed his hair, who wore earrings and cetera. Many's a pub was destroyed when a couple of Earlie Boys and a couple of Molly Men crossed paths, and for sure more Molly blood was spilled than Earlie. The more I came to know about operations, the more I wondered why the King put up with that stupid rivalry stuff. But I think now that he knew that hatred was part of what kept people lean, kept people hungry and alert.

When the ten Earlie Boys were reduced to nine, a new tenth appeared without delay, chosen from the pick of runners. You get the idea. It was not long before the Earlie Boys and their King ran everything from the city out.

I suppose we tried infiltrating them, taking them out. It's hard to know. Things were so confused and corrupt. But, before long, our job became simply to watch them. To note down their moves. To watch, and wait. To identify weaknesses, vulnerabilities. It was decided that information was good. Could be stored up and then had value somehow. Could be useful. It was that way for everybody I guess. Whether that information was true or false no longer mattered. The means—collecting it—became the end. Personally, I was more interested then in living a handy life—staying out of trouble—than any justice. And if I'm honest, I admit now that we were in the King's pocket.

Where *he* lived in my time was a mystery too—he had many houses and we never knew whether or which one he kept a family in, though we thought he did have some kind of family—but most of the Earlie Boys and nearly all the runners lived at that time where the boy himself lived: the Croke Park Flats, the poorest place in the city. The style of those flats they called Brutalism, and that was fairly fitting. Six blocks of them gathered around, hunched, in decay, joined up by a labyrinth of skyways and alleyways. Places of echoes and drippings, flappings and ghostly footfall. The blocks sometimes seemed to lean and sway, like concrete trees, the last of the paint flaking from the plaster like dead skin. Everything hung with vine and vegetation, graffiti and moss.

This was a dangerous place. Behind the rotting plywood doors and the blankets and plastics that covered balconies we heard murmurs and screams and eerie mechanical sounds. It was known that Fadinhead factories were in operation, on the STS and Blu-Sky blocks at least.

When they built the place, way back, it was supposed to be a utopian vision of the future, a place of holistic communal living. Accommodation, gymnasiums, schools, nurseries, surgeries, libraries, retail units—all was contained in the one complex. The walkways would connect people, and were wide enough that ambulances and milk trucks could service them and choppers could land on them. The blocks themselves formed an arc that opened out to the view of the bay, the ever-becoming sea, the depth of mystery that it gave us. The idea was that the Flats would return us again to that sense that we were all connected. Of course that sea view, like the utopian stuff, was lost in smog and drizzle and cloud.

At the foot of the six blocks were playgrounds, lawns, botanical gardens, a playing field. But alas...it was jungle and broken glass by then. The smashed-up, flora-drenched shell of the botanical gardens was a grand symbol of the ruin and desolation—just how ragged things had got by then...JAYPERS! Am tired now just thinking about it!

BIT CALLED

WHYS

The walls of the flat wept something serious, and the heating hadn't worked since the mother disappeared, so when he rose in the evening he lit a fire in the kitchen sink and stood over it until he stopped shivering. The fire was good. He felt close to it. Watching the stainless steel blacken, he felt a kind of shared hunger, an urge to do something. To leave mayhap. Not just the flat, but the whole city. The promise shuddered through him. Repeated on him. *I will take ye away…*

So no sooner had he dried and warmed but he went out again. Stole a few pills from his sleeping brother's stash. Took his cycle.

Made for the overpass and there watched speedboats and rivertrucks sliding underneath, headlamp beams searching a murky drizzle, forging a path down the waterway to the gloomy beyond. The rivertrucks would sail through the night, kicking up that dirty spray, engines steaming in the rain like the noses of great horses. He took a pill on the bridge and waited.

The overpass was where people came to jump, but he saw nobody this night, staring out from under his yellow hood into the beams of the river traffic—red, white, yellow, red, white, green, blue. Those beams were searching the night, soul-searching, questioning, just like him. Why had it started to rain so? What curse had come over the country, what sin committed? These were the kinds of things he thought about when he was rising. He thought it was all mysterious. And lately the mysteries of his own life seemed all mixed up by the rain. He could feel them now without pain, as if they hadn't happened to him. How had he fallen in love? How had T gotten pregnant? What could he do?

What should he do? How could he keep the promise?

He turned back from the water to watch the city. The buildings stood in darkened blocks against the cloud. There was water and there was land and somewhere out there a moon unseen. They needed each other. T was the moon; the babba was his land, but a land he did not know. Drawing him to the foreign child was T, in night moves and morning glints of hope. Over the dark of the city the roof beacons flashed white and red and he decided then to go down and be amongst the buildings, and to walk the chrome and glass and marble of the Financial District while the city workers still slept. The pharm was working well.

Δ

The conversation had continued:

/Dreamt of sunlight again. We lived in a treehouse! x/

/Mad ting. Lay off the herbal x/

/No more herbal, told you. How is the sickness? x/

/Bad. Sick always. Vomiting all morning x/

/Sorry, T. Wish I could do something x/

/Send me a line. For inspiration x/

/Lost out on the water,

A neon seagull came to me,

He showed to me a way back,

And astral teardrops falling free,

My love I'm rowing back to you,

For you're the land and I'm the sea xxx xxx/

/What does it mean? xxx/

/Dunno. You tell me! xxx/

/I'll think about it! xxx/

/Send us a pic/

[MEDIA OMITTED]

/Think mayhap it means that we're always together even if are not. Even if there are bad things, no matter that journey. If at least one of us is in a rowboat we've no worries xxx/

/Beautiful girl xxx xxx xxx xxx xxx/

72

Δ

He walked streets of reinforced glass; of concrete pillars; of tiles; of banisters; of wooden boardings, and concrete boardings. Of metal grilles. Of Helvetica. Of strip lighting. Of steel doors. Of dry-riser inlets and electricity boxes. Light casings festered with insects. They used to see each other in the Financial District because it was safe—they wouldn't bump into Earlie Boys there—and days they spent there were the best. He hadn't been able to believe how good it felt, that new feeling.

But soon came the fear of loving someone so much that you were waiting every second for some bad thing to happen. Soon, he watched how she looked at other gents, wondering did she prefer them. He waited on her next message with dread. When she coughed, he feared death. When he said something stupid, which was often, he was terrified she'd lose interest in him.

He had said one time, /Hope I die before you break this off/

/What?/ she said. /Why would you say that?/

They were walking that same Financial District and the lights looked young and lovely.

He said: /Because there's nothing to live for after you/

He could see her looking at him and knew she was thinking of his family, and his home, and his work, and knowing that he was right. But she said: /Don't be a flippen flute, there's plenty in the world/

He said: /Like what?/

She said: /Like everything. Don't say no more/

He said: /I love you/

She said: /I love you too/

But still he was convinced she would break his heart. He did not know how he knew, but it was a certainty that he and T were doomed. Every minute felt borrowed. And these feelings grew and faded, just like the happiness he had in him that time.

/Are just kids/ she said. /Relax. Let's have fun/

On his walk alone through the city he thought about her twelve months of pregnancy, and the secret they'd had to keep, and of all the ways she suffered at the hands of the Earlie King from the day she told them. All these fragments of knowing and not knowing made him want to cry, but he never did cry. They made him want to puke also, but he never did puke. He had so many Whys:

Why did I have to meet her?

Why did I love her?

Why did she have to get pregnant?

Why did it have to be her, the daughter of the Earlie King?

Why did she have to die?

Why did this all happen to me?

Cables. High windows. Chrome doorhandles. Fractals of pipes. Drains. Archways. Air vents. He turned for home, and pushed on into that night again.

Δ

/Are you sleeping? x/

/Almost. Thinking about you x/

/Hope you're in my dream x/

/Hope we're in each other's dreams x/

/See you there then x/

/Night Wendy xxx/

/Night Petey Boy xxx/

BIT FROM **THE PLAY**——

PERSONS IN THE PLAY

SISSY.....................................punter at the Pup&Pendant
KER ....punter at the Pup&Pendant
CROONER BART/the BARD....the Earlie King's right-hand man
LEG .... the Earlie King's left-hand man
MISTER VIOLENCE .... ???
SWEENEY..........................local mystic/chronic alcoholic
The EARLIE KING ....king, chieftain over the Earlie Boys
ST VINCENT DEPAUL .... vigilante, arsonist, hunter &
killer of Earlie Boys
FREDDI .... Earlie Boy
The EEL .... Earlie Boy
BARRETT .... Earlie Boy
FRANCIS .... Earlie Boy
RICE.. Earlie Boy
HOLLOWAY .... Earlie Boy
CHAN .... Earlie Boy
MIKE THE HAT... Earlie Boy
The SPANYARD.. Earlie Boy
CLEM.....................................runner for the Earlie Boys
The KID IN YELLOW....................runner for the Earlie Boys
JIM CORCORAN ....bartender at the Pup&Pendant
The BABBA
OTHER PUNTERS
THREE LADYBOYS

Most of the action takes place in the lounge bar of
the Pup&Pendant pub, a wide, square timber-floored
space with a low sagging wooden ceiling. The room
is dim, lit by overhead lamps which hang from steel
pipes. The lamps—wide shades, flat like plates—
give a weak yellow light. And they hang low, to about
six or so feet, and so the taller persons in the play
[the EARLIE KING, JIM CORCORAN] have to stoop or
dodge as they move about. Long upholstered benches

76

are attached to three walls——the bar covers the
fourth——and are broken only by the solitary double-
door entrance to the lounge and an old mantelpiece
on the wall opposite the bar counter. The mantelpiece
serves as an altar of randomly collected objects,
maintained by the Earlie Boys, both religious and
not, and at the centre of the idolatry and iconography
sits a skull, which radiates pink neon into the
room ... Tables and chairs are organised around the
perimeter of the room. The walls shorn of photographs
or clippings, floral pattern wallpaper spreads with
mathematical precision. It is everywhere continuous
and nowhere differentiable. The further out it
is traced by the human eye, the more it distorts,
as if the pattern begins to bleed into the human
imagination. In the centre of the room languishes
an ancient, tattered billiard table.

...

ACT The First, SCENE 2

At the Pup&Pendant, in the lounge. A hard rain
can be heard falling beyond the walls. SISSY and
KER sit alone in the lounge at lights up, deep in
conversation. Pints of Guin are nestled in their fists
as they count and speculate, counting and speculating
being the most ancient of human acts. Thus, amidst
the soft pipechant of unseen pints being pulled, talk
of a ferrybus scam.

SISSY.   What they're doing is they're turning
                up twenty minutes before the actual
                ferryboat for that hour is due.
KER.   As per timetable?
SISSY.   Oh, of course.
KER.   What do you mean, of course? How was

77

that obvious from what you said?

SISSY.   Right. Let me restart and be clear and
          transparent with you from the get-go.
          Let there be no confusion or murky
          areas in what I'm saying. [aside,
          'Eejit'.] They obtain the timetable,
          or <u>schedule</u> if you're linguistically
          agile, for said journey. They then
          note pick-up times from the departure
          point, which has already been
          discussed and revealed, and which, for
          reasons of confidentiality, will not be
          repeated here now. Comprende?

KER.   Oui.

SISSY.   They then use the timetable, or
          schedule, of said official operator
          and arrive twenty minutes before the
          scheduled, or timetabled, departure
          time. In this case, that departure time
          is on the hour, every second hour from
          4 a.m.

KER.   As in, four, six, eight, ten, twelve,
          fourteen hundred, sixteen hundred,
          eighteen hundred, twenty hundred,
          twenty-two hundred and midnight?

SISSY.   Are a clever mark.

KER.   Thank you. Gracias.

SISSY.   They use an unmarked ferrybus, as in
          no official logos and cetera. They do
          not advertise anywhere the destination
          of the vehicle. With me?

KER.   Oui. Right alongside you.

SISSY.   They work in pairs. One drives, one
          stands ashore of the ferrybus and
          calls out the destination and the
          fare.

KER.	One hawks the wares, the other delivers the product.
SISSY.	Précisément.
KER.	Claro. Do they undercut pricewise?
SISSY.	But no. The very thing they are doing is pretending that they themselves are offering the timetabled service. No need then to undercut, because they are not the competition.
KER.	Cash payments only, I presume?
SISSY.	Your mind is evolving at a furious paoo, and you aro indeed correct again. What they do is add to their destination call the words 'CASH ONLY...'. If pushed for an explanation, they divulge to the astute customer that are in fact the 'overflow service', as this is a fully booked service and a second vessel is needed for customers without a reservation. For this reason, they can turn away people with legitimate bookings, and therefore no cash, and take turn-up customers on a cash-only basis. Voila.
KER.	Ingenious ... So now what are the pitfalls of these gentlemen's illegal endeavour? They seem to have advanced a pretty strong business case and modus operandi, no?
SISSY.	Are not wrong. But there are other considerations. For example, how many citizens in today's world are more than ten minutes earlie for their ferrybus?
KER.	A fair point. A few but not enough for huge profit.

SISSY.	And there is the matter of insurance. Now of course all buses have insurance.
KER.	And of course it is illegal to so much as start an engine without such insurance in place.
SISSY.	Indeed. But if you are to pick up passengers illegally, are you insured to carry them?
KER.	Are not, is the answer I would venture.
SISSY.	Only last week, I observed in passing a national-service ferrybus in flames on the river.
KER.	Christ, I heard about that! At Georgie's Quay. People were hurt.
SISSY.	All twenty-one passengers died, their lives all cleared out of existence by flame. Eighty per cent of the crew also, eaten whole by fire. Only the captain of the vessel survived, and he is but crackled bacon in a hospital ward somewhere now.
KER.	Was it Vinny Depaul setting fires again? Thought he only burned the oppressors of the poor? Surely was clean ordinary folk on board?
SISSY.	Wasn't Vincent Depaul. Always claims his doings ...
KER.	And what was your role? Did you call emergency men?
SISSY.	My role was to pass by in a hurry, stopping only for a moment to observe the hideous beauty of it. Was late for a very important...thing...But you are missing the point.
KER.	Which is?

SISSY.   Insurance. That vessel was an
                official, above-water business; thusly,
                all lives and losses were financially
                covered and therefore compensation
                is redeemable ... But if the action
                of carrying said passengers was
                illegal——a scam say——and therefore
                technically uninsured ... Well, you can
                estimate for yourself the value of
                twenty-five bona fide citizen lives ...

They sup from their pints and take stock. There is a
rhythm to their drinking.

SISSY.   Where do you stand on Vincent Depaul
                then, being one of the poor yourself?

KER considers the question, while SISSY begins to
examine and prod his device.

KER.   Undecided I think. Like what he stands
                for. If I was only better able——if only
                the blood pressure would come down——
                mayhap would even take against the
                rich myself.
SISSY.   And the Earlie Boys? 'Any' enemy of
                the poor m——
KER.   [hissing] Ssshhhhhh! Ya bollox!
SISSY.   [embarrassed, changing the subject
                by nodding to his device] Here's one
                statement: 'You have reduced the people
                of Ireland to numbers, to numbers
                on pieces of paper. To [SISSY having
                trouble] bee-your-ee-cratic forms. We
                are not paper. We are people. Until you
                treat us like people, you will burn.'

| | [looking up] Well that wan was for the politicians I suppose. |
| KER. | But if he's not careful he'll burn us all one day. They say there's oil aplenty under our feet. Leaked out from—— |

A door offstage bangs.

Silvine, inglorious, enter LEG and CROONER BART. Candlewax on green liquor bottles. LEG stops to gaze into the flame of the liquor-bottle candle. On his mind, quite specifically now, is fire.

SISSY.	[standing hastily] Hallo, Leg. Hallo, Bart. We were only just going out to put a few songs on the jukey. Any requests?
KER.	[joining his comrade, hastily] Good luck to ye, gentlemen.

Exit SISSY and KER with the pints in their hands.

LEG.	Good luck, gentlemen. [when they've gone] So what you think?
BART.	Will just say it to him, plain and simple. See what he says.
LEG.	Have my doubts. Has been acting wild since the girl died.
BART.	Slut. [spits on the floor]

Enter JIM CORCORAN, with a faded blue cloth hanging from the shoulder of his white short-sleeve shirt, his dark, wide tie wagging as he lumbers thoughtfully up and down the bar. He is a tall, stooping man, and his

82

head and hands are much larger than his thin frame
would seem to allow. Thus his head appears to bobble
as he moves.

CORCORAN.   Guin?
BART.   Guin.

LEG nods.

Enter the EARLIE KING, opening both of the lounge
doors and looking to both sides carefully, before
grinning at his leftenants. The grin through a bushy
greywhite beard, still down to the navel, is a scary
thing, held too long.

THE KING.   Get me whiskey! Bring me beer!
BART & LEG.   All hail the King!
THE KING.   [utterly serious] The King is dead.
                 [then grinning, toying with their
                 nervousness, whether deliberately or
                 not it is unclear] Long live the King!
BART & LEG.   Long live the King!
BART.   Will live long too is my betting! No
                 stopping this buck-o!

CORCORAN returns and fills three Guins and three
whiskeys. He serves the men, taking no money.

THE KING.   Now, ye wanted counsel. Let's take a
                 seat.

LEG and CROONER BART take a table by the mantelpiece
while the KING walks a lap of the room before joining
them, stopping first to observe the skull on the
mantelpiece.

THE KING.	Tell me, men. Do you think it's possible for two people to end the world?
LEG.	Two people? Suppose it depends. Working together or apart?
THE KING.	Just existing. The two of them existing means the world has to end.
BART.	[pushing his broken spectacles to the top of his nose] Like the old Catholic stuff, me. Mam does too. Still goes mass. Would you be talking God and the Devil?
THE KING.	Not at all. Am talking two men who walk the earth. If they continue to walk the earth, it comes apart.

BART and LEG are clearly mystified and stare into their pints, hoping to find the answer he'll like.

THE KING.	Never mind. Think on it. Now what is it ye're afraid of?
LEG.	[shifts in his seat] Ah. Is not that we're afraid. Is a few of the boys.
THE KING.	Which of them?
LEG.	Well, Holloway mainly.
THE KING.	What's bothering poor Holloway?
BART.	Thinks he was followed by Vinny Depaul.
THE KING.	Ha! Another man lost to fear. What does he think?
BART.	Said he got the feeling someone was tailing him in the Raceways, the alleys there, and when he turned he saw a dark shadow, and the shadow lit a match at him before disappearing round the corner.

LEG.	When Holloway went after him he was gone. No sign of the fukker.

The KING appears pensive.

BART.	I say that an Earlie Boy wears his dagger, shows a front. Shows no fear. Holloway should have left no stone unturned in finding him. Showed no mercy.

LEG is looking at BART, as if he didn't expect the sudden outburst.

THE KING.	And why did ye say, 'some of the boys'?
LEG.	Well, are all a bit worried now. Afraid of getting burned.
BART.	Has been after us a long time, auld VDP, the crafty boyo.
LEG.	Are not afraid. Are asking if we can do more to find out who he is. Surely the Heavies have a file on him. Surely are clues. Surely is a dossier or something that one of your contacts could get us?
THE KING.	Goes after politicians too. Burns all the baddies, he says. And serves the poor. Or, they say.
LEG.	[shrugging] Lot of fires. Could be more than one of them doing the doings.
THE KING.	Corcoran!

Enter CORCORAN.

THE KING.	You believe that Saint Vincent Depaul is a man? Or the work of many men?

CORCORAN.	Some say he's a man, a fish-farm worker. Some say he's a group of men and women. God knows what's to be believed. Mayhap he's just a story, and the fires could be anybody's.
THE KING.	You fear him?
CORCORAN.	Fear fire! But not him, no...Whoever he is. Or they are.
LEG.	[looking for a change of subject] How is the child?
THE KING.	Leg, keep your counsel, do your job. Is all I ask.
LEG.	A'course, King. Apologies...So what you think about Vinny? Is there a way of clocking him and taking vengeance for the Earlies he's taken already? Would be just lovely to get that fukker down into the Dark Chamber and have a bit of fun with him.
BART.	Are queuing up to guillotine him. Am first in line meself. I remember poor Donovan. [shakes his head, observes the floorboards] I couldn't put him out.
THE KING.	Vinny Depaul. Serves the poor. Burns the bastards. Him of the incorrupt heart.
BART.	Would set a special stone on his tongue and send it with him.
THE KING.	Don't ye think that if someone knew who he was they'd take him out? Has burned offices, banks, assassinated politicians. We're not the only ones wanting him.
LEG.	True.
BART.	Is true.

LEG.	So what do we do? Layve it alone?
THE KING.	Am thinking.

For a moment, the babbling of the distant city
intercom, completely indecipherable, comes through.

BART.	More drink, Corcoran!
THE KING.	Not for me.
BART.	Two pints!
THE KING.	[settling on his conclusion] Have Holloway walk the Raceways and the alleyways around them, until he is satisfied that he cannot find and face Saint Vincent. If he finds him and guts him, tell him he'll be rewarded. In the meantime give Francis all of his work. All of it. Come back to me in a week.
LEG.	Clap hands, King. Right enough.
THE KING.	Send him off looking for the old artefacts.
LEG.	Sorry?
THE KING.	Nothing. Anything else to report to me, men?
BART.	Business is good, King. Life is good. You sure we can't do anything to that kid for you?
THE KING.	Not your concern, Bart.
BART.	Clap hands. But only say the word.
LEG.	Still, christening tomorrow! All set?
BART.	Love a christening, me.
THE KING.	Goodbye, men. Make sure everybody turns up sober and well.
LEG.	A'course, King.
BART & LEG.	Good luck.

Exit the EARLIE KING, the door clattering behind him.

```
BART.          [brightly] Well, is acting strange
               alright! What the fukk was that about
               two men destroying the world?
LEG.           Yea, fukk it. Get Holloway on the
               device there. In fact, better we
               remind them all to stay in tonight.
BART.          Love going to the church, me. God is
               my friend.
```

Lights flicker out and darkness grows gradually. Very
soon, only the pink neon glow of the skull remains,
pulsing in the darkness, and the garbled, static
lunacy of the city intercom grows to fill the stage,
like a kettle boiling.

                    CURTAIN.

BIT CALLED

FLATS / SWEEPS OF WATER

The reporter limped ramrod straight, up through the cobble of the botanical garden ruins to the Triangle. By a low wall where the path opened out a mangle of slugs—rat-sized, muscular, the colours of deep jungle—piled over each other and rolled against each other in a kind of gastropodal gang bang. Up through the drizzlemist he saw two blond children in clear plastic skins, and, hailing them, he stiffened his back and hastened his step.

They were Siamese twins, joined at one elbow. Their skins were not specially made for their condition but joined at one sleeve with clearfilm. They'd been kicking a slug up the path and it had coiled itself into a ball, as if to make it easier for them. Stooping over the children, he shuddered at the slime on their feet.

/Hallo!/ he said. /Am looking for the kid in yellow. Ye know him?/

They nodded in unison.

/Is he on AerCo block?/

They nodded in unison.

/Can ye tell me on which floor he lives?/

Again, nodding.

/Well? Which is it?/

The girl held out her free hand. Gnarled, and covered in pale scrapes it was, and he did not know what she wanted, until a searching, flicking thumb indicated.

/Mutes?/

She nodded and he held his device out to her.

/26/ she typed.

/Ye know which flat?/

She shook her head, and he his.

When he took his device back he lay a few coins in the girl's palm. /Thanking ye both/

The children swung back to track the slug, fixing on its slow, hopeless course.

On the fourth floor he cut in through a skyway and took a lift. They were dangerous, but his back throbbed and strictured and often spasmed, and therefore he took his chances.

The long corridor of the twenty-sixth was a muffled chorus of murmuring TeleVisio behind walls, factory songs and dry coughs, all echoing about him. Awful food smells filled his nostrils. His boots squeaked along the corridor; he wondered how he would find the right door. In the end, it was easy, for he found sprayed upon the door the terrible eye of the King, and above it the sharp yellow heart with the T in its centre.

The reporter knocked loudly, removed his hat from his head to his chest.

A youth eventually answered, but it was not the fist of yellow he had encountered before. This youth was about seventeen, skinny, tall, greasy, stoned. He had one hand on the crooked door handle and one hand in the pocket of his pantalones.

/Am looking for your younger brother?/ the reporter started.

/Don't think he's in. *HEY! HEY! Kiiiiddd?!*/

No answer. From the flat there came a strange hissing, distant gunfire.

/Not in/

/What's your name?/ the reporter asked.

The boy regarded him.

/A gamer?/ the reporter asked.

/No name/ the youth said.

/You're a gamer?/

/Go'way/

/Know when your brother will be back?/

/Go'way/

The youth went to close the door. As he did, the reporter

stepped forward, to get a foot in, to explain himself, when the youth brought the right hand from his pocket and the reporter felt a bolt of heat.

Δ

He woke in the corridor on his back, still outside the door, looking up at a mildewed ceiling, and a line of graffiti that read *I AM THE LITTLEST BIT OF THE LITTLE BIT THAT BACK IN THE BEGINNING DAYS WAS ALL. INSIDE ME → THE DARKNESS WHICH BORE THE LIGHT.* A mist had formed on his face and the floor shivered up through him.

/Fukker/ he said. /Fukker tazed me/

Turning over on his front, he pulled himself to his feet, and was jittery against the wall for a moment.

But as he traced his way back along the corridor to the lift he felt something about him was different, as if he had died and come back to life, the same person somehow evolved, somehow healed. He could not place it. That hissing sound followed him up the corridor with the factory songs and the TeleVisio murmurings, and when he saw her name scrawled above the lift he remembered when he had been on the twenty-sixth floor last. Rebecca Li had lived and disappeared here. And he knew now what was different too: the pain in his back was gone.

/Fukker tazed me/ he chuckled.

Δ

Overhead, the whirring of postal drones and the disembodied rambling of the city intercom. They sat on a bench in the shadow of the Flower: growing out of a circular clipped lawn, the structure forty feet high and twenty across, steel petal and stamen that in the old days had opened itself to the sun each morning and turned to follow the sun as the day passed. At dusk it would close again and sleep. Of course it was rusted and seized up now.

Clem had been cycling the streets for two hours and yet it had been inevitable that he would run into the kid there in the

Financial District, under the awning of a corner shop, staring in wonderment out of his hood at the mucal statue of the flower, pupils like pinheads, a white rime around his narrow lips, a bottle of NastyBoy hanging from his slack grip. Clem had shot his hands out from under baggy silver skins and showed the kid in that way that he came peaceful.

/Knew from the silver skins it was you/ the kid said.

Clem brought him to the bench facing the Flower and they shared the bottle.

/Is good news, Clem?/ the kid asked from within his hood.

/Good news you're still alive and not headless in the canal/ Clem said.

Δ

The bottle was bringing the kid around a bit. They sat in silence, lights of red, white, blue washing over their shiny skins and the slick bench.

/Why am I still alive?/

/No one knows/

/You're supposed to stay away from me, Clem. Am supposed be outcast/

/Am. Are/

/Then why you looking for me?/

/To say they christened your babba today/

/Oh/

The kid turned and shared a dreamy look. Then frowned. /Christened where?/

/Bog Bones. Thought you might like to go up there and say a pray or something/

They sat on in silence a while.

/Best go/ Clem said. /Can't really be seen with you. Run for the King now and he doesn't hang around, as you well know/

/You know what I'm thinking about?/ the kid said.

/What?/

/Am thinking about Rebecca Li/

/Who?/

/Rebecca Li. Was a girl that lived on the twenty-sixth floor, a few years older than us. When I was ten she was about sixteen. Had straight black hair, wore glasses. Said hardly anything/

/I recall now. Disappeared, didn't she/

/Last seen on Hub inflow getting into the lift on the twenty-sixth. Her family were quiet; they were religious. No drink, no pharm, no sups, no hits. The lift door opens, the angle is that high corner angle. In comes Rebecca Li, and she presses G to go down, then steals a peek out into the corridor, looking the way she's come and along the rest of the corridor too. Well, Rebecca Li starts to hide then, even though there is no one in the corridor. She looks out one more time, then ducks in and makes herself small as she can in that corner. The doors start closing and of a sudden she starts mashing all the buttons, as if to make sure the doors do not close. There is no one else in that corridor, Clem/

/How do you know?/

/TeleVisio. Archive. Have seen every angle on the floor... Next thing, she's standing again and hiding in the *other* corner of the lift, in the corner where she'd be easily seen if anyone was to come along. Hiding in plain sight, Clem, is what I mean. Then suddenly bursts back out into the corridor, just as the doors are about to close. She hangs left. The doors I would say haven't a fukken clue what's going on. They open again in her wake, and wait while in the hallway she now has her back to the end wall, straight up against it, and is looking straight up at the ceiling/

/Got to be on F or something/

/No. Post-mortem shows no pharm at all. Finally, she walks back to the lift, turning her head, taking her time, gaping at each closed door as she passes it. Whatever was making her strange has full control of her now. You can pause it for screenshots. See a blankness in her face and it's like there's no one there at all in that head. That body looks like something on remote control. Takes her time, hands hanging by her hips, a walking drone. Finally gets back to the lift and turns into it. Into the back-left corner.

/Stillness. Nothing. No moves out of Rebecca Li. Lift doors close and nothing happens. The light of the corridor is gone and Rebecca Li fades into the walls. Just a shape. Then she turns quick and presses the top button for the top floor/

/Goes to the roof?/

/Seems like it. Stands in front of the lift doors and waits. Door opens, she exits. On the top-floor corridor she walks to the end in the same blank way. Disappears in through a service door. After that there's no visio inflow. She's found floating in the water tank on the roof a day later. Like I said, no pharm or drink in her bloodstream, no history of madness or anxiety or any of that. No clues. That's the story of Rebecca Li. Mike the Hat used tell that story and I've seen the footage myself/

/Clap hands/ Clem said. /But why are you thinking of that now? Why telling me?/

/Because it's a mystery/ the kid said. /*Tommib*. Is a mystery. And I am alive and she is dead/

The kid had known Clem almost as long as he could remember the world. Apart from the brother, only Clem knew his full name. Of all, Clem had probably been let down most with T and the babba and all that. He would have caught some abuse for being the kid's pal, and they all probably thought he knew about it, which he hadn't.

/Be thankful/ Clem said. /Steer clear of them and be thankful/

/.../

/I best go. Can't be seen. What will you do?/

/Go to Bog Bones, I suppose/

/Be careful in going/

/Clap hands/

Then, in a swift, muscle-remembered move, Clem was aboard his steed, raising wheel-water in fountain rhythms and gone away up the road into the drizzlemist.

Δ

Since the scandal of the Bog Bones people weren't buried in that church ground any more. He had no idea where T was buried. Would old factory memory tell him that too? For a while the kid and Honest John skulked a path woven between the left-behind headstones, the animal stopping to chew on dock leaves, a whole day after the babba had been christened. The kid imagined them all standing about the place, waiting to go in, the Earlie Boys smoothing back their hair, winking, smiling out the one side of their mouths. They would have worn bright ties with their Kandinskees and their waistcoats, for the occasion. Runners in a gang beyond them then, sneering with the giddiness of being involved. They would have worn what waistcoats they could get their hands on.

And somewhere in amongst that small crowd his own daughter, and the King, and the woman that was T's mother.

It was spitting a high rain. They were all under the one sky right now, he thought. He could not stop thinking of the promise. He was thinking that this girl of his had had no mother or father in there to put a hand to her head, to calm her when water came. The kid himself had no mother or father around to put a hand to his back or to tell him to forget the whole thing. To say, what daughter? To say, there's more rain than blood. To say, and it's only raining—there's no need for you to join her down there in the water.

He did not pray in the graveyard, nor did Honest John; he recited instead a poem he remembered but did not understand.

/The mind works like a cradle
The body like a sieve
I am at once Neanderthal and starlight
I was made to give/

Outside in the church bog with Honest John and the old soaking headstones, he could not reconcile his life and the babba's life with all the other death.

/Go to the bend of the river, I will
 Go to the bend of the river with you/

The varnished wooden gable of the church arched above them, the curved wood like the prow of a grand boat. Oars over the double doors. /*Row me ashore, Oh Lord*/ he heard them singing. Thus he found himself floating like a ghost through the last of those head-stones and pulling his skin-strings loose just inside the door of the church and hanging them alone where a day before everyone's garments had hung steaming. Again, it all felt like something that had a meaning, but that the meaning was on the other side of misty glass. T had said to him once that he wasn't able to see what was right in front of his face. She was talking about how he couldn't see that she fancied him from the first. Was he paying heed to what the world was now showing him?

And he wandered down the empty aisle under the vaulted ceiling, between empty pews. His footsteps echoed around the old place and fell into key and rhythm with drippings. Mayhap then he glimpsed some kind of meaning, because by the time he got to the altar where his daughter had been christened all fear had evaporated from him. All doubt too. There was no choice in it. He would keep the promise, he decided once and for all.

ORBS & MOONS & BAD BELLS

/Bring me whiskey! Get me a beer!/

The reporter heard it all through the floorboards of his chamber —the King's arrival, the burst of song, the clap hands, the toasts to the child—and he thought of the weary boy, the young father.

/Out there, somewhere/ he whispered to the city lights.

Through his window, a roof buckled under the weight of jumbled machine parts, and the dying bulb of the city pulsed dimly over it. The kid was out there alright, this very night, in that mess of brick and moss and puddle and steel, but the reporter could not find him. Out there in the neon gloom he crept, alive somehow, a yellow miracle in a fallen city. Even as they celebrated the christening of his child, and toasted the lost mother.

The reporter shuffled about in uneasy rhythms. By that dim light from the city he cooked on a camper's hob a dish of beans and rice. Conception as a moment of pure light: hah! He had called upon the flat twice more but no sign, no answer.

/Maybe he is gone/ the reporter said to himself.

He ate without pleasure, his mind tracing alleyways and melancholy canals, searching every yard of high rain for the boy. He would say to him:

/Tell me about the girl/

He would say:

/Tell me how innocent it all was. How you hadn't thought the consequences through. Tell me how it was your first time. Tell me, was it a moment of pure light? Or did your mickey go where your finger found room?/

The boy might plead with him. It was true love of course.

101

They'd been drunk of course. It was not like the dirty stuff on the TeleVisio: no! Laughing, the reporter pulled on his trenchcoat and left to resume the search.

Walking through that high sleety rain, he was overtaken on the quay by a booming steamboat, bound inland. He was in many different places now though: hearing again in his mind the story of the Crooner Bartholomew killing the ladyboy; writing again the story of that woman from a Connacht island who had, it was claimed, given birth to two dogpups. He searched every wall for the sign of the kid in yellow but found only the eye of the King. He eveningdreamed:

/What happened?/ he asked the boy in a derelict hotel lobby of rotting curtains and mildew drippings and soft wood. /When the King found out, what happened?/

The kid threw rubble across his mind, and the rubble hit torn paintings and their canvases burst in damp cracks.

/He came to the Pup&Pendant/ the kid said. /*Bring me whiskey, GET ME A BEER!*... What's that song, Bartholomew? That song I like to hear?

/And Bart upped and started singing: *Hey! Hey, Polly! I wanna know-oh-oh-oh if you'll be my dolly tonight*... In fairness to Crooner Bart, he could belt out a good tune when he wasn't filling the place with his lies and pouring stout down into his belly. Then, for the first time, the Earlie King fixed his eyes on me proper. The first time he looked at me like he knew me. And by fukk he knew me now.

/BOSS! he called to me from close by.

Crooner Bart was there. Mike the Hat was there. Clem. The Eel. Freddi. Francis. Sissy, Ker, Sweeney, I'd seen in the front bar. Almost everyone I knew.

/How's the King? I said. Was quiet, respectful. Bracing for the belt I was. I nearly bowed.

/His small dark eyes came from a ways back in a cave. Were not really in his head. Remember thinking that that was how he won so many fights—how could an opponent know him when they couldn't look him properly in the eyes?

/ Will you take a whiskey, runner?

/ Won't thank you, King

/ Won't? Why not?

/ Am too young for whiskey, King

/ He hit me across the face with the back of his hand and I went sprawling back. Felt like ages before I landed. Walloped my head off the tiles too, and a splitting sound like an alarm started going off.

/ The whole place went quiet. By the use of a chair I reeled and jigged and staggered and tried to get to my feet again. No one came near to help—they knew better—and as I stood I saw the crowd in a lager light and they all sneering at me—my own people, the people I spent my days with.

/ The King was close again without me even tracking him and he grabbed me up against him. Felt blood streaming from don't know where on my face but left it alone.

/ How old are you, runner?

/ Thirteen, King

/ And you don't drink?

/ Shook my head and tried to look him in the eyes.

/ Pharm?

/ No, King

No, King, he mimicked. He wiped back the floppy grey hair onto the top of his head, wet from rain or sweat don't know.

No, King, he mimicked again. Was so close that I could smell oil off his beard. Aye, but your peeder works well enough, doesn't it?

/ And he stooped and grabbed hold of my bells and the breath went out of me. So fierce he held them that I couldn't breathe at all, and all the time he tightened his grip until I was screaming in front of everyone.

/ Didn't seem real—like a bad dream mayhap—but the pain was real. D'you know? Pain so bad spread up all through my knees and up into my stomach.

/You're my family now, he said. All a'cos you used these without thinking

/Tears from my eyes joined the blood I was pumping. Worst of all was that I didn't even try to help myself. So afraid was I that my arms hung limp at my sides and then I folded them and squeezed myself against the pain. Just stood there with him squeezing my bells like they were grapes and me with my arms folded wailing and blowing blood all over his chest and then after some time, don't know how much, there was a pop in my bellsack and I passed out there and then in his hands.

/Runner, you be good now, I heard him say in my dark dreams, and I was coming to again, still on that floor. Was lying in my own blood and my own vomit, and looking up into the light could see him standing over me with my blood all over his vest too.

/I was in the babba's pose on the floor, curled up. The pain was beyond belief, the worst I've ever experienced and worse than ever I believed the worst could be. Was like being pulled apart from the inside. Like a black hole inside. I whimpered and moaned, my pride gone.

/Then the King pulled me by the elbow and dragged me over to the door of the bar. There he left me down again. Said I was banished. Was in too much pain to even straighten/

/And why—how—are you still alive?/ the reporter asked the kid.

/Don't know/ the kid said.

/You should be the youngest. You should be on the ledger/

/What's the ledger?/ the kid asked.

/Will tell you/

The reporter found, as he told the story, that his own boots were scraping the rubble across the bare concrete floor in drab arcs.

/*Haha*/ laughed the kid when he heard. /Are spending your whole life on writing a list that nobody sees!/

The kid's surprisingly deep voice echoed around the lobby.

/Is not a list!/ the reporter cried, kicking rubble across the floor with the toe of his boot. /Is the beginning of literature!/

And then the reporter broke out of his eveningdream into reality.

And he was a dark shadow across which the neon of the market sign slid, and the different music of the market stalls all crossed him at once, drawing him fully from the dream. Calls in so many languages—the Hispanic, the Chinese, the Caribbean, the French, the various Africans, the Irish—the cacophony of rain on the tarpaulins could not drown them out, and they passed their words and their music back and forth, traded like ping-pong shots, and each stall wore its own thick smell of wood or incense or meat or herbal or plastic or lemon or wet hair or fish or curry or old leather or strong brew. The reporter squeezed his way through. Dogs barked from under tables.

He found the Spaniard with the harelip not at her own stall, but at the incense stall. She indicated to him on his arrival to pick up a large plastic container, and as he gathered it up he felt immediately its weight strain on his lower back.

/Come/ she said, beckoning him through the crowd. /Venga, venga!/

Straightening, he groaned. /The incense is making me dizzy/

She barked a husky laugh and waved away a smoky drift of cinnamon and rust.

They stitched themselves through the flow of the throng, through stalls of vegetables, sex toys, skins, herbal—an organised junkyard of everything the country had left to offer. Kumbee music blared and his hat started to come off, knocked by some squawker-joker twirling a finger in his wake. He staggered the last few feet with the container pulling him this way and that, until at last they were at her orange stall.

/Aqui! Aqui!/ she demanded, as he angled down and sideways with the box, which could only have contained pure lead, unbending as he lay it down on cobble, the pain drawing a spasmodic thread right up to his neck.

Recovering, he put a hand on the lid to see what he had been carrying, but she caught his wrist firmly and shook her head at him.

/Cuanto?/ she asked him.

He bought a dozen oranges from her and asked again about the kid in yellow. She had nothing to report.

/What about the midwife? The one your amiga spoke of. For the King?/ he asked. /Where would I find her?/

MISTER VIOLENCE INTERLUDE #1

See him now! Strutting a line between church bells and broadcasted static. Flicking a tail this way and that.

/There are too many people in the world!/ he was fond of shrugging to himself in windows. Scales and hair and teeth and yellowed eyes that cackled with laughter.

The best thing about violence was you never knew where it was coming from next. It was like being tickled as a child. You never knew who was gearing up for the jolly act. It could be VDP burning, or a vicious assault by some thug—of course!—but it could equally be a sweet little old lady coming in from her shopping and kicking the living shit out of her dear old tabby cat, or a toddler pulling a worm into two halves to see what happens next.

/Death is a creative act!/ Mister Violence was fond of reasoning, as he haunted parks and alleys and café windows. Death was change. Was creation in its purest form: destruction.

He was a big supporter of the strikes, though he was not political. He saw Saint Vincent Depaul's side of things, and yet loved the work of the criminals and the clowns in government too. Many the Heavy he stamped with, and panted with. In that way, Mister Violence was love too. Love! Love walking the lanes of night, light and shadow, from the Drome to the Pup&Pendant, from the Croke Park Flats to the Tortoni to Old Temple Bar, and even Sellafield over that watery horizon. Where would he next fall in love?

BIT FROM **THE PLAY**——

A plooping rain can be heard beyond the walls, and at
the start of the scene the HOURLY BELL is ringing.
Every few beats the distorted voice of the intercom
announcer rambles distantly, indecipherable, ignored
by the PERSONS IN THE PLAY. SISSY and KER sit
alone in the lounge at lights up, at the bar counter,
alongside each other, drinking pints of porter, each
man transfixed by the glare of his device.

SISSY.   [vacantly] They were just as they were.
KER.   Clap hands. [coughs a choleric cough,
                reaches blindly for a napkin without
                taking his eyes from his device]
SISSY.   Is giving only 92.46 per cent
                precipitation for the next two days.
                Thinnest and firmest in yonks. A bare
                tremble.
KER.   Is that statue in Dingel. She's come
                to dry us out, as promised. Listen
                to what the sculptor says about
                it. [reading from his device in an
                aristocratic voice] 'Yes, I can confirm
                that both Mary and the serpent are
                hewn from one and the same chunk of
                marble. No tricks. That miracle is
                nothing to do with me...' And here,
                look: 'I did a great trade in Marys at
                that time, but the serpent underfoot
                was not so common back then.'
SISSY.   Wind at twenty-two, not quite
                horizontal.
KER.   And here's another miracle. Taoishuck's
                survived again. The head of the state

	and everyone wanting to take his head off!
SISSY.	[sitting up straight] We'll have to get out for a walk.
KER.	Is the second time he's dodged the auld death. Fire this time.
SISSY.	Might not even take the skins.
KER.	Was his own office this time. Vinny Depaul with a bomb. Four assistants dead.
SISSY.	Nothing wrong with a bit of a wash, once you don't get soaked.
KER.	He's got to be in cahoots with someone.
SISSY.	[folding his arms] Aye, he is.
KER.	Is a wonder he wants the position at all.
SISSY.	If he is in cahoots...
KER.	The ego?
SISSY.	[shrugs] Was a privilege once.
KER.	[sighing, as if he's repeating lines he's spoken a thousand times before] Meant something once.
SISSY.	[with more gusto] It did. Fad-oh. Mayhap the statue is looking after him and all.
KER.	Stoppin the rain and savin Old Taoishuck from a sound burning.

Both men break from conversation to draw from their porter. KER draws the larger portion, and yet is left with more in his pint glass. Both men lapse into their devices again. The pink neon skull pulses gently. Enter JIM CORCORAN, with that same faded blue cloth hanging from his shoulder, and the same thoughtful gait.

SISSY.   [elbows planted on the counter,
                following the movements of CORCORAN]
                What do you think of that statue, Jim?
CORCORAN.   [continuing to sort and wipe
                methodically] I think the bark of the
                raindog makes more sense than that
                shower.

SISSY and KER share a knowing glance.

KER.   [with a grin and an elbow in SISSY's
                side] They say the pubs were finished
                before the rains came to stay.
SISSY.   You wouldn't know us, Jim. Would never
                have heard of us, only for rain. Would
                be out of business.
CORCORAN.   [sighing the words for the thousandth
                time] Rain or not, there always was
                and always will be men like ye.

Enter the EARLIE KING and LEG, swiftly through the
doorway. The KING has already pulled his skins from
his body, on which he wears an off-white vest and
brown leather pantalones, with brown leather boots
that come up to the calf. His hair cascades damply
about his shoulders, in long rain-tended curls. The
faintest beads of rainwater cling to the grey hair
of his shoulders and arms. LEG is dressed in the
more traditional garb of the Earlie Boy: a bright
Kandinskee shirt and white cotton sailor's trousers.
He has a bone nose-piercing and a dark mullet cut
out of his hair. He scratches week-old stubble when he
thinks. A knife sheath hangs loose from his shoulder
to his hip; he makes no effort to conceal it.

THE KING.   Get me whiskey! Bring me a beer!

```
CORCORAN.          Hallo, King, Leg. Are welcome again.
                   [lumbers to the cupboard and pulls out
                   a bottle]


SISSY and KER pack away their devices in their inner
pockets and stand to leave with their drinks.


THE KING.          Hallo, gentlemen.
SISSY.             Hallo.
KER.               Hallo. We'll leave you in peace.


LEG does not even acknowledge them as they pass but
pulls a table out and sits in behind it, raising his
legs wearily to a chair, as if it has been a long day.
The KING walks a lap of the now empty lounge before
collecting the bottle of whiskey CORCORAN has placed
on the bar counter and joining LEG at the table. They
sit beneath the gaze of the neon skull.


LEG.               They were just what they were. Machine
                   tenders. The Elevated, dragged down
                   into the Dark Chamber.
THE KING.          Yes, but still.
LEG.               [reassuringly] They wouldn't have our
                   spirit. Certainly not yours.
THE KING.          [breathing heavily, as if his thoughts
                   have exhausted him, arms folded now,
                   bulging] Spirit? What have I to do with
                   spirit?
LEG.               [taking shelter from the question by
                   pouring from the bottle into two empty
                   glasses] Am only saying.
THE KING.          Old age. Softening. Stupor weighs me
                   down after the hacking I've done this
                   evening. Blind stupor.
LEG.               There are other accountants. You have
```

	nothing to regret...[realising] Indeed, we ought to boast. One less accountant. One less rich man. Will please Vincent Depaul.
THE KING.	[suddenly smiling, resolved] Yes! I suppose the accountant would have hacked me, given half the chance. Though mayhap with his calculator and not his hands. VDP will be happy with us, as you say. Mayhap he'll stop chasing Holloway now.
LEG.	Clap hands. [drinks half of his glass of whiskey]
THE KING.	Clap hands. [drinks, seems content now] Beer now, Jim! [he calls out like a giddy child. He pulls from an ear a hearing aid and adjusts a setting on it] Can you turn up the country song, Jim?

The music grows, the distortion of the intercom and the steady drum of the rain drowned out.

> With shoulders worn, and tired arms
> Barrett works the fish farms
> Evenings lets the flame burn long
> Wondering where it all went wrong
> Oh let that flame burn long, Barrett
> Where'd it all go wrong?
>
> The canals run like mem'ries
> And the calls of all the old shawlies
> His knuckles bleed, his father's seed,
> Wasted like the drowndead trees
> Oh let that flame burn long, Barrett
> Where'd it all go wrong?

CORCORAN arrives with two beers to the table.

> And Barrett works the farms all day
> Sails the river, heave aweigh!
> Smokes his embers down to grey
> Oh let that flame burn long, Barrett
> Where'd it all go wrong?

THE KING.   [calling suddenly, grabbing his head as if struck by headache] Turn it off, Jim! Enough!

LEG.   Not the finest shanty we've ever shared.

THE KING.   Fukken miserable actually.

LEG refills the whiskey glasses, pulls a beer pint towards him and pushes the other towards the KING.

THE KING.   I am worn out, Leg. Lately, I am worn out. [draws from the pint, does not like the taste]

LEG.   Whereby you don't mind my saying, but you have not been the same since your daughter passed. And her child left to you as a reminder. The christening was joyous, but... You don't seem right...

THE KING.   The truth is so.

LEG.   Which is natural. [turns to speak to the KING confidentially, sincerely] Need to give yourself time to grieve, King. Take some time away. Myself and Bart can manage the business a while. Is Mike too, if needed.

THE KING.   [regarding the neon skull curiously, almost to himself] A rogue element.

LEG.	[nods, shrugs] Unpredictable, but loyal...[persistently] A terrible thing has happened you and you have not balanced it with vengeance—
THE KING.	[awakened from thought and turning to LEG] —a promise to blood...even if she was a Jezebel...is a sacred promise. I have never broken a promise to blood. [falls to regarding the neon skull with curiosity again, as if it is communicating with him secretly]
LEG.	[staring after the skull now too, unsure of himself] Yes, and so. Clap hands... You have never left Ireland... Take your wife on a holiday. We will keep the ship steady.
THE KING.	I have never left Ireland, never will. [addressing the skull now] An Irishman commanded the world into magic at Iona, and he needed a devil. And who was his devil?
LEG.	You were, King.
THE KING.	I was... But I am tired now. For the first time in my life I feel like I lack control.
LEG.	Nonsense, King! [suddenly ashamed, dips head] Sorry. But we have complete control. Doll nor bag of F nor stray organ nor wild fish passes through these waters without our knowing it and taking a cut. A Heavy won't dare disturb our work. We...you...have control. Are unopposed.
THE KING.	Yes, but. [trancelike, he gazes now at the skull and trails off]

Long moments pass, marked by drum of the rain, the
distracted intercom rambling, the hum of bar talk
from the other room.

THE KING.   [inhaling sharply] I need ... energy ...
life! [darts a glance at Leg] What is
it you think happens when you die,
comrade?

LEG.   [crossing his ankle at his knee,
considering, scratching week-old
stubble] They say there is an
underground river. Collects you,
takes you some other place.

THE KING.   We've sent enough men there.

LEG.   Clap hands, we have. They say it is all
a dream, this life.

THE KING.   And I am the monster.

LEG.   The monster?

THE KING.   In the dream. I am the monster in the
dream.

LEG.   If you say so, King ... [nervously,
awkwardly] Another beer? Have some
thirst on me this evening, after all
our hacking work!

THE KING.   Show me your weapon, Leg.

LEG.   [looks at his knife sheath] My weapon?

The KING nods and smiles. He has put out his hand
to receive it. LEG, confused, offers the KING the
handle of the blade. The KING takes it and, calmly,
and with precision, draws two strokes, one from LEG's
groin and one from his throat. LEG leans forward,
surprised, as if about to throw up, blood spilling
from his hands as he places each one against a wound.

THE KING.   [folding his arms and leaning back] You

                    must watch for the rogue wave, Leg.
                    You have been a great servant to me,
                    I thank thee...But you must watch for
                    the rogue wave as you cast. [standing]
                    Some plastic, Jim!

LEG slumps forward in his seat and rests. CORCORAN
appears at the counter and, seeing the situation,
dips to pull out a folded sheet of plastic from some
concealed shelf. He says nothing, but hands the sheet
to the KING when the KING approaches.

THE KING.   Apologies, Jim. A rare moment of
                 weakness. A momentary lapse, now
                 forgotten. An accident...but not an
                 accident, if you know my meaning.
CORCORAN.   Forgotten, King, as you say. Should I
                 call the boys?
THE KING.   [looking up at the skull again] Do you
                 remember who's skull that is, Jim?
CORCORAN.   It is MacDowd's skull.
THE KING.   Good man, Jim. I'll clean up myself.
                 [stops] Hey, Jim.
CORCORAN.   Yes, King?
THE KING.   [pointing to the body at his feet] I've
                 got a dead leg! [bursts into hearty,
                 phlegmy laughter]

Lights flicker out and darkness grows gradually. Very
soon, only the pink neon glow of the skull remains,
pulsing in the darkness.

                    CURTAIN.

                        118

BIT CALLED

RUBY

A sequence of spaces punctuated a partitioned hallway, the mahogany counter a vague constant through thick smoke. At a circular table a game of 45s was underway between six hunched silhouettes; otherwise there were only the murmurs of damaged couples and deadbeats and nightcrawlers and the distant, constant flushing of an upstairs toilet, which itself caused the regular cough, splutter and gurgle of pipework behind the wood-panelled walls.

His quarry drank Vermouth from a long glass, long legs curtained by a tartan skirt, legs pulled out to one side at the bar, her hip angled against the smokegreased mahogany. She wore a battered floppy hat; she had long feet and thin bare forearms that seemed to bend over each other like bows when she crossed them. She was an uncouth woman: when she laughed at his insults towards the barkeep, bonewhite teeth were unleashed upon the moons of bar light.

Between sips of her drink the midwife hummed lines of something; once or twice the reporter tried to finish the lines in his own poor songvoice, but that tactic did not please her. She cackled at her own jokes, and he noticed, turning his own glass nearby, that she leaned on objects—like the bar counter or the stool back—as if for their emotional support. She near collapsed herself upon them. The way she sat, turned away from everything and everybody, her back arched. The way she allowed spilled Vermouth to soak into the flattened palm of her hand … Her fingernails were painted silver; her eyes in the greasy bar mirror were silver.

/Madam?/ he asked when she went to her purse a fifth, sixth or seventh time. /May I purchase for you a Vermouth?/

He noticed everything: the knees falling slightly apart as she turned to respond to him through the smoke of her cigarillo; the blind bony fingers finding the zip of the handbag; the quick quiver across her shoulders at the formality of his tone, or the sound of his voice mayhap. He slid to the stool next to hers.

/Don't look now/ he confided, /but there's a couple breaking up at a table to my four o'clock. And did you ever notice how, when two people are breaking up, they never look at each other. They always focus on other objects. Bottles, vases, glasses, whatever... Isn't that strange?/

Δ

Hours later the two of them staggered across the rain with a sense of duty. Her chambers were not far. He hung back like a begging raindog as she keyed the code and he followed her up the stairs then, the two of them dripping rainwater from their overgarments.

/Have rarely seen such elegance in a room/ he said, running his hand across the ruby velvet sofa and then to the curtains, also of ruby velvet. There were, he noted, no windows; it was a curtained wall; it smelled musty, both alive and dying.

/Will you be recording me?/ she smirked as she fiddled with a radio knob on the low coffee table. Her fingers seemed too long to roll comfortably across a clean frequency. Her body seemed to be interfering with the reception.

/Is a modest place/ he noted, /but furnished with an old-world class/

/Thought you wanted to interview me?/

Finally, accordion music from one of the pirate stations out on the marshes drifted across the room to him. He hated Vermouth: it gave him the headachy drunkenness.

/No need to record. Have perfect recall/

/Is that right?/

/Have never forgotten a single word said to me/

/Come and sit here on the sofa while I pour us another gargle/

Ruby carpet, ruby sofa, ruby curtains; he felt as if the smoke from the bar had followed them home and loafed now about the ruby room. Was settling down like it lived there too. He turned on the main light and it hurt his eyes.

/Am not in the habit of drinking Vermouth/ he called to her where she moved about beyond the room. /Have you anything else?/

/But you said that you always drank it/ she called back.

He settled onto the sofa and the vacuum in which springs had once resisted sucked him deep. His arms pulled at the arms of the sofa to keep him afloat. The folds of accordion music rolled across the smoke.

He must have fallen asleep briefly then because the next thing he knew she was prodding him with a foggy, scarred plastic tumbler of the vile stuff. He took the tumbler in one hand as with the other he pulled himself out of the depths of the ruby sofa.

The main light was off. A standing corner lamp—tall, hunched over like herself—cast light across the tract of vague ruby. The room at once appeared vast and completely unnecessary, like a desert.

/Thought for a while you really did want to interview me/

/Do!/

/Yes, yes of course you do/

She was draped across him, her knees cutting across the top of his lap, knobbly, hard, pressing into him. He realised that his peeder was softening even as his thumb tested the hard flat of her stockinged kneecap.

Her head fell back. He worked one free hand, the other he wedged behind the lump muscle of her shoulder. They did not even kiss; their seachoppy movements interfered with the radio signal and the accordion was lost to static; his eyes hurt in the light; he wondered where he'd placed the tumbler; she was rough with him; she brought him back; she towered over him, blocking out the lamplight.

They fell back. Caught their breath.

She smoked, and wiped his seed into his own pantalones. He didn't complain. The light bulb flickered out and she started to cackle again in the darkness, as if they were the butt of some joke.

Later, he asked her, /What is the weirdest birth you were ever dealt then?/

It was as easy as that to get her talking about the daughter of the King, and she spoke without fear of retribution, as people often do late at night. /Keep it to yourself/ was all she said by way of warning.

The pregnancy had in fact lasted twelve months. /You hear about these freak pregnancies now and then. You expect the child to be born with teeth, or gills. You expect them to be huge. This wasn't really the case. But the mothers rarely survive anyway. I knew this one wouldn't survive. Though I didn't tell *him* that.

/Did not really deal with him actually. Dealt mostly with the mother, and she did not even speak to me. She gave her orders in nods, shakes of the head, device messages. Or she told the girl herself, who told me ... That girl was a brave one though/

The silhouette of the midwife's head shook in the dark.

/She did all the talking. Was such a small little thing. Am no fool, I know girls her age have babbies all the time now. But fair play to her. She asked me all the right questions. She ate well. She spoke well. She didn't feel guilty or ashamed or anything.

/I would be picked up by the one they call the Eel. He would collect me here, blindfold me, take me out there. He was a poor lover, if I'm honest. Oh, you know nothing bucko! But he was never rough with me. Not rough enough. Every time they took the blindfold off me I was in this bright blue room. Had one of those light fixings that mimicked the sun, running on a track from one corner of the ceiling to the other as the day passed. Was gorgeous sunlight, just how I imagine it used to be.

/She directed the whole thing, that girl. Was only fourteen, you know? Had them do the place up like that. She did everything, and she kept her spirits up in the worst of times. Don't know whether they treated her poorly or not. Twelve months!

There's no manual for that, you know. But she knew. She knew alright. *My baby is special,* she said.

/She liked to read a lot, but less and less could she read. The looks of distress towards the end were horrible. She tried to hide the pain and the fear. Was as if she was being eaten alive by the thing inside her. Her belly skin looked as if it were about to burst. She was not the vessel for that babba, and it is God's curse that she wasn't allowed to live to be the fine mammy she would have been. You know she did not cry for her daddy or mammy once?/

He saw only the glowing red rock of the stick of herbal she had lit. He had not put his peeder away even, and it lay shrivelled and empty by her rough hand.

/What about the father?/ he asked, begging a toke. /Did you ever see him?/

/Did not. Was a boy her own age, from the Flats/

/Think I know him. Is a runner for them/

/Was/

/Tell me/

/Tis little I know really. He was never spoken of. She did it alone, all of it/

The spark flared. She exhaled a grey stream into the dark and he heard fluid on her chest.

/She did mention him once. Some comment I made, some throwaway thing that annoyed her. She said, *Don't make what happened between me and him dirty. Was not. I love him. His child will be with him, I know that.*

/Well, I didn't know what to say. I apologised and she huffed and tutted and said it was fine. That was the only time I ever heard about him/

/Don't know how he wasn't killed/

/Clap hands/

/But he wasn't/

/Wasn't/

/Why?/

/Don't know/ Already the midwife's face was changing in his

memory and the darkness. She could've been a mother herself, but she had said there were no children.

/Am compiling a ledger you know, of all the men and women they've ever murdered/

/Good for you/

He sighed. Pins and needles swarmed along his arm. /I should go/

She cackled gently then. /Was that my interview?/

/Go to sleep, guapa/

He rose stiffly from the couch, freeing himself from her.

He realised she was weeping.

/Am sorry/ he said to the glowing tip. /No, I *like* you/

/Is not fukken you/ she sobbed to a finish. /Ya dope! Is that sweet girl. She never met the baby she carried .../

/Am sorry/ He fumbled for his hat and trenchcoat at the metre-drain hooks.

/Have to let you out of the building/ she sighed, and he heard her get up to follow his silhouette.

His boots swept through pools of groundwater, down the pavement under a row of sentinel streetlamps that flickered and twitched the course of his footfall. He was bone-tired, and felt certain now that he would never find the boy alive. He needed a proper drink.

BIT CALLED

BACK TO THE CINDER PATH

/You want a coke?/ he had asked T once.

/Would murder one/ she'd said. /And would you get a gin in it too?/

/Are too young!/

/Go on!/

/But will be killed for getting you drink/

/Fella, you're dead anyway if anybody finds out about us now/

That was the night.

Δ

The kid in yellow slept even less now. He walked the city streets with Honest John to aid his thinking. He told the pony about T for the umpteenth time. He showed the pony pictures from his device: of T sitting in a window; of T smiling in the Financial District, by a traffic light in the rain; pictures she sent of her belly growing. He read to Honest John the messages from her he still had. The pony didn't care, but quivered and swished to warn off the flies. They forgave each other their differences, the kid and the pony.

He met Sweeney at the Jolly Bridge, he who sang to the flame and rambled of his dreaming, and complained about his work at the fish farm, and was heard to say he would drink Ireland out of existence.

And to ease his mood the kid chimed to the drunken mystic:

/A mermaid jumped a swimming lad
Picked him to the bone.

Lashed her body to his knobby,
And screaming dragged him down.
Forgot he in his happiness
That lovers too can drown/

/Dirty!/ Sweeney laughed. /Go home, moc/

/Tell me again of the salmon of old and old factory memory?/

/A great fish/ Sweeney lamented, snapping the flame on his
lighter. /Mighty, wise. Travelled long ways/

/Is sad to think of them now, fenced in/

/It is/

/Will we free them?/

/Will we what! People need freeing before the fish. Give me
some more poetry, moc. If you're going loco you might as well
phrase it nice/

The King's voice echoed in the kid's mind: /There's a lot of
fellows around saying, *Am the King of the Gypsies. Am the King
of the Townies. Have the best dog, the best house.* But these fellows
are fighting with their mouths, and with the things they persuade
folk to tell about them/

Was it the Pup&Pendant? With Earlie Boys drooling, respectful; him with the runners listening in from the fringes of the
lounge?

/But very few fight proper/ came the echo. /With their whole
selves. I fight with my hands, my eyes, my stomach, my teeth, my
voice, my heart, my memory. I'll fight any man in the world and
because I fight with everything I'll never lose/

The kid sang a little sea shanty for Sweeney then, about roses
red, and chasing whales around Cape Horn. He was in great form
again after that.

/Would you have liked to go to sea?/ he asked Sweeney.

/Might yet. You never know what's coming next/

On the café radio they listened to a special programme about
the statue of the Virgin that had spoken. The statue was in the tiny
citadel of Dingel, a mystical place everyone said, and the statue

had turned to a teenage girl walking home from factory work and told the girl that the rain would end and that God would return. Already people were flocking to see the statue, and the radio voices were talking about whether the rains would end.

/We've been through these false prophecies before/ one voice said.

/But the start of the rain was prophesied/ came an answer. /Why would the end of it not be prophesied?/

The idea of the Virgin giving birth confused him, and brought him back to the mystery, and gave him pain. But the kid had his own things to be doing.

/Fukk the statue and fukk the prophesy/ he laughed.

And when he said goodbye to Sweeney the older man looked at him like he was mad.

Δ

He went back to the flat. The brother was asleep on the couch, still in his skins. There was water everywhere, a smell of piss.

/Fukk's sake/ he said to the brother. /Haven't you your own room to soak?/

The brother only turned on the couch. /Some fella has been calling for you/

/Sweeney?/

/No. Fella in a hat/

And back into the herbal daze.

The kid went into the brother's room to kip but the bed was putrid. Damp, mouldy. And so he lay his own yellow plastics out on the floor in the hallway and curled up into a ball. He would only need three or four hours.

He dreamed of a café that was closed. Was a big dark café with a terracotta floor and long rows of shelves down the middle, separating the tables. Each row of shelves reached to the ceiling and each shelf was adorned with big glass jars, and in each glass jar was a light bulb that was lit. So it was a very beautiful light in the room, and outside the windows it was pitch-black. But it was not raining. And it was not *not raining*. And who was there in the café with him but the Earlie King, and they sat at the same table and both had cold coffee. They were friends, the King and the kid. There was no badness or fear.

/Can I tell you a secret?/ the King said.

/Can/

/I'd like to put out each one of these light bulbs, until it would be dark/

/Why?/

/Don't know why/

The King shrugged. Seemed ashamed or amused, the kid could not tell.

/Don't like them either/ the kid lied.

/Can we so?/

/Better not/

And he woke up to the sound of rain, and the hourly bell, and left the flat for the last time.

Δ

He looked for Crooner Bart in the covered markets first. Everybody leaned into each other and squeezed past each other as deals were made. The songs of different countries blared from stall to stall, and the rain on top of it all made a great and many-layered sound. He let the crowd carry him through the many smells and looked to see could he spot the Bard on his rounds. Men the kid saw with all gold teeth, and cat's eyes, and ladies dressing from head to toe in fluffy cotton, with great big umbrellas under their sheep's arms, and ladymen in all sorts of rigs too. No sign though of Crooner Bart.

The Mon O' War he tried next, but they said the Bard'd already collected and moved on. Spic Norbuck was polishing glasses and said that the Bard was in very good form.

It was only spitting that morning, and there was a brightness behind it. Cause for optimism. He was the last on a busy river micro and went three quays along to the place where there were three pubs in one square block. Off the waterfront side there was the Pup&Pendant, and around the corner, one below and one above, were the Standard Sanchez and the Rose Red. On a Thursday Bart was known to visit all three on the earlie, mixing business with pleasure, and as the kid in yellow looked northeast upon the Croke Park Flats, streaming in the far distance, he knew well that he would find his man, and that there would be no turning back.

Δ

Found Bart he did, in the Rose Red. Above the door were painted bright-red petals but inside it was a dark place, thorny. The first time the kid had been there—Mike the Hat brought him and Clem on a jolly one evening—they had seen two men drinking with each other in silence. The men bought each other rounds but never spoke. One of them wore cowboy boots; he had long hair and never took his brown skins off the whole time. The other had hung his skins by the door and was stripped down to jeans, sandals and a vest. They drank the same rum, the same way. They smoked in turn and, eventually, after about two hours drinking together, they stood up at almost the same time and went for each other. Blood sprayed across the polished timber of the place.

/Off they go/ Mike had said.

The kid remembered those words as songlike, but the Hat had a very sing-song style about him.

On this morning, he stalked down the back to the karaoke section and when the Crooner saw him coming he looked away as if he hadn't seen. Sitting at the back bar he was, by the karaoke booths, alone, and the kid sat down along from him.

Bart leaned away, stroked his goatee.

/Barty, how are you?/

/What do you want?/ he said, watching the other punters. Taking names, clocking witnesses.

/Need a favour, Barty/

/A favour? Are lucky to be alive you traitor cunt. Are lucky I don't cut you right now/

133

His anger was for show: he was interested was what. Nervous but interested.

/Is grade in it for you/ the kid said. /Bart, I always respected you, and now I need to ask something. And I'll pay for it, like anyone else/

/.../

/We always got on. You were like an uncle to me/

Truly, the kid hated the Earlie Boy. But now the other did look at him. The other sat back, breathing hard over a heavy body, and had a good look at the kid through his specs. There was no friendship or goodness in his eyes, but plenty of curiosity.

/Into the music box/ he said, and he squeezed out from the stool and went panting into the second karaoke booth.

The booths had upholstered benches all round, and the sound-proofing meant the punters in the pub could see the occupants through the Perspex but could not hear any singing. The kid went into the booth first, and waited while on the touchscreen the Bard picked an ancient trance beat. Then they took up opposite benches and forgot the crowd beyond, and leaned in close, elbows on their knees, the only way one could hear the other over the blare.

/Fukk you want?/ the Bard said.

/Some F/ the kid said.

Bart smiled. /You're a fiend now, is it?/

/For a party/

/Lying nappy... How much?/

/A full bag/

/A full bag! Is a party or a funeral you're organising?/

The kid in yellow did not answer.

Bart spat on the floor and zoned in to the music awhile. This was his way; the kid waited.

The music boomed so loud he felt it in his lungs.

/Will cost you/

/Can pay/

/A hundred and ninety will be the price. Am adding tax for what you done on the King—if you don't like that, go fukk yourself/

/One-ninety is fine/

They made the arrangement, and when the kid got up to leave Bart caught him by the collar and pulled him close. Even this earlie in the day his breath smelled like vomit.

/Now/ he said. /King probably wants you dead anyway, and I don't know why he won't let us kill you, but swear to God if you tell anyone you got this from me I will cut your bells off before I kill your brother, your fucking pony, and lastly you. Fair enough?/

/Understood/ the kid said.

This time the threat was not put on. The kid had seen Bart kill as many animals as he had sunk pints. One time he shot rats coming out of a drain one after the other the whole night long. The kid had seen him with women, trans, kids…all sorts of violence.

/You made the big mistake/ he suddenly bellowed. /Anybody but the boss's daughter!/

So suddenly bright in the face was he: /And everyone liked you too!/

The kid turned to leave the booth. /Only hope that one day I can right the wrong I done/

/Never!/ the Bard giggled. /No way ever/

The kid pulled open the door and left Bart bopping along with his song.

Δ

He had a couple of hours to kill and he didn't mind that. After collecting Honest John, straight inland he walked with his pony along the canal, and for a while it was all housing estates and back alleys, and then it was industrial yards that never slept, all connected by rusty light-rail tracks and lakes of steaming water that ran off all ways. No matter the hour of the night or day, a yard light was always on somewhere along here, shady deals being done, hush-hush couples doing the juicy in dry dens. The Earlie King and his boys weren't the only ones with secrets in that city. Mayhap—the kid thought—deep down in the oily sewers beneath the city's gas caverns and leaky repositories, there were things far more secret than what we thought we knew. He'd heard talk once of cloned ones shipped out as slaves, and many dead before they reached their Asian and South American destinations. There was so much in the world that was mysterious, all of it held just beyond the rain, or piped just beneath the city's surfaces.

It was raining down hammers, and that suited the kid's plans fine because it meant the tide would be good and high and fast. After the yards there came a tall ditch of jungle briars, and behind that was a set of proper train tracks. Those rails went all the way to the west of the country, and the squalor and the marshlands there amidst the islands of Connacht.

Old red-brick walls had somehow survived along that path, just a couple of feet high.

/The men who built them lived in a different world, John/ he told the pony. /Would've been good at building walls, I would. Would've built walls up and down the country all day long. Come home at night to my girl and my babba and you. Everybody fed and dry. Would've had money for proper outings, to faraway places/

He had been on an outing only once, to the town of Mullingar, as a boy with his parents. He did not remember his brother being there. They were to see a circus his father had become obsessed with, because a performer in the circus claimed to be able to make gold out of gull feathers. It was rumoured that the performer did the trick in plain sight of the crowd, and distributed true gold to the front row once the trick was achieved. Of course that man with his mother wasn't his father, but a nameless man friend of his mother's, and they did not get into the circus—they forgot all about it after an incident—and the kid remembered being dragged along a pavement and seeing only a poster of some elephants with painted toenails, and all the elephants seemed to have big wet fearful eyes. He stopped on the canal and Honest John stopped a pace ahead. He pulled his spray from his skins and made her sign on the red brick. Uncertainty was trying to creep in but he would not let it.

Bald cypresses and drab willows: all wept when the kid came to say goodbye to his pony.

/Can take you no further/ he tried to explain, in a hill field where he hoped a kindly person would stumble upon the animal. /Is too dangerous/

Rain beaded the ditches, and a network of waterlogged estates spread out below. He hid his tears in views of oxbow lakes and mangrove copses and a sagging wetland dump.

/Are the best, John. The best…/

John followed him back to the edge of the field as if nothing was changing, and simply stood there watching when the kid locked the gate, separating them forever.

/Am sorry/ the kid wept, turning his face away, clenching his two fists.

Honest John went to eat at some tufts. The kid pulled his hood up and trudged on.

Λ

He caught an Ardaithe back into the town. The city intercom blared through the carriage, and between the distortion it seemed to be talking about the statue in Dingel that said no more rain, and about the attempted burning of the Taoiseach. But it was no use. He was thinking of the task at hand. He did not feel ready. He'd said goodbye to his pony but not to his brother. As they came back into the city, the bad bell was ringing the hour of four.

On Garrigues Dock, with the sky dark, the rain smacked down onto the boardwalk, assaulting the old wood relentlessly. Hardly anyone was out, but a ways down from him was a big lumpy pile of plastic on the bench, which was a homeless too drunk or blissed to move. The boats were moving through, steady as always. He watched them from inside his hood, through sheets of rain, each cutting a path, smoke and diesel smell and beams of light marking its way, and they all sounding horns to each other.

The disembodied intercom voice crackled over the city, persisting, the voice of a madman talking to himself as a city full of mad people walked around talking to *them*selves.

He did not hear the cycle coming, so lost was he in the rhythm of the rain and the traffic and the intercom. In his ruined silver skins, Clem leaned the red-yellow Xer against the bench and sat down next to the kid.

/Me lad/ the kid said over the rains.

/Me lad/ Clem said.

They did not look at each other but watched the boats.

/What's all this about you wanting a full bag?/

/Ah, Clem, don't worry about me. Is for a pal/

/You have no pals any more, so don't spin me that yarn/

The kid put his hands out and felt the rain. /Okay, is to get the brother out of a spot of bother he's in. Am not taking it I promise/

/Up to you what you do. Truth is, if you're taking it there's people who don't mind/

/Is that for true?/

/Is. Not me. Am for you even if I'm not allowed be. But don't go against the King, don't try and do business yourself. Promise you will be killed then/

/Like so many others/

/Don't, lad/

/Let's talk about something else/

/Like what?/

/How's your mother and father?/

/Same as always/

/Will you tell them I said well/

/.../

/.../

/... Lizzy's up the pole/

The kid laughed. /Up ya boyo!/

/Is not funny!/

/You'll be an uncle!/

/.../

/Good for her. What's his name?/

/Is a dandy. Name is Oliver and I ought to cut him/

/Arra now/

And then a couple of silhouettes whizzed by on mountain cycles and the boys looked to see who they were.

/Better get this done/ Clem said. /Is a flap in my sleeve elbow here. Take the bag and put the grade in it/

The kid did so, then waited for Clem to pull the money into his skins and count it where it was safe.

/Clap hands/ Clem said.

/Tell me before you go/ the kid asked.

/Tell you what?/

/How is the work?/

/Is grand. Busy as ever. I run all the time now, nearly always for him/

/Are my replacement then … Is he still putting on the whole show from the greenhouse?/

The kid could not see Clem because his eyes were on the water, but he heard the plastic shiver of his friend turning to look at him. /Why you asking?/

/Just miss it is all. Am just wondering/

Eventually: /That place scares the shit out of me. He goes out to town less and less now. Too many enemies I suppose. Is going mad I think. Am always getting summoned to that fukken greenhouse/

/He ever mention me?/

/Never/

/You ever see my babba?/

/Never. Forget about her, me lad/

The rustle of skins again was Clem getting up, and now he faced the kid and put out a hand that the kid shook.

/And don't do anything stupid with that/

/Won't. Take care of yourself and Lizzy and that new babba and your ma and da/

/Will/

/Peace out, river trout/
/Over and out/

Δ

He came to the flooded NO-GO zone on the north side of the river. It was said the water was contaminated, and the slick air, and you had to row across vast networks of submerged suburbs to get to the hill of derelict houses where the King had made his real home.

His thoughts lost in the white noise of fear, the kid wore silver skins, bought to mimic Clem, and took the runners' boat from the same hide as always, in the dense rainforest of ferns and bald cypresses and paperbark trees on the south side of the Kilbarra Basin. A vile wind swept across the shivering grey, carrying drenched sandpipers off to Suriname, and as he rowed with care he traced the remembered path through the wide-lilies. Beneath him, he felt the ghosts of the suburbs, and saw, poking up here and there, the chimneys of two-storey houses. Calm, well-ordered streets he had seen on the TeleVisio archive, people moving in droves as they commuted to work under umbrellas, and boys playing football on wide greens, in sunlight, and skateboards tracking the smooth tarmac, and cars reversing into spots, and crows picking over the carcasses of shiny crisp packets that danced up and down the road. All drowndead now, by time and sea and rain.

Parts of the east and west side of the Basin were hilled and some large houses had survived the flooding. Rampant flora now gorged on them. On a terraced hill, the King had ignored the health warnings and rebuilt a walled property surrounded by a marshy mire. Watched by a few edgy salamanders, the silvery kid came to the place the way of a runner or an Earlie Boy, up through the mire from the lonely mooring platform to the back wall. The way was secret: down a short alley of ferns and into a trench which was a shallow creek under a ditch. There were a few such creeks running down from the top of the hill, they kept water from running through the King's garden. You got into the back garden by typing a code into a keypad on the huge brick wall. The small iron door clicked and the kid went through without pausing.

Δ

The cinder path ran up through the long grass to the greenhouse and to the back door. It was on the cinder path he'd first seen T.

What would you say is the best story you ever heard?

Dunno. Probably the best one hasn't been told yet.

Can't wait to tell my babba stories at bed-time.

Will be a grand mammy.

Stop!

Δ

He crouched for a while in that same long grass. The lights at the back of the house were out and the structure loomed over him. The jademossy and wide steamy windows of the greenhouse were filled by strange plants with big colourful heads and stalks like arms. The grass sighed over his head, and he heard the achy bending of the yew trees in the margins. Water ran all over him. It was dark. He was outside the scope of the perimeter light yet.

The King was a mysterious man, but the kid knew also that he was a man of routine. Evenings after dinner, he tended his orchids in the greenhouse. He always had a big glass of milk after he started, to wash his dinner down. He listened to no music, no radio, but smoked tobacco and quietly tended. It was thinking time. Many orchids died on him but he did not mind death.

Out he came now, out to the greenhouse, pulling the back door behind him and triggering the perimeter light. The kid moved right alongside the greenhouse, keeping low in the grass. In that light he flickered like an upriver salmon amongst the reeds.

The King moved about inside the greenhouse, a blur of grey-white beard and shoulder. The kid's heart—hidden inside him where he crouched beneath a slab of upturned pots and bags of compost—was pounding so much that he thought the King might hear it through the glass. Some said he was the seventh son of a seventh son, and had strange senses because of that. Some said he came from nowhere to rule all evil people in Ireland. The kid was going to do something this night that condemned one of them forever.

Rain rolled down the roof and cascaded over him. There was a rusty barrel to the side of the greenhouse door—he got as far as that, and stopped again and crouched.

The Guin blimp came overhead on its way to the city, making big noise and lighting the garden and the rain like a searchlight. The yews bent back, cowering. These felt like the last things he would ever see. He felt the bag of Fadinhead come into his hand.

Δ

The King's routine was to brew a cup of hot milk and bring it to the greenhouse with him. He would emerge from the back door, enter the greenhouse, put the milk down next to his pipe. He would leave it there to cool, then set up his utensils—clippers, gloves, a number of sprays. When he had everything kitted out and ready he would go back into the house for five minutes, always under some pretence. Perhaps there was some utensil he had to collect; perhaps it was to seem unpredictable, or to show the family that he wasn't so far away; perhaps it was a routine of the bowels or bladder. How did the kid know this? From running? Or had she imparted this routine to him, long long before he'd need it? Or was T, his beloved, giving him what he needed even now, from some other place? Did he even know himself how he knew this stuff? Well, all that mattered was that it was the plan, and the plan was working.

Because the kid heard him moving about, heard him coming back to the counter inside the door, and heard the light thud and soft scrape of his hand tools landing, of instruments being dragged.

And then a pause.

And then the door of the greenhouse clattering open.

And then the ratchet and close of the back door.

From his huddled corner the kid saw only a glimpse of the daemon turning on the kitchen light.

The kid had pulled off his skins and stuffed them behind the barrel. He took his chance.

Δ

The light hurt his eyes. It took long seconds to get his bearings.

Already he had taken too long.

He was dizzy; he couldn't see anything.

His whole head ached with the light.

But then formed out of the light's glare the mug of steaming milk, and he brought forth the bag of Fadinhead and was not scared any more. He emptied the whole thing into the mug. As he emptied he stirred with his finger and scalded his finger. He stirred for as long as he could before he would slip back out to the garden.

Then he heard the ratchet and swing of the back door. It was too late.

He turned towards the back of the greenhouse.

Fled to the end, orchids glaring at the rush of him.

Δ

Under a long table at the far end he hid, behind pots that had long thick stalks coming out of them. Through the stalks he could see the colourworn cotton trousers of the King and the tail end of an untucked shirt. How did the kid feel? Did he pray that it was a dream, or any other thing?

This vision of the King's legs stationed itself at the counter by the door for a long time. The kid could only watch through the stalks and the leaves as the King came up the aisle halfway, and then turned and went back towards the door. The way he turned, the swivel, it was almost like he danced.

There came the sounds of work then, tools picked up and put down. Was that the blunt stamp of the pint glass on wood? The kid hunkered down low. He would either live or die now, he could do nothing about it. His bowels quivered.

/I knew it was not Clem/ the King suddenly called out. /You do not move like Clem/

/.../

/Maybe because you do not have his bad habits with the pharm/

/.../

/Are you going to come out, runner, or am I going to have to come and get you?/

/.../

/Will come out/ the kid said then.

/Watch the plants coming out/ the King said.

The kid crawled out and waited where the King could see him at the end of the aisle. The way the King stood side-on, spraying, the kid could not see the milk.

The King half-turned, looked out of the corner of his eye, from deep in his head. The way his lips pressed, turned down at the corners—he was holding down fierce anger.

/I wondered whether you would come ... And I thought lately that you would not/

/Am here/ the kid answered. /Am taking our babba away with me/

/Who is *our*?/

/Me and T/

The King continued to spray the leaves of a plant. He had thick plastic gloves on. The rain beat down on the greenhouse roof.

/The promise I made her/ the King said, /was that I would not kill you or have you killed once you never showed yourself to me again. That promise is null and void now/

/The promise I made her/ the kid answered, /was that I would come and take the babba away from you, and give her a life of good and not bad/

The King laughed and small teeth shone in the glare of the light. It was a warbled laugh, distorted by anger. /You knew I would not allow you to take the child, so how did you reck you would come? Have you a weapon?/

/Have no weapon/ the kid answered. He glared at the King now.

/You have not/ the King concluded. He put down the sprayer and rolled up his sleeves. He seemed to be looking at his reflection in the dark glass, or listening to the thrashing rain beyond. Did he too see Mister Violence out there? In his own reflection even, waiting giddily?

/And do you know what will happen to you now?/ he asked, turning finally to give the kid his full face.

/You will kill me/

/I will ... Are you afraid?/

/No/

He sauntered towards the kid, who stood on the spot. The King gulped, and he stroked his beard as if it were a comfort to him.

/Am not afraid/ the kid answered, /because I know/

/What do you know?/

/Know that you will die too/

/We all die/ the King agreed. /But I'll die a long time from now, and you'll die tonight/

And then the kid recited:

/To enter the ring with the storm, to grapple and clinch,
To enter the jaws of the shipwreck and never flinch,
Over me comes a mist, the moon muffles her light,
The lamp goes dark. The air goes damp. RED BEAMS FLASH!/

With a tilt of the head, the King stopped to consider his quarry. Faltered for the first time.

/Face your death honourably, runner. Don't spoil things with lines you don't understand/

/Over you is coming a mist/ the boy said. /Your strength is leaving you. Life is slipping out of you as we speak here. Oh, look at the empty glass!/

The King turned to observe the milkcloudy glass on the counter, all but empty, the rime of some powdery residue within it.

/That glass of milk you have drank in full—in it was a bag of Fadinhead. A whole bag! Which would kill a horse, as you know/

The King caught his breath. /I am no horse, runner/

The King walked towards the kid and the kid retreated. They circled the island of plants in the middle of the greenhouse, but the King's steps were now full of doubt.

/You will die, certainly/ the kid said.

The King eyed him like a suspicious child, then fell to his knees. His wide eyes rolled up to the milk glass, all rimmed with the milk froth.

/Your time has come/ the kid said. /You will very soon be the late king!/

The kid laughed, though it was a put-on laughter, that of a boy in a schoolyard.

/You hear me?/ the kid said.

/I am going to stop you talking now/ the King groaned, putting his hand out like a blind man, pulling himself up.

He stumbled forward.

With that amount of F he would be hearing the rain hammering all round on the glass of the greenhouse. He would be hearing his own heart pounding.

The kid stepped back—keeping his distance—and spoke louder as he looked down at the King:

/Your time has come. The reign of the Earlie King is over. Am taking my daughter and you cannot stop me/

The King laid his head on the panelled wood of the floor, as if the words were undoing him. He seemed suddenly drained of colour.

A beam of light from the Guin blimp strobed the greenhouse as it turned. Sweat came down off the King in torrents. He shielded his eyes from the light with a rough, whitening hand.

/Down you go and go in peace/ the kid called. /Is over now. You can pay for what you done in the next life, so you may's well relax now/

The King was quiet.

Reaching for something that wasn't there.

He might have whispered something, but his face was dignified.

By the time the kid got to the door of the greenhouse, the other was curled up like a babba on the floor, his beard all caught up in his arms as he held at last only himself.

/Boy/ The word squeezed out of him as from an accordion. /Boy/

The kid pulled the greenhouse door shut and locked it from the outside.

Δ

/Okay/ he said to himself on the path.

/Okay/

A deep breath and he turned the handle on the back door of the King's house.

The kitchen was dark. Shadows of things.

Clutter: many trinkets, and looming, darkswollen nooks and crannies. In the back of his mind a voice was saying that this kitchen would tell you stories, but he was already through it, into a tenebrous hallway. He heard the sound of the TeleVisio coming from somewhere, a woman's voice making vague threats. Light came only from a room at the end of the hall. The kid crept up the stairs, the heart pounding still.

He wished so badly that T was waiting here too. A voice in his head suddenly spoke to him that the babba meant nothing to him really, that T meant everything, and the promise to T. Did he even want the child? Only later did he think about the voice and that feeling, for it was his own and not another's.

On the landing he stood. Big breaths in and out. Light came out from under the third door. Dim paintings in frames on the wall: he could make out animals, dark woods and bonfires. Dizziness.

He knocked. He didn't know why he knocked. He went in.

It was a beautiful room that he crossed the threshold into, one he would never forget. Some kind of light in the corner was the high sun, and four blue walls like a clear sky under sunlight—just like on the TeleVisio—made him feel like he lived in a world where it did not rain. And birds: paper birds hanging from the ceiling, their shadows making more birds—horizon birds—where blue skies and a few white clouds were also painted.

The sun cast shadows on the wall. Shadows of a cot and a chair, and toys, and above the toys like a giant was a figure standing over a rocking chair.

/Have come for the babba/ he said. /Like I promised your daughter/

Her face was grey, gaunt, her lips cracked, her hair wet. She was in pyjamas, and had the babba in her arms.

She looked at the kid, her mouth open like a fish's. He stood there: skinny, shivering and dirty. Music played somewhere, a fiddle dancing. He began to panic.

/Have heard about these sun rooms/ he said casually. /Have never seen one though/

She gawped at him.

/Have to go/ he said. /One way or the other. Should I leave the babba with you?/

T's mother looked at the quiet child, in a bundle and sleeping he presumed. She seemed high on something, but it wasn't obvious what it was. When she let the babba down into the cot he remembered the promise. He didn't want it now. Had he only wanted vengeance on the King, and not to take his own child? How could he take that child from the cot and away into the wide-open world? It seemed impossible all of a sudden.

The mother had been writing on a pad that he didn't know where it came from. He was sure she was on some deep pharm. The words she had scrawled she held out for him to see.

WHERE IS DADDY?

/Daddy's gone/ he said.

Like a bird caught indoors she clattered off the wall and the sides of the door before she got through it and fled the room, her dressing gown twisted and swinging behind her.

Δ

He found himself at the cot, looking over a sleeping child. She was fair, with soft blonde hair and chubby, blotchy cheeks. Her white cotton tummy rose and fell.

/Promised I'd take you somewhere else/ he whispered. /Promised your mammy/

He thought he sounded like a character from a TeleVisio soap then. And he saw himself loving that babba and watching her grow, and there they were in some house in the country, living a life, eating meals together, her asking him questions that he had the answers to, and ... He suddenly looked to the windows and the doors as if the King might come flying through them.

/We have to go fast/ he whispered to his daughter. /Because I don't know what else could happen ... Am sorry I didn't come sooner. Broke my promise, but am here now,,, Don't even know how to fukken hold you, do I/

The babba was not as light as he'd thought she might be, the soft bundle of blankets weighty in his arms. There were two shoulder bags in the room and he hadn't time to look through them so took them both.

Downstairs he could still hear the TeleVisio, people laughing. He thought that the Earlie Boys would already be on their way. Somehow he was sure of it. His heart blasted through his chest. It ached. Every sound seemed to be the front or the back door, but nobody came.

At the front door he pulled on a set of dark skins that was far too big for him. Everything went under them, the babba, the bags. All the time the child slept. When his mam had sent him for eggs as a young lad he was always afraid of them breaking and he

149

took so much care of them. Holding this child was like that, like holding one big egg, and thinking that if the egg dropped on you the whole world was over. With his bundle held close and gentle under his skins, and bags dangling from him, he went out the front door of the King's house.

Δ

The rain gushed, relentless. Back at the punt he scanned the dark-blurred horizon for lights on the lake. There were none.

/Are in the clear I think/ he said to the bundle beneath his skins, that was contracting now, moving itself to test his hold. For a last time he looked over his shoulder and scanned the slope for moving shadows on the mire. There were none.

/Away/ he said. And over into the boat he slipped, the rope unmoored and between his teeth.

Away he began to row only a moment later, in dark skins spilled wide across the boat, an oar gripped in each hand, and the babba poised in a nest he made with his two skinny thighs, knees pressed together.

/Away!/ he said again.

MISTER VIOLENCE INTERLUDE #2

BURD, Teresa. 50s. From North Barrier, mother of five. Higher Executive Officer for Census Division of civil service. Insulted the Bard in a pub [Mon O' War?] after a drunken disagreement. Murdered by Bart [method unknown] on the street somewhere in Smi'Field. No witnesses. Night, 20/21.12. Family informed.

MASTERS, Inigo. 33. From the Midlands area, possibly Athlow. Casual dockworker, fond of a pint. Debts accumulated; recovery deemed unlikely. Guillotined by Crooner Bart/aka the Bard at the Dark Chamber/Death Bag, Docklands [exact location of which unknown]. Several Earlie Boys in attendance. Night, 13.03. Family informed.

MURKOO, Leroi. 24. From the Croke Park Flats. A marketeer from George Street area who refused to buy into protection policy. Guillotined in his own home by Holloway, with the Bard and Leg in attendance. Day, 07.04. Family informed.

MOOLAN, Dan. 21. From South Barrier. A Molly Man, boat mechanic, who met and traded insults with five Earlie Boys [Chan, Rice, the Spanyard, Freddi and Francis] on the boardwalk. Murdered there by knife wound—each of the Earlie Boys present claimed the kill, suggesting several knives were used. Night, 14.11. Family informed.

STROUD, Gunther. 40s. From the Croke Park Flats. Production line manager at Lepping Fish Farms, Grahán. Was a witness to two girls being abducted from a maquiladora nearby. Guillotined by Mike the Hat somewhere outside Grahán, after pursuit and beating. Earlie Boys [several in attendance] say they don't know if he was even alive when guillotined. Weekend of 19–20.09. No known family.

MOOLAN, Fiona. 39. From the South Barrier. Talked around town about the murder of her son by the Earlie Boys. Tried to contract somebody to murder Rice. Caught. Guillotined by Rice at the Death Bag/Dark Chamber, with Chan, Leg & the Spanyard witnessing. Night, 25.01. Husband informed.

MULLIGA, Garód. 40s. From the Highlands, Meath. A crooked accountant, had laundering duties from Earlie Boy pharm and doll money. Worked out of Leeson Street. Suspected of siphoning larger portion of funds for self than due. Had his throat cut by Leg at the Dark Chamber/Death Bag, or possibly somewhere en route, between Garrigues Dock and Docklands. King also present. First oral evidence of bodies being fed to cormorants. Evening, 02.06. Family not yet informed.

LEG [real name unknown]. 35–37. Earlie Boy, long-serving. King's leftenant, along with Crooner Bart. Reason for killing unknown. Possibly suspicion of usurping/betrayal. Possibly paranoia of the King? Murdered by the King in the lounge of the Pup&Pendant. Jim Corcoran did not witness the act but was there in the aftermath. Cause of death: knife wounds. Night/evening, 02.06. Cannot inform family.

GREEN, Tanya. 17–22. From Inchee Ker. Tanya was good at school. Left at 14 because family couldn't afford to keep her on. Worked Dunboy fish farm for a couple of years. Fell into street work. Met the Earlie Boys; fell into their 'care'. Relationship with the Eel led to death. Suspected of infidelity; no proof. Strangled in her own home, in front of mother and sister, by the Eel. Francis witnessed. Evening, 24.06. No need to inform family.

NAME UNKNOWN. Late teens [?]. From the Croke Park Flats. Gamer [?]. Guillotined by the Bard with several Earlie Boys in attendance, in the unnamed's own home. Morning [?], 03–05.06. Details to be completed—waiting to hear more.

The reporter read his own work with curiosity, with a fervent unknowing, rediscovering his own words as if they were the work of another person. He was in awe again of the detail, fascinated, feeling again the dark attraction to dark words and terrible deeds. Stooped over him, Mister Violence read too, with that Cheshire cat grin, and grey-black church steeples for teeth.

Bit from
WORD OF WARD—

Fire! It spreads afore my eyes in flowers. The footage starts with an aerial view over the dark baywater. I see the sea black, like oil, and steam over it like a great fog, and a dark cityscape aflame. Believe it or not, it was a Tuesday. The ground began to melt earlie on the Wednesday morning, from under the very feet of the people trying to stop it. The boats all left the docks as the flames ran riot, much of it hidden by then in great pillars of black smoke. Then the explosions started, and half the city was evacuated. Fire swells in the TeleVisio screen. Its purity, its heat under the rain. It was clean, and true, and ate up every human thing it crossed.

But no, wait!

Go back.

Our involvement with all this—O' Casey, the kid in yellow— it all started with the head. Pure bad luck. Wrong place, wrong time.

You see, me and Roe were used to staking out industrial yards and street corners: long boring evenings in delivery boats, taking turns pissing. Watching the people we'd been assigned to watch. Accumulating surveillance. Data for data's sake. And we were happy to keep our slate clean and our mouths shut. I don't know about Roe, but I went for the rank of Detective only because I needed the extra money, and my experience fit the profile for promotion. See—we didn't want to be heroes. We just wanted to stay out of trouble and not see anything out of the ordinary. But wasn't it the pure ordinary way of the thing, and our terrible luck, to be calling on those flats on that morning...

We were following a lead, which was not half as exciting as you might think. A particular runner, a young lad we watched on a weekly basis who was close to the King, was seemingly on the outs. Hadn't been seen in a while. And after a certain period of time 'unseen', you had to check if the mark was still a 'viable operative'. So what we did was we went door to door, for five flats around and including the mark's, and mayhap we had a photo-laminate of a few Disappeared for residents to check. But Roe and me, wanting to keep out of trouble, made these calls when we were least likely to get in trouble. At ten in the morning, when nobody would be home, or out of bed, or ten at night, when they were in the pub or on the job. And this is how we got to the twenty-sixth floor of the AerCo block at the Croke Park Flats.

The corridor was dark; the walls were bawling water. You'd get pneumonia ringing the doorbell. We were calling to each flat, with no one answering doors so far, which was topping. Things were going to plan! But on this day in all of history this kid's door was splintered and ajar.

Now, doors were ajar all the time. Neighbours broke in, fights were had: doors never got repaired. We could still have walked away. But there was the sound of voices inside, and Roe was suddenly knocking louder. I don't know why! The voices didn't break or pause, so it was the TeleVisio mayhap. I turned to walk away and Roe said in my wake:

'You think we should have a look at this one?'

I remember this all so well.

He stood by the door, adamant for once. I didn't want to go in of course, so I said to Roe:

'Do *you* think we should?'

He shrugged. I was hoping for a Suppose Not.

'Suppose so,' he said.

Okay then. In we go.

Those doors were flimsy, treated ply, and black and peeling, and they all had a stencil sign that said: EVERYTHING OF VALUE

HAS ALREADY BEEN TAKEN FROM THIS DWELLING. This was from the first phase of dereliction, a political decision which had of course been reversed when the city's population went haywire. Roe knocked, and called out was anyone home.

'Routine call—nothing to fear!'

Whatever voices we heard—excited, cursing—did not respond or react to our announcement. Still, it did not sound like TeleVisio. These are the kind of moments you think of putting your hand to your weapon, and think then further about how you've never even fired your weapon. The hallway was nervous, one bulb flickering. The walls were covered in mildew. Old skins hung from the grate hooks and there was a musty smell.

Down the hallway we crept, Roe in front.

'Hello? Hello?' we called all the way down. 'Guards on the property. Routine call only.'

The voices ran on uninterrupted from a room on the left, goading each other, warning each other, planning manoeuvres, and when we crept through the door we saw that a computer console was in game. Whoever else was in the network group, they were talking away to each other while their avatars shot at things or ran from things. The room was dark bar the glare of the screen, and there was no one in it. Clothes all over the floor, and a bed that you wouldn't let a stray cat on.

On the screen I could see an avatar on his back—some kind of operative. I listened long enough to hear one of the voices say, 'Where are you, Shells? Fukken gone plonkers again? Shells, you cunt! Am getting riddled here!'

Roe turned the volume down and we carried on up the hall.

They didn't have much. No family photos, little furniture. Religious things hung on the walls, a picture of Jesus on the cross, and the statuette of Mary with her foot on the serpent's head. This place was like a cave, I was thinking. The floor was littered with cans and packets, the carpet squelched. There should never have been carpet in these buildings—I always said this—but I suppose it was the cheapest material in the country then.

A St Anthony's necklace hung over the entrance to a living area, and we passed under it quietly. A sodden couch and Tele-Visio bank spread to the right. A dirty sleeping bag and some old pantalones and shirts were all that remained of the kid in yellow. To the left was an island dining unit. Beyond that was a galley kitchen unit, and there, planted amongst cans and plates and food packets, the head.

I touched Roe's elbow.

'Ah, Jesus,' he said.

Head of a teenager, greasyspotted, greasymopped, wispy facial growth. Eyes closed, tongue falling out over the bottom lip. The irony of the dead avatar on the computer screen did not escape me.

'Will call it in,' Roe said, and he pressed on his earpiece to talk to the office.

Well fukk Roe anyway for asking the question, is what I was thinking.

'Where's the body?' he said when he was done.

'Would imagine it's up here in the kitchen,' I said. I'd a ten-dency for sighing all the time; Joolie never let me forget that.

Sure enough, we stepped up that single step and there was the body on the lino, belly down, crumpled where it had been rolled off the counter and landed.

The open neck was harder to look at than the head. There was a lot of blood.

'They did it on this counter here,' Roe said.

'Sure,' I said.

There were the usual bad smells, but no sign of a struggle. I saw footprints, fresh, in the sodden carpet. Many feet. A curtain directly opposite the hallway entrance hid a fire escape, and I could tell by the slight move in the curtain that the escape was open. I heard distant laughter, and screeches of excitement, like they'd always been there. I noticed all these things, but never did anything about them.

The call made, Roe sat up on the arm of the sodden couch and switched on the TeleVisio. Started watching some programme about life in rural villages. He found it immediately, as if he knew it would be there. See, if Roe ever spoke to me, it was only about his homeplace, some rural bogtown, and the injustice of closing his old barracks there.

I found myself looking at the religious trinkets around the flat. Four framed illustrations of Jesus and Mary were hung in the hallway and living room, and again I noted that statuette of the Virgin with her foot on the serpent's head. They weren't unusual in themselves—many had them—but they were unusual in the context of the two teenagers who'd been living there. Mayhap these boys were squatters; mayhap they were brothers and they'd once had a god-fearing mother or father.

I took myself to the curtain and pulled it back. Sure enough, there was the door to the fire escape, ajar. I stepped out. I looked out over an urban rainforest, a ruined port, a dire sea. Is hard to describe now.

In my dreams I still hear that intercom voice, chatting gibberish over the city. Like a voice in some fallen world that speaks to keep itself company in the vacuum. You see, none of the information—the intercom, the constant flow through devices—none of it meant anything. We were drenched in words and numbers and none of it was real. It somehow kept the masses docile or confused enough to control. That was it. But there was something else in it that night. Closer than the intercom. I listened, and heard distant, rapid-fire conversation. Four or six voices. I leaned close to the railing and as subtly as possible looked over.

Down in the yards, through the rain, I saw five men. Two at least I recked as Earlie Boys. I couldn't see the others clearly. One was concealing a large object under his skins, and from its bulk and shape I had little doubt that it was that notorious portable guillotine. We could only just have missed them.

All you had to do was stop and wait and listen and see. I'm talking about letting the world reveal itself to you. You do that, and you won't miss anything. All the badness and all the mystery

159

comes to your feet and stretches out and lays itself at your mercy. What was clear to me from that moment was that the Earlie Boys had beheaded this lad in the last few minutes. Mayhap three had held him down, while one kept watch and one did the job. Was clear also that neither the body nor the head, despite being held stretched out on the counter, had struggled or resisted. No tables or chairs were overturned. The dirty crockery and empty cans and tins hadn't even been knocked from the side. He had not fought the brutality: I came to believe he had welcomed it. Now, I don't know whether he cried grief or relief, but cry he did; this was clear from the drying tracks of tears on his cheeks. There you have it.

But I let them go. I went back inside to Roe, who was marvelling at rice paddies on the TeleVisio. He pointed to the screen.

'See this?'

I could see beyond his shoulder one of the many sunken towns of the Midland Lakes, a common enough shot of the church steeples and bank roofs poking out of the water, with the houseboats of the people who could never move on from the town tethered to weather vanes and the like.

'Is my own old homeplace,' he said. 'Where I was stationed for thirty-two years.'

'Right.'

'Godawful shame.'

I know, I know. We were fierce bad then. *I* was fierce bad then. There's a lot I've to be guilty for. An awful lot. But I feared for myself and so I neglected my duties. I *do* feel shame, as it happens.

The What, How and When didn't give me the Why though, and that is the next job of the detective. Why did this happen? Motives were quick to come to mind, the usual ones: revenge, debt, altercation. Further out lay the context, the histories: all the minutiae. These things I would have hidden in a closet to avoid, but thanks to Roe we were now already thinking about having to compile. All these real parts of a real person's body and life were already transformed into admin—like that, this boy was an online matrix to be completed.

Δ

Only six of us attended the briefing in person, though everyone in the unit was supposed to at least log in. Many were using the Vincent Depaul investigations as an excuse at that time—the whole force was supposed to be looking for a man who went by scores of descriptions—and of the few that did log in to the briefing, no doubt they had us muted. At some points on these calls you could hear snoring. This was normal.

The six of us who did attend just stood around the screen and the arrangement of desks in a briefing room with our hands in our pockets, a guy named Sheaf popping painkillers with his coffee and groaning.

Roe eventually sighed, and said he wouldn't keep us long, and flicked on the link-console—that familiar hum and whir is lost to us now—and accessed our own database. If you could only see that database now, there's so much you'd know about our country...

Of course our home screen—Roe's and mine, that is—was a shambles. The couple of insignificant cases we'd stumbled upon were marked Unsolved or Pending, and Roe clicked quickly through to the case he had labelled, 'Head/Croke Park Flats/26th Floor, AerCo.'

'Have been tracking a young lad known as Kid Yello for about three months—'

'—Real name?' Maxwell asked.

'Unknown,' I said. 'Are not a hundred percent sure he knows himself.'

Maxwell pondered this. An officer named Gates looked out the window.

'Is a runner,' Roe went on, 'who's quite close to the King, we believe. Has been running for him for a while.'

He pulled up a graphic of the kid in yellow: skinny, cowlicked, freckles, always in yellow skins. His tweed waistcoat, seen in one photo beneath the open skins, was shabby, second- or third-hand. He was no Earlie Boy.

'We usually see him twice a week. Standard pick-ups and drops. Known to drink with an old-timer from the flats called Sweeney. Hangs around with a couple of other runners. Knows how to disappear—we haven't yet figured out where.'

Truth was we didn't care and hadn't been pushed to find out.

'A while back there was no sign of him at a standard pick-up on Sorrentino Dock, and he seemed to go offline after that. Still spotted around but didn't seem like he was working. Then, a few days ago: thin air. We were following up on the non-conformity when, at the kid's supposed address, we found the head.'

Gates's sigh was that of a man in pain.

We were so, so good at excuses, and the silence of our colleagues was no surprise. What did I care, I was getting paid and staying alive. I'd a wife who I cooked with and we were fond of each other. Was a possibility that when she came around to the idea we'd have children. What did any of us care, for that matter. We were all at it. Or not at it, I suppose. It was the modus operandi of the whole organisation at that time. The whole country.

Roe pulled up the graphic of the Head, and then of the body, both of which were currently in a lab somewhere down the hall, peppered no doubt with the biscuit crumbs of our resident WhiteCoaters.

'Is not Kid Yello?' Maxwell yawned.

Roe confirmed that it was not.

The talk then ran to the Earlie Boys, and the myths and facts about them. The stories about that crowd were like the horsey rides at the merries: they came and went and came back around. The chain of thought was obvious: that the Head—as all beheading victims came to be known until they were identified—owed the Earlie Boys money, or had crossed them some other way, and that he had received the punishment from them, as with others before and after him. They took pride in making examples, did the Earlie Boys, and this was the way of their King. Kid Yello's involvement was unclear, but seemed significant.

'But something's up,' Maxwell told us. 'Have three marks lying low. No pick-ups the last couple of days.'

'When the King's not picking up money, something is brewing,' Gates said.

Now, administrative procedure dictated that we had to make an action plan, and sadly for Roe and me we would have to follow it to some extent. In case we were audited. My memory of this whole time is weighted by a generally bad feeling in my stomach. I knew it was bad. I knew we were getting into something. If I'd have known then what I know now—fukken HELLFIRE—I might have walked out the door of that meeting and never come back.

Yet... we said we'd go door to door again at the Flats. We said we'd get a lot from the ID of the Head. We said we'd need to have the place checked for prints. We said we'd check the gaming data. We said we'd talk to your man, Sweeney. That would be our start, and in our start was probably our end.

LIGHTS & CONVERSATIONS

Who strode so late, through the rain and the wind? The boy did, the kid in his yellow skins again, with a bundle under those skins, a baby in a bundle whose cries into the shimmering night went unheard.

The kid held the bundle in his arm, warm and small and not without strength, as postal drones flung overhead on missions and late-night engines were drawn towards the great vessel of the city. That bundle felt strange, like an animal he had never before encountered. It spoke a language he did not understand—gurgles and spits and moans and giggles and wails—and it moved in ways he did not expect. It began to cry, to make itself heard against the rain of the night.

/What can I give you?/ the kid reasoned. /What is there here on me for you?/

He switched the babba from one tired arm to the other.

/Your mother would have known what to do. My mother too. We'll find someone to help us. The world needs more fukken mothers!/

He put a hand inside his skins to touch the babba's forehead.

/You are warm and dry at least/

And then the kid cried again, for everything that had happened to make the future look the way it now looked. His tears were lost in rain the moment they left his cheek.

/*Tommib*/ he whispered. /*Tommib* and happy and babba and nappy/

A loud noise came from behind, a long hiss in the rain.

The kid had a sudden fear, and heard echoes of the Earlie Boys. As if when he turned round everything would be over.

He turned.

Only a wisp of fog rolled across the canal behind him.

/Christ, girl!/ the kid gasped. /Am so fukken nervous!/

That night, on the side of a tundra pond, beneath the knees of a towering cypress, they slept in hiding, out of sight of the Hub and its drones. They were in the sticks now, southwest of the city, its orange orb humming in the distant sky. It was here, by the light of his device, that the kid went through the babba's two bags, trying to interpret what things were and how they were used. In the first bag he found two babba bottles, a half-dozen nappies, some sort of fold-out mat, wipes, an opened packet of biscuits, three different tubs of creams and a bag of white formula that looked like Fadinhead, and which he threw out. In the second bag he found an assortment of babba clothes, spare babba skins, and a vast sum of cash—more than enough to see them through a few winters. The gleeful kid showed a wad of the money to the babba—/Granddaddy's death gift!/ he laughed—and the girl put her nose to it, then tried to suckle the money.

Δ

In a country ferryboat terminal he listened for his name, for reference to the girl, but they were safe here, two days' walk from the city. He inspected the new clothes he had bought for them with satisfaction, and the bulky packet of formula, and all of a sudden couldn't really remember anything about his life. And he just felt like he was missing something.

But he had their babba. He had their babba, he had money. So really, what else could have been missing?

Honest John.

And T of course.

For a while then he imagined that T sat across from him there in the terminal, all soaking wet from the rain.

/Can't believe you came and got us/ she said.

/Said I would/

/Saying and doing though.../

/Only wish I'd done it sooner/

/... Did you kill my father?/

/Think so. Sorry/

/Don't be sorry. Don't know why am sad. He was a bad gent. He deserved it/

/Did he?/

/I know he's killed people... but sure you know more about that than me.../

/Clap hands/

/You know all about him I suppose/

/Suppose/

/Did you ever kill anyone before him?/

/Only him/

/And did you ever. Y'know. Was I the only? Y'know/

/Were the only one. Love you, T/

/Love you too/

/You scared?/

/Yea. You?/

/Not any more/

/Why not?/

/Don't know. Just feel okay. Feel like no matter what happens now I've done my best. If I die now will die peaceful, so there's nothing else to be scared of/

/.../

/.../

/What are we gonna do?/

/Fukk it/ he laughed. /Am scared! Didn't think this far ahead/

/We'll hide?/

/Yea/

/New names?/

/Didn't think of that/

/What should my new name be?/

/Dunno. Can only think of you as T/

/What do you want your new name to be?/

/Don't know/

/Fukk. I feel so weird/

/Will be okay/

/Look though: we're free! We're out of town, we've money, we've our babba ... Are a family!/

/Clap hands/

He noticed then blood oozing from her belly, crimson flooding her grey sweat-top. His heart sank. She continued, unaware.

/But what will happen with the Earlie Boys? Will they come after you?/

/Don't know. Bart will want to. Was the King's main man. He loved your Daddy like a Daddy. Will want to send drones out. But the others I don't know/

/But what if Daddy isn't dead?/

/.../

/.../

/Don't know. Is dead am sure/

/But if not? What if he couldn't die?/

/Nobody could survive that much F. Is dead, T/

/But what if not?/

And their babba seemed about to cry then, so the kid tried to speak to her instead. He said to her a few times, /Am your dad/, but she didn't understand him.

He said: /What you think about all this? Have heard that in the salt lakes of Munster they have green and pink dolphins. Would you like to go see the dolphins?/

Yet the babba would not reply to him. She looked around her with big eyes, mayhap trying to make sense of something that didn't make sense. He had lots of decisions to make, but he couldn't think straight at all, and the babba simply looked around, mayhap thinking ancient thoughts or mayhap having all the answers but not the tongue to pass them over to him. He loosened the carrier and balanced her on his knees, bobbing her up and down.

The babba rolled her lips against her poking tongue and bubbles of spittle erupted and slipped down her chin. She smiled then, arms dangling like a puppet's the way she was held out by him.

/You like that?/

She smiled again at the sound of his voice, moved herself against his hands. She liked being spoken to. But then she wriggled and pounded on his shoulder, longing to be free.

He said a poem for her:

/I went down to the hazel wood,
  Because a fire was in my head
  And I couldn't hear the hazel water
  I put a berry on a thread
  And when white moths came out to sing
  And mottled stars were flicking out
  I popped the berry in the stream
  And caught a little silver trout/

He realised then that she was staring not at him but beyond the window, transfixed by the changing of the traffic lights outside.

/Hello/ the kid said.

/Yoo-hoo!/ he called, and her nose wrinkled as if an itch came upon her.

/Alright. Will just keep quiet/

She had big black eyes and a soft round face like any other babba, but somehow he got the impression that she was tough. That she understood what was going on and was giving herself time to figure out whether he was man enough to carry the whole thing off. After a while he couldn't remember any longer which one of them was the older and which one was the younger.

/Will not let you down/ he promised, and her head juddered back to him and her face changed and she began to whimper.

/Look!/ the kid said, pointing at the cluster of traffic lights beyond the window. /Reds and greens and oranges!/

They looked at each other properly then—mayhap for the first time—and it was okay. The babba looked at the kid, trying to figure him out, and the kid looked at his daughter, trying to figure her out. And after that she turned to the traffic lights, and he watched her watching them.

Bit from
WORD OF WARD—

The six blocks of the Croke Park Flats loomed above us like sentinels. Nobody—of those who opened their doors at least—said a word. One bright Fadinfiend asked us were we Angels of Death, and was disappointed to hear that we were not.

And it was Sweeney we met next. The old weirdo that some called a mystic, others a daft drunk. His rickety punt coughed its way downriver as Roe and me waited at Garrigues Dock on a thundery evening. This Sweeney was one of a kind. Greasy-waxed patchwork skins—they said about him that he was over eighty years old, and yet in his dark skin he looked fifty or sixty at most. They said he'd Aboriginal blood. That he spoke fluent Irish even though he hadn't a good word to say about the country. That he could write in ogham, and commune with the rivers and ditches. He was wiry, strong, ageless mayhap, hauling a sack up from the boat, and he showed no surprise or worry at our approach. Through a curtain of rain he called to us in a broken voice.

'Sorry?' Roe shouted back.

'Suppose 'tis me ye're waiting on, moc?' he repeated, approaching the awning.

'Is.'

'Can we ask a few questions?'

'Only if ye take me home snappy. Have to feed me slug.'

I may as well confirm to you that it was not the custom of people at that time to keep slugs. Grotesque, formless beasts they were, many as big as rats, some even bigger.

'Will take you,' Roe said. 'Just come on in out of this thunder.'

△

Sweeney too lived at the Croke Park Flats, the AerCo block also, so back we went, to a particularly... decrepit unit, with sagging walls and bare floors and old maps and building plans in collapsing piles. It was a junkyard of knick-knacks: piles of old solar panels and small old satellites were stacked high on the balcony. A rail of old jackets, wax and leather for the most part, ran along one wall in the living room. What tiles remained were blooming in some breed of greenbrown mould. There was such a stink of petrol that you could nearly taste the place. And he did indeed have a pet slug, kept in the bathroom, where its slime had hardened and created a lime-green crust all over. Four tentacles stood hard and searched the air when we came in, and curled and shrank as the bulging, rippling, silvine seagreen creature retreated to a corner. It was huge.

'Why a slug?' Roe asked as Sweeney spread a bland fish-food mix in one corner.

'Slugs are territorial. So he keeps other slugs out of my dreams.'

'Your dreams?'

'Yes. This might be the physical realm of the slug, but it is not the natural realm.'

'No?'

'No, that's why he's so slow. Is why he leaves the mucus trail. Observe him. His dreaming is elsewhere, away with our dreamlands, our collective unconscious. Henceforth, moc, he protects me in my dreaming. Other slugs will slobber all over your dreams. Other slugs will feed on your dreams. Is why you can't remember them, mostly.'

'Oh yeah?' Roe grinned. 'Tell me, did you have a few drinks before you operated your vehicle this evening?'

'Think! Why do you wake up and say to yourself, *I feel sluggish?*'

Roe found himself lost for words.

'What is the slug's name?' I asked.

'How in fukk am I supposed to know?' said he.

Sweeney did not offer us a seat; we stood in the hallway and he folded his arms. With his skins off he wore only a vest and faded, colourless shorts. He was covered temple to toe in the markings of some tribe: mystic flames and ancient animals and maps and ogham markings.

'Now,' he said. 'Ye seem to have important business, but I too have plans this evening, so mayhap ye could please cut to the chase?'

'The boy,' I said. 'Kid Yello. We've been tracking him a while and now he's disappeared, and I'm afraid we are now in the possession of a human head, and, separately, a human body.'

Sweeney considered this. 'Is that what ye call him?'

'We would be interested in speaking to the boy about it,' I went on. 'And we know you…hang around with him sometimes…Do you know his whereabouts?'

'So it's not the head of the gasúr?'

'No.'

Sweeney flexed a wrist back and forth while he thought; forearm muscle bulged.

'Do not know the whereabouts of the gasúr.' He seemed surprised.

Roc piped up: 'Were you not in some class of cahoots with him?'

'Depends on your reck of *cahoots*,' the old buck replied. 'I saw him now and then, in bars and other places, especially after the Boys sent him away. He was good with the poems and the songs and that. The gasúr was my friend…mayhap…'

'Why did they send him away?'

'Don't know, do I. Never said.'

'When did you see the kid last?' I asked him.

'A matter of days ago, I suppose.'

'And what happened then?'

'We got drunk.'

'Where?'

175

'The Jolly Bridge. Or, possibly, the Clubhouse. Or it could have been the Mon O' War.'

I said: 'Sweeney, do you have any role in this transaction with the kid?'

'I do not, moc.'

'Where do you believe the boy is now?'

'I believe he is in a place unknown to us. Vanished ... And may he stay vanished.'

'Why do you say that, Sweeney? Do you know something we should know?'

'Not I.'

I found myself at a loss. I do believe that was my first-ever interview.

'Gentlemen,' he continued, 'unless you wish to detain me I am a busy man.'

I pointed to a g-ball insignia on the wall. 'Stars fan?'

'All my life.'

'Am a Seals fan myself.'

'Sorry for your troubles, moc.'

'You ever go to the Drome?'

'Every chance I get. Matter of fact, will be there tomorrow night.'

'Enjoy the game,' I said.

Exhausted of questions, we turned to leave, and Roe squeezed out the door ahead of me.

Δ

'Jesus,' Roe said when we were back in the vehicle. 'Didn't do so well there, did we.'

'We didn't.'

'Are about forty other questions we should have asked too. Am sure of that.'

'There are.'

'Jesus-fukk. You think he knows more?'

'Sure look. We're not used to this craic. We can ask him more later. Besides, I don't think he's guilty of anything.'

'Clap hands.'

It was shortly after eight in the evening. We went to Brod'rick's for fish and eggs and after that Roe went away home.

I went home myself, and drifted around the apartment, thinking, noting all the lovely things Joolie had done to the place that I always somehow missed. Things like picture frames with photos of us in different parts of Ireland. We'd even gone on a sun holiday once, you know—to Libya, at great expense—and this was something Joolie was very proud of. You know, I've seen with my own eyes the ecohomes of the megawealthy, on a calm oceanic horizon, low and perfectly symmetrical, like tents in the distance ... Joolie said that she was okay coming back to the rain, but that the sun was something everyone should experience once, and not just in TeleVisio shows or UV booths ...

Anyway, on my own then I started thinking about that beheaded boy. You know, it wasn't the gore that got to me. It was the loneliness of it. This kid was alone when he died, surrounded by ... men holding him down, cutting him apart. More than likely, they were laughing. These are deranged types of men I'm talking about. And this poor kid, who didn't even have a name that we could call him, was looking up into their faces, and his last experience of life was that. And the worst thing? Is I believe he welcomed it. Death.

Listen, I'd gotten through my life to that point and, if I'm honest, I don't know how I got there. Didn't know how I'd become a guard. Who I was. It was like I'd just kept turning up, or I'd kept rolling the dice, and this is how far along the board I'd gotten. You see, my life didn't add up. It was one long fragmented distraction, or avoidance of truth. Of purpose.

But never mind. I went to the balcony then and fell asleep, and woke into the rain. It was impossible to tell whether the rain was one thing, a single natural element, or a trillion things happening at once. It was the same with the world, and people. There in the rain were the Croke Park Flats. I took them in. I saw a whole dirty world at work. A trillion things happening at once. Festering. And I decided then and there that I wanted to solve the crime. Whether for the kid or for myself I didn't know.

I was watching the Flats and thinking on Sweeney when Joolie came through the front door calling hallo.

'How was your day, sweetheart?' she asked when she found me. She started sweeping the balcony, moving little plants around, pulling dead leaves from them and so on.

'Oh, it was fine,' I said. I felt… optimistic almost. For the first time in ages.

'Anything to report?'

'Not a bit. Business as usual. Patrols, paperwork. Repeat.'

'Aren't you very lucky? They're talking in work about another beheading.'

'Ah, yes. Creepy stuff.'

She arched out her back with hands on her hips and groaned. 'Are you in long?'

'Only five minutes. Was just taking a drop of air.'

'Is everything okay?'

'Of course! Everything's fine.'

She finally landed that kiss on my forehead. I miss those.

'But tell me, love,' I said. 'How are you? How was your day?'

And she proceeded to tell me all about it, while in the background the Croke Park Flats gathered and mobilised against the port and the mist.

BIT FROM THE PLAY——

ACT The Second, SCENE I

Note on Finance: This opening scene of Act the Second
is to resemble the ancient 'mummers' play' or the
'wrenboys' play' of lost Ireland. Despite the lovely
dancing and moralistic acting-up, the main function
of these plays is to secure money from the audience.
There will be an opportunity to do so, as outlined
below.

Note on Costume:
——SAINT VINCENT DEPAUL wears shimmering black skins
that hang from him like monk's robes. A long white
shirt collar protrudes from the neck of the skins. His
head and face are wrapped in medical gauze, so that
he cannot be recognised. When not hooded, he is seen
to wear a wide black skull cap over the medical gauze.
——MISTER VIOLENCE wears a black trenchcoat.
Red handkerchiefs hang from various parts of the
trenchcoat, like pockets turned out. He wears a bowler
hat, with cormorant feathers around the brim, and
a cormorant mask (with long beak) covers his (red-
rimmed) eyes and nose. Beneath, his chin is dark, both
hairy and scaly. Over his shins he wears skull-bell
pads; his clothes shimmer and drip an oily substance
as he moves.
——The EARLIE BOY wears a bright Kandinskee and
waistcoat, and pink cotton pantalones. His hair is
shaved into a Mohican.

Curtain up on a pitch-black stage, a <u>womb</u> of darkness
and silence. Gradually, barely, light increases,
until the dimmest of spotlights——almost no light at
all——illuminates the hunched figure of SAINT VINCENT
DEPAUL, who is seated at front of stage, right. His

180

back is to the audience. He is at work with a number of
vague implements. He is making a petrol bomb.

MISTER   [from offstage, in a gravel-soaked
VIOLENCE.   sing-song voice that lisps on the
              sibilant sounds, as if spoken through
              a forked tongue] All things be done
              with charity. If Vincent's loose, the
              fire's free!

SISSY.   [offstage also, echoing, as if the
              voice is a memory] They say he gets
              the petrol from underground deposits.
              They say the whole city's riddled
              underneath the hood.
KER.   [offstage, as above] 'Tis a jalopy of a
              thing, this city.

A single drumbeat sounds, as SAINT VINCENT DEPAUL
finishes one petrol bomb and begins another.

INTERCOM.   [warbled, fuzzy, barely making sense]
              MANY EYES MAKE SAFE...EASYGRAIN——
              EASY! GRAIN!...forecasting at
              fifty, seventy, and, later, easing
              to twenty-two...Fire-warning. Fire-
              warning. Fire-warning...Curfew... last
              curlew...FRESH FISH AT LAST...
KER.   ...Returning to the sea.
SISSY.   ...Drenched in petrol and oil...
              A jalopy, this world...

As another drumbeat sounds, another petrol bomb is
completed, and SAINT VINCENT DEPAUL rises from his
seat. At this moment a second spotlight——brighter, but
still dim——finds stage right.

Enter MISTER VIOLENCE, though his voice will
continue to come from offstage.

MISTER   Enter trouble,
VIOLENCE.   Who likes RUBBLE?

                [changing the rhythm]
                For a shekel, little more,
                Will set a fire, very WARM!
                For a little more, you'll get
                A song of fire, never BET!

A third drumbeat begets a rhythm, and MISTER
VIOLENCE begins to dance, something between a Morris
set and a tap dance. He is skilled in his endeavour,
and the skull-themed bell pads on his shins toll in
time with the music. The dance and the music mirror the
actions of SAINT VINCENT DEPAUL, who, on the opposite
side of the stage, is becoming more active. He is not
only making petrol bombs now, but pulling maps and
plans into the light from an unseen stack. He moves
back and forth across the stage, in time with the dance
of MISTER VIOLENCE but never aware of his presence.
He climbs unseen ladders, pulling down unseen tools
and ingredients to further his preparations.

MISTER.   [voice offstage, singing to the drum
VIOLENCE   and bell beat]
                Watch in the fire what melts away!
                  Melts away! Melts away!
                Watch in the fire what melts away!
                  Melts away! Melts away!

Enter an EARLIE BOY, stage left, strolling in the
direction of stage right, under a much brighter
spotlight.

SAINT VINCENT DEPAUL immediately spots him and
ducks, sweeping around to front stage left to get
behind the EARLIE BOY. A mime commences, in which
SAINT VINCENT DEPAUL, hunched of back, stalks the
EARLIE BOY in the spotlight, who is visibly spooked
in his efforts to get from stage left to stage right.
MISTER VIOLENCE's dance with music increases in
tension and tone with the mime of the stalking, until,
eventually, the EARLIE BOY panics and runs offstage,
with SAINT VINCENT DEPAUL throwing a petrol bomb
after him.

SAINT VINCENT [laughing, returning to his work.]
DEPAUL.   Vanish in flames, moo!

MISTER   [voice offstage, singing to the drum
VIOLENCE.   and bell beat]
               Watch in the fire what melts away!
                Melts away! Melts away!
               Watch in the fire what melts away!
                Melts away! Melts away!

Actors (preferably children, or short adults) dressed
as cormorants now begin to move through the audience
(appearing from the back, blocking the exits too)
holding out feathered bags for donations. They must
remain silent, or, at most, squawk at audience members
for money. When they have finished collecting money,
the cormorant actors join MISTER VIOLENCE's set
dance on stage.

Still singing, MISTER VIOLENCE now produces two
flares from his sleeves, which he lights. Everything
builds to a peak, in which SAINT VINCENT DEPAUL,
still completely unaware of MISTER VIOLENCE's
presence, inadvertently uses one of the flares to

light his own, which he carries to stage left, before
securing on his back a sack full of fire-making tools
and petrol bombs. The sack says FRESH FISH on it.
Stage left, SAINT VINCENT DEPAUL climbs a ladder to
the top of the curtain and drops into a small punt
there.

Shaky visuals are now used to show landmarks of the
city——the Centre, the Drome, a pub full of Earlie
Boys, the Financial District, the Docklands——moving
from right to left on a slow reel. From above them,
SAINT VINCENT DEPAUL drops petrol bombs (which
are actually flares, releasing also smoke), and the
visuals of the city landmarks and various symbols of
the city's rich, or the city's corrupt (the Ardaithe
going into the hills, courtrooms, etc., police
headquarters, etc., the graffiti sign of the King's
Eye, political billboards, etc.) are then spliced with
images of fire, as if they are burning, until all the
screen is fire, and MISTER VIOLENCE is singing and
dancing and laughing at a furious pace, in a frenzy,
and the cormorants dodge the flares, until smoke
fills the stage and the cormorants flee and all, all
of a sudden, is darkness again. MISTER VIOLENCE's
laughter echoes.

MISTER   [offstage, echoing]
VIOLENCE.   All things be done with charity.
                If Vincent's loose, the fire's free!

                    CURTAIN.

BIT CALLED

INTO THE SHIV'RING

Down past sodden riverside shanty towns they travelled, and down past towered towns too. Through jungles of tufted sedge and willow forests, parting lagoons of duckweed and bladderwort. They saw rubbish heaps ablaze, and factories pumping smoke into the rain. They saw wild fireworks, and shimmering elevated rail lines, and lights on hilltops.

/What would you have?/ he wondered as the child moaned.

He'd bought cola, and chocolate, and an orange. Kids liked cola and chocolate. In a plastic container he'd found pieces of soft potato and so he bought those also. He'd put cola in a bottle he found in the babba bag and fed it to the child. The child had winced, drank, winced and drank. She had cried out. Her face was soft and round and swollen and her cheeks pink. Snot burst in bubbles from her nose and he squeezed the snot away between his finger and his thumb.

Then he crushed the pieces of soft potato in his free hand and held them up to the babba's face. The babba only cried and pulled her head away. Then the cola came back out the babba's mouth, only more oily, and she sicked it down her clothes and the kid's skins. So, cursing, the kid took the babba out to the rail again and held her out now from his skins over the ferry's wake.

Churning, thrashing, the wake below consumed the babba's brown strings of vomit. The rain on the dark river came thin and slow, in snaking waves, and the waves and the firmness of them gave everything a rhythm like music. They called that kind of snaky rain the Shiv'ring. It was a mystical rain, and such it was on this night, the world shifting aft and afore in sound and vision. Even at his arms' length his child seemed lost in that Shiv'ring.

While she wailed and vomited, wailed and vomited, he noticed from the stern a view of a town above jungle leaves that flapped. The lights were orange and gentle and spread about like the galaxies he'd seen on the TeleVisio. Like the stars of old they hovered, watching over the people of the town. They were friendly lights, though he could not imagine a friendly town.

/Why won't you fukken hold anything down?/ he asked the babba, when she was nestled in his skins again.

He kissed her cold harsh cheek and with a small dirty towel he stroked her wet head and back and legs. For only a moment more his eyes were given to the town lights and then they were lost and there was only the steady Shiv'ring, dark foliage, the echoes of waves and engines on the river, and the electric transmissions of ghostly machines unseen.

/Let's try again/ he whispered to her, and so, waves and night-calls lost to them, they stepped back into the ferryboat bar and under hanging lights began to tack back and forth across the muggy heat and the mansweat stench of the room, finding their seat in the corner still unoccupied.

At the table he tried to feed the girl yoghurt, but she wouldn't open her mouth wide enough for him to get the yoghurt in, so it kept going around her lips and chin. She hadn't been eating at all really, though she always seemed to have something to sick up. She looked a hollower child than when he had found her, more ragged. Though she slept often, she had purple clouded bags under her eyes, and her skin was pale and dry. He tried as gently as possible to force her mouth open but she started to cry. They were not getting on great these first couple of days, though the kid tried everything he knew or could find out on his device.

/Will open it when you're hungry/ he eventually counselled his daughter.

He said to the blonde woman next to him: /Do you know what am supposed to do here?/

But she didn't hear him.

He said: /Have you something I can sort of wedge her mouth open with?/

The febrile tremors of the engines he felt still below the accordion music. It was deep night at this stage and people were flootered and starting to roar. The accordion spiralled up and down all the while in the background of the shouting and laughing and scolding and the old river pushing against the helm and the engine chugging away as the night turned its own wheel. They were southwest-bound, stopping everywhere on the way; it would be a good way to get lost, but he'd never imagined it would be so busy.

/I feel one hundred years old this night/ he said to his daughter, who was falling under the spell of the boat's rhythm as the poetry of a thousand voices careered around them in slurs and spats and vicious prayer, foam of beer spinning back and forth over the laughter, threats and protestations. A musician sang; elsewhere a group of women and men roared at a g-ball match on a corner TeleVisio. The kid's table shuddered, the empty glass upon it rattling. Sea legs wobbled and collapsed into tables and benches and panelled walls, but all the people there seemed to be comfortable with each other, to be armcrawling across each other's shoulders and calling out for each other.

/Ballinatrá!/ yelled the deck boy as the convulsions of the table increased, though beyond the window the kid saw only darkness and mist. He wondered what the smells of gargle and meat would mean to his child. For she seemed to be making her own investigations all the time, and this strange person who held on to her, his only significance was that he got in her way, pulled her back from carrying out all sorts of worldly studies. And her eyes. He felt like they were ancient in some way. Like everything about those eyes was in him from the day he too was a babba, before that even, and so what happened to him could only happen her, and then he was thinking, oh my girl, my girl, my girl! And the babba sneezed then and woke into a crying state and he picked

189

her up close and hushed her and decided once and for all that he required a beverage to take the edge off his fear and worry.

/Come, babba/ he said. /Go for a walk/

Δ

Ambling to the ferry's warp and weft, he jostled with her unhappy squirms and sporadic fits of whinging. He tried to tell her the story of the troll and the bridge, but she arched backwards and stretched out her arms, short blonde hair spreading out in fall. On tables he noticed statuettes of the Virgin—her foot planted on the serpent's head, like the ones his mother had left behind—and he smelled coils of incense. People were set up for a mass it seemed; mayhap this whole rabble was an ark cult on the move again. What the kid was looking for was not religion, or prayer, but an unguarded drink. The flavour did not matter.

/Last call for Ballinatrá! All alight for Ballinatrá!/

And here, around the corner from the main boozing hall, all flecked with beer and liquor as it was, he found a few tables underlining a dark window. And here, in one corner beneath the dark window were three fans of hair on three pairs of sprawled elbows, elbows covering the mystic corners of the ouija board. All three were asleep, or entranced. One snored.

Between a thumb and a finger, the kid quietly collected up two of the six glasses from the table. A single nerve-wracking clink.

Viscous rum-red liquid: when he turned at the entrance to the hall one of the séancers—ginger, bug-eyed—had awoken and was regarding him, and so the kid hastened with his daughter to lose himself in the accordion journeys and crowdmurmur and tumult of the main hall, and drifted throughout until he found their table still free and began to drink.

Δ

/Yurt!/ he cried to the tune of the Meltin Bogs.

The blonde at the next table finally answered him. Said: /You cannot feed the child that!/

She was slim and wiry and standing at a queer angle he thought. A rare blonde, like the child. /Where is the child's mother? That you are poisoning your sister with chocolate. Know thee nothing? And you chatting away to yourself all night. I *seen* you/

/The child's mother is not available/ the kid replied, peering up into her tightness with a zigzag smile across his face. He sang along to the song. The yoghurt was on the floor now and the babba chewing on her own hand, looking after it with vague interest.

The blonde warrior was down on the upholstery with them then, holding out the child's bottle, full of milk.

/Hello there!/ he laughed.

/Is not yoghurt but milk/ she scolded. /Here, give her this/

His mind ran on several tracks: over the sea and under the rain; across the accordion music; back and forth through sad tides of memory; it told him, some voice at least, that if he got up and ran now he could be rid of the child and start afresh.

/Hold her properly, like *this*/ the old blonde lizard was telling him from somewhere. /Milk, a mashed spud. Beans, warm but never hot. Check the heat always. No chocolate, no cola no more. No crisps or biscuits... Give me those... Less yoghurt... Cream for that rash—here it is in the bag.../

And all, all, all of a sudden: hush. All quiet on deck. Only the steady engine and scratches of rain beading on the dark windows. A cough here and there.

/Is that God then?/ he gasped.

Standing at the top of the steps by the bar, a blurred figure, one grey arm wielding some downward-held shaft of golden light. Words called slowly, like: /momentum/ and /purse's clearance/.

Prayer followed, wavelike, all along the heads.

The kid cocked his eyes up and down, tried to focus.

A head of white hair and an ashtray face—half a sailor, half a priest—talking to the crowd, a steady arm on the shiny brass railing. They listening with their heads bowed, dipped.

Below the kid was the babba, suckling on a plastic bottle, looking well, peaceful. Looking peacefully to him. The red explosions on her face were smeared in a cream. Sadness bolted through the kid, a leaden shock. Everybody, the whole boat it seemed, was praying. And the babba of his peaceful at last. And the blonde woman with her bony claw around his shoulder. And a pair of red-freckled bug eyes watching him from across the room.

/Hold this!/ the kid gasped, thrusting the babba at the blonde.

Δ

Bug eyes in the gloom. The lights and riverbank fires of the brasser camps and the dark shapes of the factories beyond. The ever-breaking wave against the cold steel bow. Everything—the riverbank, the wake, the fuzzy lights—melted into the Shiv'ring.

Eyes streaming, acid mouth, difficult to swallow. Bitter taste.

/Was that?/ the kid groaned.

/Was absinthe/ Bug eyes above him, a broad silhouette, a woman's voice. /You okay?/

/What?/

/It was absinthe that you took from us/

Lurching of ferry, the word waking some unknown stomach memory. The word implanted now in the mind.

/Rotten … You! Are huge!/

/I know/

/Like a wrestler!/

/People say that/

The kid coughed once more and wiped his mouth with the sleeve of his skin. The rain tasted fresher here on a country current.

/Got to get my babba/

The broad, bug-eyed ginger woman did not keep pace with the kid but pondered a moment more the darkness of the river. Then, casually, watching the night sky, smelling the air, hands crossed behind her back like the wise old oystercatcher, she followed the kid in, whereby amidst the prayers of the whole bar the kid found his girl again, and took her from the blonde, who wasted a scowl on him that he did not notice.

Everyone's chin was pressed to their chestplate. There was a circle cleared near the sailor-priest at the top of the steps, whose voice was warbly and high, not as rough as his face or his skin or his old woollen jumper, as he said, /…faithful now is a different thing altogether. We look for answers *beyond* the pale. We open our gates to dark waters, in search of *that* which is out *there* in the darkness/

A murmured wave of yeses and amens rippled. Bug Eyes wandered through to watch their leader, her arms folded, head and shoulders above the crowd.

/*That* which reaches out from the depths. *That* which is yet lost in the darkest rain. But not gone. Not gone!/

/Clap hands!/ they all agreed.

Accordion music swelled up out of nowhere and then they were belting out a chorus of /Rowing Ashore/ and the sailor-priest was dancing a jig at the head of the crowd.

Bug Eyes arrived at the table, stooped to the kid: /Alright now?/

Then Bug Eyes laughed, and dropped a heavy hand on his shoulder. A soft hand, pale and freckled, that of a young woman.

/*Seasickness* gone?/ she laughed.

Δ

She placed a bottle of UpYaBoyo before the kid and a bottle before herself.

/Here is a more normal drink for you/

Holding her like the blonde had shown, the kid fed the babba the remainder of the milk. The room still spun, but less with each deep breath. He had some control again.

/You stole the wrong drink/ Bug Eyes laughed, shaking his free hand and introducing herself as Jeri. It would have been easy to mistake her for a man in dim light, with her size, with her prominent skull and meaty jaw, an old jumper and jeans stretched across the girth of her. But her careful voice and calm way were female. He felt safe with her like he hadn't felt safe for months and months.

/Portboo!/ came the call like a wave breaking.

/Where's your mother?/ she asked.

/Are going to meet her off the boat/

/And it's just you and your little sister on yeer own?/

/Is/

Her eyes said she'd let the lie go, for now.

/You're a brave young lad!/

/What were ye doing at that table?/ the kid asked. /When I took the drink? Ye were all asleep I thought/

/A séance/

/A séance? Chatting the devil?/

Jeri took a pull from her bottle and shook her head. /Not exactly, no. It's doing like Father D said and opening your gates to dark waters. We're looking for answers, you see/

/I don't get it/

/Did you ever hear the story of the man and his key?/

/Don't think so/

The babba coughed and spluttered a moment and then continued to drink. Soft sounds of sucking and glugging and deep chest humming were beautiful to him now.

/Okay. A man commutes back to his island home every evening after his work on the fish farm. The island is small, with only one road up to the village, and only one working streetlamp, which happens to be just outside his house on the outskirts of that village. Hear me? Every evening the man docks at the tiny pier, walks up the one road, takes his key from his back pocket, and by the light of that streetlamp lets himself into his house/

She paused for another pull.

/But one evening he puts his hand in his back pocket and the key is not there. Neither is it in his other pockets, nor is it in his skins. He goes to the road and starts to search the lit path beneath the streetlamp. But cannot find that key.

/After a while a neighbour comes by and when she hears the problem she helps the man to look. They search every inch of the streetlight until the neighbour finally says to him, Are you sure you lost it here? To which question the man casts his arm out to the dark world—the island and the sea and the wingspan of the rain beyond—and he says, No, I probably lost it out there somewhere.

/Then why are you searching here? she asks.

/Because, he says, this is where the light is/

Jeri looked up from a table stain that she couldn't clear with her sleeve to regard the boy. /Do you see what I mean?/

/...Not really/

/No? You see, people have lost their way. They've been looking into the light for answers. Like that pool of streetlight. We have looked only at what we already know. Science, books, data...And all that time things just get worse. Life gets worse. People act worse towards each other...We can't get *home*. So, some of us are looking for answers in the dark. Some of us are out beyond that streetlight—in the dark of the island and the sea—searching for an end to the rain...and other things.../

The kid looked down to the babba, who had begun to doze. He was embarrassed.

/You should burp her before you let her sleep. She'll be upset before long/

/How do I burp her?/

/You don't know how?/

/Not really/

/I...It's like...You slap her gently on the back/

Smiling, her whole face changing in the smile, Jeri fixed her big round glasses to the top of her nose again. /You don't really know what I'm on about, do you? With all this key and dark stuff?/

/Understand a bit. I think.../ the kid laughed again. He took a swig from his bottle, let the baby sleep on. /Where you all going?/

Slinging her arm back over the bench, opening her gaze and her body to the room and the music, Jeri stifled a long yawn. /We're all headed south to see this talking statue/

/What about it?/

While Jeri searched for words the babba did begin to stir. She forced herself long in the kid's lap, still sleeping but already beginning to moan, turning her face away from the light and back into it, her face wrinkled up and reddened. He watched her, prepared for the tears.

Jeri shrugged. /To see what she has to say/

/But is a statue. The talking is surely all a crock?/

Those bug eyes closed and the ginger freckled head shook solemnly. /Not at all/ Leaning, she put her arms across for the babba, who had begun, yet sleeping, to cry. When Jeri had her, she began to pat the babba on the back, the child held over her left shoulder, tiny in comparison, like a little loaf of bread. /Like this I think/

With the child's back to him, the kid had that sinking feeling again. The failing feeling. The lost feeling. Jeri rubbed and patted the grey cotton of her back.

/If you think like us then you look beyond the obvious. This country is slowly disappearing. The whole world is falling to pieces. Time is accelerating and cracking apart, and after almost three thousand years of praying none of the organised religions has been able to stop that. None of the sciences either/

The babba suddenly belched, frightening herself into a further torrent of tears.

/There!/ Jeri laughed. /Now you try/

The kid took his girl and tried the same.

/But a little harder. Firm is the word ... But who knows where God is. He or she or it is out there, I know that. And something is happening to our souls, I know that. But he or she or it is locked up. Or insane. Or asleep, or in a trance of ages. Or a coma. And maybe we're only in his or her or its dreams now. God is suffering from a terminal bout of nostalgia or amnesia, and in it, in that locked room, we're some weird distant image. A half-remembered thing. Only we're living in the now. We're stuck in limbo. You know? Wait, you don't, do you ... But what I'm saying is maybe some part of him or her or it, in statues, in séances, in rain, is trying to talk to us. Trying to send us a message for help. Or giving clues to help us find him. O*r* her, *or* it. You ever look into a Shiv'ring, like there is tonight, and felt mystery?/

The kid nodded.

/Weird isn't it? So shimmery. It's like it's got some vision or message for you beyond the curtain. Isn't it?/

And it was. As soon as the other said it, the kid agreed.

/So we're going to see/

/Are you a priest?/

Jeri laughed. Drew a final swig from her UpYaBoyo and with her mouth full shook her head and swallowed. /No. I'm a student. Of theology/

/What's that?/

/Like God Studies. I'm not enrolled any more. I'm on the road now/

The babba belched again and began to rub her face against her father's shoulder.

/Good!/

/I know lots of poems, you know/ the kid boasted with a sudden proud smile. /Am good at remembering poems/

Jeri sat back and folded her arms. /Say one for me/

The kid paused, recited:

/Trees closed their leaves into needles
And closing his frown he saw the four horses
Neanderthal saw the north coming down/

Jeri said nothing. The length of her stretched hand pressed her flat upper lip in calm thought, her gaze away over the wide room. The kid, burping the child the whole while, couldn't read the other's look, and so gave her another verse, one that pleased people more:

/The raindog's loose—what means you?
The rum pours free—what means me?
WHAT'S IT ALL GOT TO DO WITH A TREE?

Take a sup—what climbs up?
Rums all round—what falls down?
WHO'S BEEN FLOGGING LADS ALL ROUND TOWN?

THE RAIN! THE RAIN! THE RAIN!
THE NEVER-ENDING TRAIN!/

/Next docking, Bracknoor!/ came the call.

From the corner of his eye, beyond the dark-beaded window, he saw the neon signs of riverside camps and accommodations. Jeri remained pensive. The babba would not belch again, and the kid smiled dumbly.

/Where'd you get that first one?/ Jeri asked.

Δ

Silver morning rain broke on the vast lakeland beyond his rust-weeping porthole and shades of grey brightened the cabin. The ferryboat chugged on.

He woke before the babba and moved carefully to get out of the bed and see out the porthole. She woke and watched, but did not cry.

Green dolphins swam alongside the vessel, rolling over the surface.

/Would you like a hug?/ he asked his girl, stretching and yawning.

/Baa/ she replied, stretching herself. Yawning. Looking around her like she knew nothing of the world, or had forgotten all that she had known.

/We are not so different/ he said. /But you are a special child, and are going to live a very special life. Your own mother was a princess, the daughter of a king and my own true love. I only hope you are all the good of her and none of the bad of her father/

She listened away to him, chewing on his hand with hard gums. They were getting used to each other now. She did like being spoken to.

/You know also that you escaped a very, very bad life up there in the city? And that you have in these last days travelled more than me or your mother ever travelled yet. But I think you will see amazing things and places in your life. You will see the sun, I know it. Will go to school until you are eighteen, I swear it. Will get off this miserable mossy rock of a country. Will go to university somewhere. Be a student, like Jeri. Will become some kind of great person. Will only be good to people/

The kid sat with her then and told her again Jeri's story about the man and his key and the dark.

Λ

When the story was done the kid went to his device, to see again how nappies were changed, and found himself again reading through the messages from T. She lived on in the messages.

He had not changed the babba's nappy the first day—until a woman in a ReetPlex had told him that his child stank, needed changing. The rash on her bottom and legs had not disappeared since, but he thought it was looking cleaner each day. She was patient with him this morning, while he lifted her legs and wiped her. He wished she could tell him all the things she needed and felt, so that he wouldn't always be failing her.

/Jeri says they're going to Dingel for answers. You think we should go that way too?/

She rolled her head from side to side, testing her neck, continually discovering her physical potential. He left her on the bed and went back to the babba bag for the bottle.

/Mayhap we could speak to the statue and find out about your mother? Mayhap she could tell us what to do. Where to go. How to live. What she wants for you .../

Sat up in his lap, the two of them rocking with the ferryboat's rhythm, she took her bottle easily. He was trying to burp her again when came a knock on the cabin door.

In the same colourless jumper and jeans, Jeri rubbed crust from grey eyes with her knuckles, before replacing her glasses.

/Had fun?/ the kid asked. On his shoulder the babba craned her head round to see who had come.

/I've been walking the moons of Sheba with fallen angels/ Jeri said.

The kid grinned but Jeri did not. /And what they say?/

The girl produced bubbles of drool on her chin as the young woman and the boy regarded each other in hope of understanding something that was just beyond them.

/That ye should come with us/

The following evening I went looking for Sweeney at the g-ball. The Drome was inland, west of the city, out in the middle of a network of canals and raised roads. The sound of car and boat engines filled the rain, and all the fans in their teams' skins marched the footpaths to this low glowing core in the distance. It was all industrial yards and fenced-off marsh between the canals. That whole part of the city was sinking, was one of the first parts lost after…

In those days a Heavy could show his badge at Gate 27 of the Drome and get goodish seats for nothing. The gates were like spokes in a wheel, all bright corridors full of snack and memorabilia booths, where you could buy programmes, jerseys, hands, hats, skins, SLUSH, Dynamite Sticks to eat, any class of drink… They had QUIKEASY tattoo parlours to get your team's emblem done. All class of things, and at the centre of it all was the court. And the size of the court always amazed me—it was so small in such a vast building, like one small piece at the centre of a 500-piece puzzle. Thirty thousand seats around and some Tele-Visio screens that were half the size of the court itself, all there to watch thirty fellas hammer lumps out of each other for an hour.

I got to my seat in good time for throw-in. On one side of me the seat was free; on the other an old hooligan sat with his wife. I looked at the programme and knew none of the players. Neptune, a team from the south, seemed to be going well, and so it was billed as a tough game for the Stars. The court was busy with pre-match entertainment, mascots firing skin packets into the crowd from portable cannons. And dollies came up and down the breaks in the aisles offering snacks and drinks. They had mannequin bodies but their big old bellies were hot boxes for nuts and hot dogs and whatever else was going. I remembered hearing that there was a way to hack them so that they gave out free food, but apparently the programmers had blocked that, for now. The echoed calls and the squeals of the crowd as the teams got some final practice in made me quite nostalgic. This is before nostalgia became a serious illness of course. I was sparked by youth, and excitement, and mayhap a sense of possibility. It was like a feeling of waking up—remembering dreams or ideas from years ago—as if some hopeful part of me was waking up under the lights of the Drome and the calls of the crowd for their teams. I was relaxed, you know, smiling, getting into it. By the time the klaxon went and the two teams were throwing shoulders into each other I was clapping loudly and bouncing in my seat. I was happy out!

Δ

By the end of the second quarter Neptune were up by a few points, and the Stars didn't really look capable of pulling it back. Two or three guys had gone off in stretchers but nothing too brutal really. I took a toilet break and who did I meet in the push for the drain—only Sweeney, all decked out in his Stars colours: hat, scarf, jersey, the lot.

'Seals aren't playing tonight, Sergeant,' he said.

'Am no sergeant,' I said. 'Call me Fran.'

'Are you enjoying the game, Fran?'

'Am. Is my first in ages. Hasn't really come to life yet though, has it.'

'Ah, we're shite, moc,' he said. 'Clane useless. We couldn't get wet in rain!'

We were shuffling forward in the surge, closer and closer to the troughs.

'There's a half to play yet?'

'No, no, it's over. It's only going to get worse. We need a new

202

centre, a new coach. Too much. The whole thing's corrupt, like this city, like this country ... What are your seats like?'

'Perfect,' I said. 'Orion's Belt, right on the centre. You?'

'All the way up in the Pleiades. Only rooting seats I could get this night.'

'Seat next to me is free?'

I could see straight away his dilemma: sit with the Heavy in the good seats but have to talk with him, or stay with his lot and risk a nosebleed.

'You're a gent, moc!' he finally grinned. 'It would be a fine thing you'd be doing for me.'

Δ

Neptune ran away with that game, and many more after it. If you had record books you'd see that they dominated the national game for a decade at least, or until everything sank into chaos and waves. Yes, the Drome and Neptune and all their trophies sit under great tides now.

After the swarming crowd started to thin on the canal networks I asked Sweeney if I could stand him a drink somewhere.

'I know what you're looking for, Fran,' he said. 'But I don't drink with Heavies.'

'Ah,' I said.

'I'll tell you what though. Let's go for a walk back along and you can ask your questions. None of the men you and me are worried about go to Stars games ... Will you smoke a keen dart with me?'

He held forth the herbal. I took it. The nostalgia was on me.

'Moc, let me ask you a question first,' Sweeney exhaled. 'Did you ever get shat on?'

I thought I'd heard wrong.

'Shat on?' he repeated.

'No! I can't say that I've been shat on ... Should I have been?'

He cackled away. 'Ah. Is an old Earlie thing that I heard about. Sometimes a Heavy is caught alone by the crew, down in a dockyard somewhere or a quiet corner, and they hold him down and someone shits on him. Idea is that he goes back to work and is too ashamed to tell anyone, so they have that over him. They get away with it, apparently.'

I accepted another toke, told him that I'd never heard of that happening—but then again, if the theory was true I wouldn't have heard it, would I?

He agreed with me on that.

'Never been shat on by an Earlie or burned by Vinny Depaul,' I confirmed.

'Lucky you,' he replied.

Riverlights flared out, and the rusting yellow cranes were so many lonely shorebirds on the lookout.

'But you seem honest,' he told me.

'Am honest,' I said. 'Am not lying to you.'

'And you're not on the take either.'

'How do you know?'

'Is easy to tell the ones that be on the take from the ones not…' We waited to cross a canal bridge and he regarded me with curiosity. 'But if you're not on the take, and you haven't been shat on, that makes you a lucky one.'

'I guess,' I said. 'I suppose I don't exactly stick my neck out either though.'

"Til now.'

'Am I sticking my neck out now?'

'Sure you are. With the question you're about to ask me, *yes* you are, moc.'

'What's the question I'm about to ask you?'

'Where is the boy and what did he do?'

'Correct,' I shrugged. 'So…?'

Well, Sweeney stopped in his tracks. 'Tell you what… Rather than tell you, I'll show you.'

Δ

I was worried about the direction we took from the start, along the north side of the river, past Garrigues Dock, inland then to Smi'field Square where people used to trade.

'Here,' Sweeney said. 'On this cobblestone square is where people first came to know the Earlie King.' He looked sideways at the road. 'I was here. A younger man then.'

'I know the folklore,' I said.

'No folklore, moc. Like I said, I was there.'

'This isn't a safe place, Sweeney.'

'Let me say this, moc. Tonight, you are safe with me.'

'I'm not going to get shat on?'

'No.'

And I followed him down a narrow laneway, pocked by stacks of pallets and piles of rubble, a big hole of open sewer filling up with rain. Across the road then we went to a block of three well-known pubs: the Rose Red, the Standard Sanchez, and the Pup&Pendant. These were Earlie houses, in every sense of the word. If a crime was reported in one of these pubs—any emergency at all—we waited a long while before we waded in to clean up. I sensed a trap; I berated myself for trusting the old native.

'Sweeney,' I said, 'I'm not falling for this.'

And I turned to leave.

'Relax, moc,' he called after me. 'Am not one of them. Am something else entirely... And nothing's going to happen to you. Except answers.'

And I did swing to face him a ways back up the street. I did turn back towards him.

You could see the neon lights of the Rose Red stretching along the roadwater and the shiny cobbles so that it looked like everything was streaming away.

'Don't be afraid,' he called.

And, you know, I wasn't then. I was relaxed all of a sudden.

'Moc,' Sweeney said. 'You're looking for the kid, and I want to show you something, because if I only tell it you will not believe me.'

Something was changing, in me and outside of me.

'Come on so,' I said.

Δ

The Rose Red was near empty. An exhausted-looking barman, a fellow with a crown of thin black hair and a shiny dome, was pressed to the counter reading a newssheet, a white shirt hanging loose off him.

'What've you done with them, Terry?' Sweeney announced as we took off our skins.

Terry raised his head to regard my companion. 'You'd know better than me, Sweeney.'

I hung back as Sweeney bounced up and down on his heels at the counter. I was waiting for something to happen, but nothing was happening.

'Right then,' I said to him in a low voice at the table, two rums between us. 'I'm going to be honest with you. I'm here because, of all the crimes perpetrated in this city on a daily basis, I have decided to do my very best to solve this one. To find this boy and arrest the killer of the head in that flat.'

'In your line of work are you not supposed to solve *all* crimes?'

'Well, I have not been so good at that part in my career to date. But let me add this: taking into account what I have just said, know that I am very nervous at being in this pub, a known haunt of the Earlie Boys, and I *am* afraid of being shat upon, or worse. I know that worse can happen in places like this. So could you tell me why we are here, who wants to hurt the boy, and who killed the poor buck in the flat? Or anything at all that might help me answer those questions?'

'Right, right,' he said. 'Calm down.' He took a big sup of rum. 'You've hit the nail on the head. Look around you: what do you see?'

I looked around and shrugged. 'A pub free of leaks, with a strong fire. The rum is cheap, but thin. I see empty karaoke booths streaked with grime...'

206

'And you mentioned that it is a known haunt of the Earlies. Can you see any now?'

Of course I couldn't.

'But it is Friday night—where are they?'

'I don't know. Another of their pubs?'

'Let's see.'

With a second draw Sweeney emptied his glass and started to gather his things to leave.

'Hold up! Hold up!' I said to him. 'Are we going somewhere else?'

'Like you said, another pub.'

'Can we not?'

'At least come and look.'

And off we went.

That night was a rainy sulphuric haze. Through the bright windows of the Pup&Pendant we cupped our hands around our faces and peered in. No Earlie Boys.

'So I see now,' I said. 'There are no Earlie Boys around. Message received. But why? What has this to do with the boy? With the Head?'

Right at this point—I see him now still—a small, fattish man pushed past us, wearing an old trenchcoat and hat. He had keys in his hand. It was the first time ever I saw O' Casey.

'Okay, see,' Sweeney said when the stranger—the reporter—had passed. 'Now I will tell you that they—the Earlie Boys—are looking for the very same gasúr as you.'

'Why?' I asked.

'They are looking for him because he has done two things.'

'Right?'

He pulled me by the skins to the other side of the road and we stood up against a stack of pallets on the canal's edge. He was very close; his skins smelled like herbal and petrol from his boat. He looked up at me with mad eyes.

'The kid has *killed* the King, moc. And he has kidnapped the King's granddaughter.'

It was one of those slow, vivid moments. Everyone has two or three of those moments in life, where everything … is dream-like. And yet—and yet vivid, more real than reality, every detail a photograph … I remember clearly a punt full of fruit gliding past us on the water, guided by a low-lying Spaniard, and the plastic on top of it rippled in the rainsulphur breeze. I remember a siren a block or two away. I remember the warm wind changing and blustering as we stood there and I processed what the old native had said.

'He's what?'

'Some days ago, the boy went to the King's house, put him down, and took the child, whose mother died in childbirth. The child's mother was the daughter of the King.'

'Why would he do that?'

'So little you know about your mark! He did *that* because *he* is the father of the child.'

I stood there, trying to get my head round it.

'Now if you'll excuse me,' he said. 'Thank you for the drink, but I've things to do.'

And he spun off into the night, looking all around him.

Δ

As I made my way home on the Ardaithe, sharing a carriage with a few executives from the Financial District and a couple of arguing homeless, I had this feeling of time flipping—of past, present and future spread out in front of me on a flat surface. I could consider them all at once, and I saw the kid waiting at street corners for drops that never happened. I saw him cycling with no message to deliver. No purpose. I saw the subtle changes in the routine; his shoulders slumped and his hood searching the wet pavement. I witnessed again in memory the edgy glances, left, right, over the shoulder, that were nothing to do with us—he was expecting someone to come for him. That boy understood so little about the world, but understood that people were going to kill him for what he had done. And what had he done? Done the juicy, mayhap fell in love, like someone he saw on the Tele-Visio. You read these stories about too young parents that you never believed.

And then one day he was gone, lost in the country with his daughter, and a whole kingdom laid to waste behind him.

And I needed to find him.

And the King—him of no known origin, no age, no name. Despite the trillions of terabytes of information floating around our heads, nobody could pin a single fact on him. And now, apparently, he was dead and gone. At the hand of a young kid.

I got off the Ardaithe two stops from home and switched platforms. Went instead in the direction of HQ.

Δ

The boys at reception grinned when I passed on the way in—they'd never seen me darken the door of the place an hour after my shift, let alone after midnight. Is looking for a decent brasser on the Hub, is what they were probably thinking.

I found an empty HubbleRoom and started my search.

In those days, you could pick a street and a time period and you could search the visiomatter for any IP—Identified Person, that is. We pulled our vigilance from the chipcams and dot-phones all over the city, the Hubble's patrol drones... infinite sources. An authorised agent could start with a cigarillo packet receipt for example, and they could pinpoint the time and place the transaction was made, and they could then follow that IP using a combination of financial, social, user, audio, visio and thermal data from the Hub. And once your mark got on a boat or a plane you could follow them to any other part of any network. But IPs were easy.

Which, well... It was not so easy with UPs—Unidentified Persons—and these were either people who'd never been registered on the network—rare—or people who'd had their details purged from the system deliberately. This was an illegal act and came at a high price on the black market.

The system that the Earlie Boys had was that, rather than being completely purged and becoming UPs, they would show up as different IPs at different times. The user ID was constantly changing so that you could never, bar with visuals, confirm that such and such a person was in such and such a place. They could do whatever they wanted, and you couldn't track them. They were ghosts with human qualities. Or should that be the other way round?

What I did was I went way back for inflow of the kid in yellow making a drop on a particular street where we'd often watched him. I copied the image stats and saturated them, and then looked for a match at the Jolly Bridge.

IPs and UPs fled back and forth across the screen, but I found him, eventually, going up the fire escape steps with purpose and staggerfalling down them a few hours later.

And what I did then was I followed the kid in yellow to the next street and the next camera, and from that camera to the next, until he got home. And I sped up the inflow again until he was seen coming back out of the block and heading off again. I followed him in triple-speed down alleys and along canals, into the Financial District and the Rose Red, and beyond. Everywhere he went, my eyes tracked him, how he cycled, face twisted up to the rain with concentration. I framed that image, reframed it, saw the skinny face, cheekbones strong, lightning blue eyes fixed on some action or some future point, some grain of tarmac on the road that was not tarmac but was his dream of the King's death, some paving slab or flow of rain that was not rain or slab but him holding his daughter. Even being so much older, I could not know or understand the way he felt.

Once the kid had travelled too far north of the city, into the NO-GO zone, our inflows became unreliable. The last visio inflow ran out in grass wetlands and he was lost to me, cycling into undergrowth. I did a sprint trace across the Hub but he did not return that way. Joolie called and I did not pick up. It was morning. I cannot explain to you how I felt at that time.

Somewhere, during the middle of that same night, the one they called the Bard showed up, taking the same route into the undergrowth, and within thirty minutes he was followed by the one they called Mike the Hat, and then others, carrying a punt on their backs. Inflow through to the next morning, the next afternoon, did not show the kid re-emerging from the undergrowth. Mayhap they'd killed him after all. Mayhap Sweeney was wrong.

I located map folders for the lakelands in that part of the NO-GO zone and decided on seven other places this kid could have exited the lake system. I did sprint traces of each one, for every single camera angle. I copypasted that image of yellow in every camera archive on the northside system. Four hours later, with people getting through their morning's work at the station, I found him on a half-sunk ghost estate to the west. Patrol-drone visio. There in a high field he began to move west. In the folds of his skins the thermal view showed a small, warmglowing entity. What happened in the days after that happened very quickly, and in a blur for me. I slept very little from then on.

BIT CALLED

DINGEL

Dingel was the westernmost place left. Iron boats crashed against steep blue-slate mountainside and it took them three hours to dock at a treacherous harbour inlet.

When they were safely ashore, the kid and the babba looked out to sea from a dark granite pier and, seaward, saw mountains of wave moving behind curtains of cloud and rain. It was as if that wild, angry place was a wall up to the sky, shutting them off from the rest of the world.

/We're trapped/ Jeri called over the hard hammering of the rain, watching the same unfathomable blue violence.

/Doomed/ said the kid. /But I am a wind in the sea; I am a seawave upon the land. Open up to me, Ireland, you bollox!/

/Where'd you hear that?/ Jeri laughed.

The kid shrugged. /Some poem/

/Rains *hard* here/ called the sailor-priest, who struggled towards them, adjusting a large rolling pack over his shoulder.

The sailor-priest was a wandering man, Jeri had said. White-stubbled and scarred, he was ill-tempered, and stopped now and then to scrawl frantic messages in a paper notebook that he kept in his breast pocket. The kid had seen one such message, on the deck as they attempted to dock for the twelfth or thirteenth time. It said: /BEWARE THE BROKEN WATCHES/

He saw also what seemed like names written thereunder:

—MISTER DETH
—ÓISÍN
—KILDERKIN

—ST VINCENT DEPAUL
—BLICKER
—FOXY JOHN

/Who does he write the messages to?/ the kid had asked Jeri.

/Or who does he receive them *from*?/ came the reply.

But the sailor-priest—or Father D as the others called him—was not a drunkard, or a leader. He drank tonic water, and was always somewhere in the middle of the caravan they set in chain, going up the mountain pass towards the town proper.

Δ

The town was indicated by pillars of smoke that rose from behind a hilltop into driving rain. A thousand or so people were left, the kid had heard, people who dived for lost treasures in what had been Kerry, or were ruin tour guides, or scientists studying the mutie sheep, or drunks, or old-towners who knew nothing else, perpetually failing farmers. It was a town, Jeri said, that was just about treading water, on the verge of drowning. The countryside and surrounding villages had been swallowed by the ocean, which continued to try to swallow the rest.

/And yet it's been that way up here for a hundred years or more, and will probably be so forever/ the strange one concluded.

On the way up the path the kid saw and showed to his daughter the mutie sheep: black, slick, hairless creatures with huge black eyes, a few with spare limbs or heads sagging from them. They gorged on the lush mountainside grasses, barely noticing the new visitors. They moved awkwardly, like arachnids.

/But the six-leggers, you'd want to see them jump—oh boy!/ said a small, stocky member of the congregation to the kid and his daughter.

With an hour's walking, they crested the pass and came down into a view of the town from the north. It twitched light amidst a cloud of rain, and had its own small hill, on which sat a dere-lict fire station, and winding lanes and low terraced houses in a cluster. A large aquarium and a few other small factories or laboratories marked the lower end of the territory, and there the sea encroached again, so wild and high that the pier could not be seen. To the west and east of the track to the town, a few larger hillside houses perched and surveyed the madness of the ocean, but there was something faded and ruined about the grandeur they might once have claimed.

/Where's the statue?/ the kid asked the stocky man, whose name was O' Leary.

/Out beyond the town somewhere. South. She'd want to be fukken worth it/

The babba sang to herself on the kid's back and the kid adjusted her weight on him. /What'd you hear happened?/

/Heard that two young girls were coming along the road past the grotto and that for a few moments Our Lady glowed and the rain all around the grotto stopped. And they said that the glow was actually a shaft of sun and blue sky shining through on top of the grotto, and Mary said to them, *I have stopped the rain once. I will stop it three times, and after the third time it will rain no more*/

O' Leary spat, and the babba crowed at the sound.

Rain came down loud as ever, in mockery of their dreams. The kid realised suddenly all that he did not hear: the city vessels, the intercom, the hourly bell ringing, the drones passing overhead.

/What'd you hear then?/ O' Leary asked.

/More or less the same. Only the way I heard it there was something about the serpent too. That it wriggled free of her foot and escaped. Or that she let it go and smiled at it/

/Fukk the serpent/ O' Leary spat, the babba laughing again.

The path was stony and uneven and hard on the feet and ankles. They fell into the trudge of their boots a while, and O' Leary spat for the girl a few more times, until he said, /Is your sister?/

/Is/

/Lovely girl/

/.../

He shooed a gnarled finger at her face. /Can I carry her a while?/

/Can/ the kid said, and he stopped to unravel her from his back.

/Lovely girl/ O' Leary said to her in a babyish voice, cradling her between bicep and breast. /She have a name?/

/Em...no, actually.../ The kid grinned awkwardly. /Don't know.../ He laughed. /Is complicated/

/Ahsure. Names only cause trouble/

While the kid fixed his pack, O' Leary pointed out to the girl the many glistening trails of slugs that criss-crossed the mountainside grasses.

As they drew closer to the town they could make out pubs and laneways and swarms of people milling about. It seemed to the kid so busy, like he imagined festivals, like the merries, and that was strange to witness in the middle of nowhere, between mountain and sea.

/Had two grandchildren/ O' Leary said, between coo and tickle, while the babba squealed with exhausted delight.

The kid did not ask what had happened to them.

/What is that redness seeping out of the ground?/ he asked.

/Machines. They buried their machines here. In fields...back gardens...Is the rust seeping up/

Δ

They set up camp in an old merries on the outskirts. The Big Wheel and RocketRide rollercoaster rattled in the wind. Rusty bones of them. Prizes still drifted back and forth across the ruptured tarmac, amidst branches and broken glass. Bumper cars were islands in an overflowing water feature now. Two dozen large sea containers had been left strewn across the southern entrance of the site and they began to occupy them in groups. A man in a pub had told someone that some big buck had come to strip the merries and transport it, but left halfway through one of the storms.

/The storms here.../ he'd apparently said, and made a big explosion with his hands.

There was a House of Mirrors, but when the kid idled in with the child to look about the glass was all broken and jagged and leering. When he went to the Horror House the skulls had all toppled from the skeletons and rolled in shifts across the puddled floor.

They hadn't been there two hours when the forecasters said big storms were coming in.

/They *are* bad/ Jeri said. /They come in now and then and last a couple of days. We best get in and lock up/

/We didn't even get to see the statue yet/ the kid moaned.

Everybody took portions of food, spare bags for everything else. The wind picked up and rain turned from hammering into something else. Something stronger than he'd ever witnessed before. Something dangerous. It began to sound like the sky was opening up.

The kid lit the lamps in their container while Jeri worked the door shut and lined the bottom of the entrance.

/Don't worry/ Jeri said as she stood again, now in the kid's lamplight.

/Am not scared/ the kid said. /Is only raining/

Bit from

WORD OF WARD—

The thing that I keep saying about surveillance work, you see, about police-detective work, is that it was boring. You spent all your time submitting, processing or searching for data. But when that kid was gone, he was gone. He transcended data. This occurred to me after days of searching Hubble and checking journey times and staking out Earlie Boys over long hours with Roe.

'What are you thinking?' Roe kept asking, as if we were partners in some TeleVisio drama. 'What's with this new pattern?'

But I didn't tell him what I'd done, what I knew or what I was thinking. About Sweeney or anything else. I shrugged. And anyway, he was more interested in the Vincent Depaul case at this point, after a warehouse had been burnt down.

'What he's doing now,' he informed me, 'is he is targeting data stores. Trying to destroy the information. You see, he realises now that data is used to control the poor. Or so they say…'

But I *was* watching.

The one they called the Bard, or Crooner Bart, seemed to be doing the rounds as normal. Pulling up his eyeglasses to scratch at his red eyes, he shuffled from pub to pub. Taking the river micros as always, talking to no one, wiping his hand on his nose, ignoring the untied laces of his boots, pulling up his skins so that he could adjust sagging pantalones as he walked. He seemed glum—no doubt. He was possibly on the device a little more, but he offered no clue. There was no panic in his eyes, only process.

On the third day, with moonbeams breaking through the cloud and softening the rain, we parked up a hundred yards from the Pup&Pendant, and began the long, quiet wait. It was a business-as-usual sort of night, people on the streets hauling themselves to their places of work or rest, a numbness to the calling of the hawkers and the shifters.

Neither of us noticed him until he was at the glass of our vehicle, tapping on the pane for me to bring it down. Stupidly, feeling Roe suddenly tense in the seat beside me, I did so.

The Bard leaned almost right into the vehicle. I remember there was a smell of vomit off his breath.

'Go 'way,' he said. 'Stop following me.'

And away he went, pulling his pantalones and skins up all in two handfuls. We did not follow him after that.

But that night I did notice that someone else was interested in the Bard. Leaning from a window above the Pup&Pendant, and peering over us as the Earlie Boy left us in his wake, was a dark round figure, hard to clock by the drizzle between us. Then the white headlamp of a riverboat burst on him and he was round and dazzling. I recognised the face from the night of the game. It was the second sighting. It was the first night I cogged that the reporter—O' Casey—might be involved too.

BIT CALLED

STORM PASSES

/Give me a verse/ Jeri whispered over the babba's soft snores. /To pass the time/

The two of them existed as two stooping faces, floating in an ocean of darkness, in the calm space under catastrophic waves. The device pressed out a shallow dome of light between them, in a container they couldn't see the corners of.

It had not been so bad the first hour, but then a terrible feeling came. A wrenching came. It was as if they were in the jaws of some leviathan, and it was dragging them across the merries yard, trying to lift them so it could throw them into the bay. The hammering on the container was deafening, that of a thousand strong arms pummelling with a thousand lump hammers at the tops and sides of the container. It would have killed them to be out in it. But, for some strange, happy reason, the babba loved it, and lulled by violence fell straight to sleep. Jeri said it was no wonder, because it wasn't so long ago she was in a womb.

Jittery of nerve, the kid thought of some verse.

/She ate monotonous food and thought the world was flat
  She knew the things that moved at night was neither dog
      nor cat
  But hobgoblins and dark-face men,
  And she was sentenced in the end.
  And so she clenched in brittle hands
  A world she did not understand/

/Powerful stuff/ Jeri sighed. /How did you come to that one?/

The kid shrugged, trying to settle against a wall of the container.

/Don't remember/ he said, when he realised that Jeri couldn't have seen him shrugging.

/Where are all the women in your life?/ Jeri asked, later.

/Just have that one there now/

/Where do the verses and sayings come from?/

/Don't know. Some I learned at school. Found a hard drive once, in a skip, and there was loads on it. Have seen them on graffiti, on the network. I stayed in a library for a bit…/

/Fascinating. It's as if you were born to store them/

There was a fizzy crack and Jeri held forth a bottle of Up-YaBoyo across the light. She was either smiling or grimacing, a glow running beneath her bulging eyes.

/She's not your sister, is she?/

After a second, he shook his head. /No/

/Stolen?/

/No/

/Then what?/

/My daughter/

/Ah/

/…/

/Wow. How old are you?/

/Thirteen … I think/

/You seem older… But not that much older/

/Amn't sure when my birthday is/

/How do you know you're thirteen if you don't know your birthday?/

/Me and my brother had birthday parties at Christmas. Know when I was nine—is when my mam went—and have counted every Christmas since/

They drank in silence, until Jeri said, /Can I keep asking you questions?/

The kid shrugged to the half-light again. /Sure/

/Where is the girl's mother?/

/Died. Giving birth I think. Or shortly after/

/Ah. I'm sorry for your loss/

/.../

/What was her name?/

/T/

/For?/

/Just T/

/.../

The kid started up then. /People try to put filth on what happened between us, but it wasn't like that. Wasn't like that at all/

/.../

/She loved her reading. Loved how I knew all these verses and words. Even taught me some of them/

/.../

/Was like we were meant to find each other. My knowing the words, her knowing the meanings .../

/She understood them?/

/Mostly, yea. She did. We'd walk and she'd tell me what she thought they all meant/

/What did she say?/

/She said that people lost themselves and some tried hard to find themselves, and most of the words added up to that meaning. She said the rain was a veil in Ireland, like in a wedding—that was very clever—and she said one day her babba would see the face behind the veil. But only if I took them both away .../

The kid trembled in the candlelight as he squeezed back the feelings.

/Away from who?/

/A bad man/

/Who?/

/Her father/

/Ah/

/But I didn't. Was afraid/

/But you took the baby/

/Too late .../

Big bottlegulps now. Squeeze. Silence. Light snores of the babba in his lap.

/You think I could mayhap speak to T? If we did one of your séances?/

Jeri did not answer.

/If she's out there, mayhap I could reach her?/

But her eyes were averted in thought, brows bent in, off in some deep state, turning to darkness, some far possibility.

/You think?/ the kid asked.

She turned back into the half-light. /Mayhap. Let me reck it/

As if in excuse, or a plea for understanding, the kid then opened up entirely. He told Jeri all of it—about the Earlie Boys, about running—and he protested his innocence in every way.

Then, later, he dreamt of fire—a dream full of suffering and terror.

Δ

By lamplight they ate crabmeat from plastic bags. The babba's sleep had been deep a long time. Cosmic cracks of thunder tore holes all round the darkness, and great howls loitered, gone and returned, gone and returned. The storm was building into jaws again.

/Were you in Dingel before?/ the kid asked.

/Yes/ Jeri said. /For research. I was studying some old papers, artefacts, and they were only available in an archive here. It's gone now. *They're* gone/

/What were they about?/

The kid went confidently for two more bottles, cracking them open with a coin from his pocket.

/Ever heard of Faust?/

/No/

/Well, it's a story about a man and, well, I was trying to write a book about him then. It was going to be called *The Unfinished Encyclopaedia*, and it was going to be about how the Faustian Age was ending/

/That was a time in history?/

/In a way/

/When?/

/You see, the story of Faust is about a man making a deal with Mephistopheles—the Devil—in order to have all the knowledge. To know everything that could possibly be known about the world. He exchanges his soul for that knowledge, believing that it will make him happy, or powerful, or godlike mayhap…

/My idea was that we live in an age where the average person has done that—has sacrificed their soul to live in a world of information. To know everything. The answers to any question were in your device, and you were born with a comm-code, and access to all of that information. We could control the whole planet with technology. It was all about power.

/But, as with the story of Faust, that age, that quest, that desire was coming to an end in failure. All that knowledge didn't *produce* an answer as to why we couldn't find peace. Why we were here. I wanted to say that this quest for total knowledge was a mistake. And that… essentially… is where I thought we were at. And I wanted to say that we still just about had time to grope our way back to God. You see, Faust's final delusional mistake was that he believed he was in control. Like we do. Even though we're drowning…/

They drank. They scratched themselves. The kid did not admit that he did not understand.

/Lots of words I remember/ he said.

/Yes/ Jeri said, suddenly sullen. /I know that/

Both were quiet then. She wiped her eyes and nose. Was she laughing or crying?

/Are ye not a cult?/ the kid asked.

/Us? Not really… I don't think so. We don't have any answers you see. We are a wandering question mark/

The kid shifted his weight from one aching buttock to the other.

/Why do you tell me all this, when I'm just a kid?/

/Because I think you'll remember it all … In case anything happens to me!/

Old Bug Eyes started laughing then—guffawing—loud and sudden and scary. /I'll see about the séance/ she said.

BIT FROM **THE PLAY**—

Act the Third, Scene 3

Evening in the lounge of the Pup&Pendant. Hum of
banter from the front bar. Clink of glass. Heavy metal
is playing on the jukebox there and an argument is
taking place as to whether it should be allowed to
continue. In the lounge, MacDowd's skull glows on the
mantelpiece as ever. SISSY and KER are seated at the
same two stools, looking at their devices as ever.
Occasionally the tortuous lurching crank of riverside
cranes can be heard over the music and clamour of the
pub. From offstage, JIM CORCORAN is refereeing the
jukebox debate.

CORCORAN.   [offstage] He paid his money, Mick, so
               he gets the fukken song. What happens
               next is up to ye.

On a TeleVisio programme in the corner behind the
bar a reporter gives the facts of a nineteen-week
strike at postal-drone facilities around the country.
In official broadcasting skins he describes the boxes
piling up as 'mountain-high'. Neither SISSY nor KER
appears to be listening.

SISSY.   [focused on his device] Says here on
               LocalNews that a study has proven that
               the average temperature of human blood
               has fallen a whole degree in the last
               fifty years.
KER.   Are becoming a cold-blooded people.
SISSY.   Snakes and lizards.
KER.   Returning to the sea.
SISSY.   You know I never learned to swim.

They both drink from their pints of stout. SISSY, seated on the right, drinks with his left hand, while KER, seated on the left, drinks with his right hand. They have precisely the same amount of stout left in their glasses.

SISSY.   Did yer old man follow the sea?
KER.   [eyes away from the device and to the ceiling to consider the question] They said he might have descended from desert people, so uncomfortable was he with it. Never went near the water that he could help it. Never worked it nor sailed it. Looked to the mountains but never got near them either.
SISSY.   What did he do then?
KER.   He ate. Ate and ate. Drove lorries on the last working motorways. Died young and fat. [drinks] A blessing, the way things were going.
SISSY.   [drinks] My old man was a diver. In lakes. Cunt never taught me to swim, and I begging him. Was as if he wanted me to drown.

Enter CORCORAN.

CORCORAN. Lads, am wondering on a scoreline and have me hands full with these metallers.
SISSY.   Which one?
CORCORAN. [pulling three pints at once] Otters—Stars.
SISSY.   Will check. [squeezes painfully at his back and hyper-extends it]

233

Exit CORCORAN.

Offstage: sound of a banging door and then clamour-
hush from without. Metal music dominates. Enter the
BARD. Hood of his skins down, he looks fretful, ill-
tempered. He comes to the counter in the lounge with
his skins on and dripping. Rain beads on the grey
plastic. Of a sudden he remembers the skins and pulls
them off roughly. When they are tucked under his arm,
still dripping audibly, he pulls a fistful of coins
from the chest pocket of his Kandinskee and begins
counting them back and forth, and piling them neatly
on the counter, still with a sullen, bothered look
about him. Only when he has built a small tower of
coins on the bar does he see the two regulars.

THE BARD.   Well, lads.
SISSY & KER.   Well, Bart.

Enter CORCORAN with a thin black box, a little larger
than a match box, which he slips across the counter
to the BARD, who retrieves it and tucks it into his
pantalones pocket.

CORCORAN.   Porter?
THE BARD.   [checking his tower of change] Guin.

A loud note pierces the stage——that of a clarinet, the
note played a high G#. It is an overwhelming note,
held too long, used to jolt the audience into a feeling
that the moment is bad, significant. When the noise
fails and fades, the BARD and the two local punters
have already established conversation. Time seems to
have passed. The BARD has a line of small pebbles of
different varieties and sizes lined up on the counter.
SISSY and KER listen obediently to his lecture.

THE BARD.   [holding up a particular pebble
               between forefinger and thumb] This
               one now. Got this one on a mountain
               in Cork. Is a good two hundred miles
               from here, given all the byways
               and highways. [scratching his chin
               earnestly] Yes, two hundred and four I
               think, via the sunken hole of Thurles.
SISSY.   You stop in Thurles, Bart?
THE BARD.   What? Did I fukken what? Sure there's
               fukk all there. No, you sail straight
               on.

Prompted by the BARD, all three drink.

THE BARD.   Saw sparrows there. The sparrow,
               you see, is a migratory bird. Roundy
               auld head on him. You find them only
               in Cork now...Maybe the hills around
               Waterford too.
KER.   You been to Waterford too?
THE BARD.   Have. Waterford now would be closer
               than Cork. Down the coast on a
               clipper——a hundred and twenty miles.
               Problem with Waterford is where to
               land.
KER.   Right.
THE BARD.   Would tell you a story about
               Waterford, only you wouldn't believe
               it.
SISSY.   What story then?
THE BARD.   Aht.
KER.   Go on, B. Tell us.
THE BARD.   Doesn't end well.
SISSY.   How so? Do tell. Are bare broke for
               stories here.

The BARD considers this. Scratches his goatee.
Begins to finger a particular greyblue stone, smooth,
round, a blazing white marble streak bisecting its
greyblueness. The two local punters' bodies are erect
in anticipation of the story.

THE BARD.   See this one. Got this one in
                   Waterford. On a job that I can't say
                   what it was. They have green and pink
                   dolphins down there, coast to coast,
                   all the way from Dingel to Hok. And
                   I took this stone from the mouth of
                   one——a green one——not ten minutes
                   dead, washed up on the roof of an old
                   school we ran across. [sighs]

Realising that this is not the story they were to hear,
SISSY and KER relax their shoulders and slump again.

Beat.

Beat.

SISSY.   Awful wild stuff happening down there
                   in Dingel all the same.

Enter CORCORAN. Checks pints, begins to fill a fresh
round.

KER.   That game was the Otters', Jim. By
                   twelve. All done.
CORCORAN.   Just my fukken luck.
THE BARD.   What is that now, in Dingel?
SISSY.   Wha——oh. The statue. That miracle
                   there.
THE BARD.   The miracle?

KER.   The statue of the Virgin that appeared
              to two old men saying she'd stop the
              rain.
SISSY.   Rake of people down there now, praying
              for all sorts. They say one fella
              went down in a wheelchair and came
              strolling back up. [leans forward on
              the counter and looks to the BARD for
              approval] Cured like.
CORCORAN.   [sceptically] Cured is right.

The BARD only drinks, makes no real response. The
outward impression is one of sudden boredom, of
disappointment with the answer to his question. But,
nevertheless, his mind is beginning to tick over.

SISSY.   Ever been to Dingel, Bart? Is a wild
              auld spot, they say. Full of mutant
              animals and the like.

Beyond the pub [offstage] you can suddenly hear
the hourly bell. As if awoken, the intercom fuzz
and rambling begins again. Random, outdated and
irrelevant bytes of data and statistics are spewed out
over the city.

THE BARD.   Never been.
KER.   How would you even get there? How
              many miles would it be?

It becomes apparent that the two men are filling the
silence out of fear.
THE BARD.   [shrugging, not bothered] Dunno.
              Shannon Barrier I suppose.

Beat. Awkward. Filled by the drinking of the men.

The BARD rubs his nose clean and dry with the heel
of his hand. With a lift of his head he suddenly has a
renewed sense of purpose.

THE BARD.   Lads, is a few bob there to put into
               the jukebox if ye wouldn't mind. Have
               a bit of business to go through with
               Jim. [calling] JIM! JIM! Will you show
               two pints at the front bar for the
               lads? Have to talk to you.
SISSY.   No problem, Bart.

CORCORAN enters as SISSY and KER stand to leave.

CORCORAN.   [humming] Not a bother.
KER.   Any requests?
THE BARD.   Hah? Play them ones I like. The dear
               auld ones.

Exit SISSY and KER.

THE BARD.   A word, Jim.
CORCORAN.   Always.
THE BARD.   What do you know about this statue
               they're on about?
CORCORAN.   [tilting the head and frowning in
               consideration] Ehm. Know it happened
               about a month ago. Mayhap more. Way
               I heard it, 'twas four sailors looking
               for accommodation she appeared to.
               Apparently their names were Matthew,
               Luke, John and Mark. I wouldn't know
               about it. Although, apparently a
               hundred thousand have gone visiting
               there.

CORCORAN pulls the pints. Despite two free stools now, the BARD continues to stand.

THE BARD.   What about the healing? The lads say
              people are being healed?
CORCORAN.   Same as them I heard it. Nothing more,
              nothing less.
THE BARD.   You believe it though?
CORCORAN.   [with one pint left to settle, he
              begins to pour the second while he
              considers the question] Honestly, B,
              don't know whether to believe nothing
              or everything any more. Don't know.
              [smiles, well-practised] Sure what does
              the innkeeper know only the margin on
              a pint and the distance to last call?
THE BARD.   [angrily] No! No. No pub bullshit
              tonight. Have troubles on my mind. Am
              thinking.
CORCORAN.   Sorry, B. Meant no harm by it. Only to
              say that I find it genuinely hard to
              know.

Exit CORCORAN with two finished pints.

THE BARD.   [aside] Am not myself. [his head is
              drawn down, his face fallen into
              his two hands, elbows perched on the
              counter. Turning slightly, doubled
              over almost, he looks back to the
              pulsing skull on the mantel.]

Enter CORCORAN, warily.

THE BARD.   [looking up at him] Am sorry, Jim, for
              shouting at you in your own house. Am

239

	not myself. Have troubles on my mind.
CORCORAN.	Not at all. How is he, B.? You been up there?
THE BARD.	Is not well, but no longer in danger. I worry. Is not himself either. And when he is not himself, I am not myself.
CORCORAN.	I didn't want to say anything.
THE BARD.	Is haunted. He went somewhere we don't know and does not seem to think he should have come back. No longer seems invincible. If I could get him the kid, and the child...

CORCORAN pulls down a luminous green bottle, and pours them each a short drink.

CORCORAN.	Any sign of the kid?
THE BARD.	[shaking his head wistfully] Disappeared into the rain. [beat] Fukken punk. Terrible things I would do to him.
CORCORAN.	[raising his green glowing glass] To the Earlie King.

The BARD salutes and drinks.

THE BARD.	But what if there was something to this statue thing? What if I went down there and did a bit of praying.
CORCORAN.	Could you get himself down? If there were miracles to be had...
THE BARD.	Never. Sure he thinks he is God.
CORCORAN.	Mayhap he is.
THE BARD.	Clap hands. [beat] But I could get down there in three or four days. Say a few prayers. Get out of this

                            cursed arsehole of a place. Get myself
                            a stone. Maybe that's why I've been
                            collecting them all these years, maybe
                            there's some magic behind them that
                            will help him.

Beat.

CORCORAN.   [trying to bring the conversation
                 back to reality, subtly] How far would
                 Dingel be?
THE BARD.   In my own vessel? Mayhap three
                 hundred mile. One-forty to the Shannon
                 Barrier at least. [firming up his
                 notion] Mayhap a stone from Dingel and
                 a prayer to the statue might cure him.
                 Get him back from wherever that mind
                 is roaming. A bit of magic, aye?
CORCORAN.   Pray that you find the boy and the
                 child too. Mayhap the healing's there,
                 in vengeance.
THE BARD.   Clap hands. [cheerily] Either way, have
                 no stone from Dingel yet. [downs the
                 remainder of his pint] Yes, am going to
                 Dingel to pray. That's it now.
CORCORAN.   Well Godspeed to you, go easy and
                 safe. Will hold on to any collections.
THE BARD.   And will celebrate the fact now with
                 my little Chy-nee favourite. She'll get
                 the goat of Barty before the bad bell's
                 next ring. [goes for his skins]
CORCORAN.   [smiling, flipping a towel between his
                 hands, relieved to see the other go as
                 always] Well, go easy on her now and
                 all.

Exit the BARD. CORCORAN is left alone on stage and
as the lights dim and the sound fades, the pulsing
glow of MacDowd's skull on the mantel grows stronger
and stronger, to dominate the darkness and the
stage, until it appears as a pulsing neon beacon,
accompanied by a pulsing electric buzz, and the
growing note again——G#——of the clarinet.

CURTAIN.

BIT CALLED

THE STATUE

Somewhere in the depths of what he guessed was an afternoon, the storm began to relent, and soon the Wandering Question Mark emerged like worms unto the warm rain.

The kid and his babba came out into the light from the depths of the container and, discovering the pipemetal sky outside, and the tabula rasa of calm sea below, sure enough she began to cry.

Others stretched, called out; some cried for joy and leapt about for a short time. One even stripped and pranced around, embarrassing the kid so much that he went back inside.

When he did come back out they'd erected a huge tarpaulin on aluminium poles in the centre of the clearing between the containers. Under the tarp they set out a large asado, made from some other metal and held down with gathered rocks. The kid and his child watched all this from the shelter of the bumper platform, where they played with stones. A troop was sent to town for beer and bread. Jeri took charge behind a veil of silver smoke and crabmeat was emerging from packs and skins.

/What you think?/ the kid asked the babba. /Are they all fukken mental?/

The girl sat up on her legs, back straight, ankles tucked under nappy-wrapped bum, and with gusto she swung a fist to the sky. She stared at his belly with a furrowed brow. No sound did she make, but with her sermon delivered she clapped once and roved off on her knees.

After that, he spent a deal of time keeping her from scratching blood out of the rash she discovered on her legs. He then soaked the same legs in the white cream from the babba bag, then tried to keep her from eating the white cream that gathered on her hands as she tried to scratch her legs, so that, by the time O' Leary came with some burnt crabmeat for them, the kid and his daughter were grappling, and it seemed like the kid had more cream on him than the child had on her, and if it really were a grappling match it seemed too that the girl was winning, and O' Leary laughed so hard that he spilled half the crabmeat from the plate and fizzed the beer in his free hand. Then some skulls from the Horror House suddenly landed on the asado, causing everyone to scream. It was as if the storm had been chewing on them and spat them back out.

Δ

That evening, they all stood in a triangle and held hands, for a reason that the kid did not understand, and after a few strange prayers they set off to see the statue.

They marched like a platoon through a horizontal rain, growing heavier. Their boots dragged in the sludge, back to the outskirts of town and east then at a lonely crossroads. People chatted about what they might see, about dreams they'd had during the storm. One of the ladies showed him how the bundle pack he'd had on his back could be altered to go on the front, so that the babba's head poked out of the kid's skins and they faced the same way. She was fascinated by the world, watching all the heads bobbing and the shoulders bouncing, and squeezed funny noises out of her mouth and chest. She seemed much more a person than when he'd met her first; an easy child, people said when they trudged alongside to say hello. She was the only baby amongst them.

When he fell into step with Jeri, the kid asked again about the séance.

/It's been on your mind?/ Jeri asked.

/It.../

But the kid just nodded. Pulled the hood of his skins forward, put his finger to the babba's mouth so that the babba sucked and chewed on his finger.

/Okay/ Jeri said. /I'll see about it. Let's get tonight's fun out of the way first/

Soon they began to meet the crowds: scores, soon hundreds, then unquantifiable. It was chaos, like the Patrick's Day crowds but so much more claustrophobic on the narrow boreen, between encroaching ditches. At every field and marsh gate chip and candy vans had been set up. Hawkers meandered through the crowds, selling cans and cigarillos and miniature Marys and crosses and binoculars and rosary beads and pills and temporary skins and beans and mussels and crabmeat.

They had repaired this stretch of road: it was slick and clean and pressed. A few of the trudgers drew beads from inner pockets and chanted decades of the rosary as they came closer and the crowd thickened. You could sort of see something through the thin rain, up high on the bank. A light.

/Hail Mary, full of grace, the Lord is with thee/

Where *was* God, the kid now wondered, thinking of all that Jeri had told him. Now he did feel a sense of something important happening. This felt like what it meant to be part of history. There were people everywhere. The road was clogged with them.

O' Leary drew up alongside him, caressing the babba's cheek with a finger. He said, /Feel a deep sense of peace and protection here in this place/

The crowds swelled, and the Wandering Question Mark started to lose each other. They had to press to get closer to the grotto, high up on a rocky bank that grew on the right as the boreen wound downland. Stone steps zigzagged up to the grotto, but these were cordoned off and the crowd gathered below, heads craning up the slope to see the statue of the Virgin in her cave. By the time the kid got close enough to see her with his own eyes, he was alone with the babba, surrounded by locals and shawlies and sailors and boy racers and groups of old, old priests, and every other type of person he'd seen in the world, and the rain had grown heavy and enveloped with its musty iron aura the air that they all shared.

The foliage around the grotto grew densest green, large flat alocasia leaves with lighter maps of olive on their surfaces. Out of the foliage the grotto emerged, large chips of limestone held together by smooth chunks of concrete. It was deep enough that there loomed a sense of great darkness. Framed by that depthless gloom, she bathed in the small bright tongues of many candles, her hands held together before her, white eyes blank, pale lips pursed with a serene sense of purpose. She was just a statue. A normal statue. No more than five feet tall.

But in the flickering candlelight she did seem to be gently rocking, or turning, hither and thither, the shadows moving on her white face so that you couldn't tell if she was looking at you or someone else.

/Look at her now/ a young sailor said, a dredger of western seas perhaps. /Her head is moving now/

An ancient whiskered tomboy whispered to a companion: /Will she speak?/

/The rain … Is it dropping off now?/

The kid heard so many decades of the rosary, and the muttering of so many people, and the patter of so much rain on the plastic skins of the people. He gazed up at Mary until … yes, yes …

Yes, there *was* something.

Something.

/A lady two days ago was cured of blindness/

/Three days ago that was. On the same day that *she* came out towards me. Out from the cave just slightly, into the rain, as if to say that it did not bother her, and would not bother us much longer/

Her pale face, shadowed and yet bathed by firelight. Her soft white hands.

/Heard the Angelus, though it was not time/

/Wives are returning to their husbands/

She was breathing, he thought: that was it—she was *breathing*! She was alive, like them.

She was here. Present.

The Virgin Mary was present. She had come to them.

She was doing the most important—most human—thing: she was breathing, her chest pregnant with wet air and falling then, full and falling empty, growing again. It was gentle, but undeniable: he could *see* it. He filled his own lungs.

/She's breathing!/ he cried.

As one they drew in breath and ejaculated gasps of wonder and low confirmation. /Yes! Yes! She is!/ These sounds rippled like a wave down and up the boreen—/I see it now! Watch her chest!/—and the babba chose that moment to add to the cacophony, breaking into jittery tears, hungry to be fed, or changed, or cuddled, or released from his chest, or crying mayhap from tiredness, or from thirst, or with some pain of tummy or itch of the red blotches. Within seconds she had built her little cries into an agonising siren, the dirge that gave pleasure to the chest at first, that felt good to the child because it was the child announcing herself, and her complaint, but soon grew out of control.

But the kid could not even hear his child, because he was speaking to the breathing statue directly, her with her foot on the serpent's head.

/Why?/ he said, shifting his head out of the babba's wet way, searching those grotto-trapped blank white eyes for answers. /Why did you do this to me? Why did you take T? Why did you give us the child when we did nothing? How could you ruin us?/

The babba bawled.

/You bitch/ he said to Mary. /You fukken whorecunt. You murderer. You give life to evil and you take love from us. I hate you. And I don't care about rain, or miracles, or anything else. Let the innocent live. Take the damned. Take me. Take the King. Take Bart. Take anyone else, but give T back. Give her back to this child. Let your miracle be that. Do right by innocent people, you fukken bitch!/

The child gasped and choked on her own tears, hoarse from them, in the state of weeping that was a whirlpool, impossible to escape, impossible to remember the reason for, emerging from the cycle only when she had enough breath and energy to scream. The crowd were too caught up in the breathing of the statue to notice or hear. Rosaries were incanted now at a multitude of volumes, speeds and rhythms; they sailed in armadas through the high seas of the air. He found O' Leary before he found Jeri, and he said to him, /Please, take her from me. Cannot help her/

He had already unwrapped the child from his body and thrust now the red screaming thing into the bewildered man's arms. O' Leary did not say anything, only looked stunned. But he turned the child to him then and held her up, and before anyone knew anything he was cooing and shushing, pulling the girl into his skins and embracing her, and the kid had fled.

MISTER VIOLENCE INTERLUDE #3

Follow him now, the fukker! With his brick teeth and his tarpaulin shroud! You'll know him by the engine steam pouring from his nostrils—follow that steam! Follow the smell of diesel! Follow the oil dripping from his arsehole, from subterranean depots, slipping from busted pipe to sopping sewer. Follow it west, inland from the city, to find this monster at work. This purifier. In along the grand canal for twenty miles, *He* rows, while Mister Violence chugs along in his shadow, one and the other, the two of them joined at the feet. Beyond the first fish farms and before the last is where they dock. A rickety punt rocks on a dark slipway. Prehistoric jungle leaves have returned, and flap over the black windy road up. The air is pungent. Watch them: they come to a blank, dark building, where on the first floor, one door, marked ACCOUNTING, always has the light pouring out from around its rim. Twenty-five, seven. The light never goes out. And he is scheming violence. Twenty-five, seven. He has lists and documents and plans. He lights matches. The light never goes out on his planning. Success or failure he returns to the room and dreams of burning again. *He* is the one Mister Violence likes the best, or at least just as much as any other. If the light is on he is planning to burn. Each match has a target. The light *never goes out*! Mister Violence leaves his friend there to plan.

/Take your time, moc/ he mimics, because he knows he won't be let down.

So he leaves him to his work. This chap knows what he's

doing! Or is it *they*, as many believe? Well, Mister Violence doesn't have a care, as long as someone's hurt by the end of each drenched day.

I did a background check on the address above the Pup&
Pendant and I found out that this O' Casey was a reporter. Small,
incidental stuff for various Hubble media and newssheets. Short
stories of note from the city and the provinces. He was writing about the talking statue, about Vincent Depaul, and all
sorts of other junk. He was a passable writer, nothing too flashy
or expansive. He had come across our path a couple of times:
always drink-related.

I read an interesting transcript with him though, after he'd
been picked up for indecent exposure one sodden midnight. His
complaint started with the usual:

/Why don't you pick up the people who are really doing
damage? Why don't you tackle the serious crime. What's wrong
with taking a rooten piss in the canal?/

/Is against the law is what/

/Is all fukken piss anyway. If anything I cleaned the godawful
stuff/

/Okay/

/There are *serious* crimes going on out there. And I can help
you. I *know* things/

/What do you know?/

/Know who Vincent Depaul is for a start/

/You do?/

/I do/

/Well, the mic is on. Tell us and we'll get to work on it/

/Well.../

/Well, what? We're listening. The computer's listening. Now's your chance/

/Well … he's a man, and it's hard to tell his age. Maybe fifty. Or sixty. Ish … Wears a cap/

/You have a name?/

/No … But he sails a punt into the city along the Grand Canal. A banjaxed auld thing/

/An address? A mooring?/

/Well, he comes in from the Grand Canal/

/So VDP is an oldish man who comes in from the Grand Canal in a jalopy of a punt/

/Exactly. He wears black skins, and covers his face with cloth/

/So, we're looking for a man in a cap, with an old boat, no name, no address, no mooring, no face/

/Yea. But I think he might live in the city too. The Flats mayhap/

/You can stop there/

/Have done my research!/

/You've just described half of Dublin. You know nothing/

/Is something else. I have a list!/

/Yea. You can stop there/

/A ledger of the people the Earlie Boys have killed!/

/A fine will teach you to keep your peeder in your pantalones, and if you waste another minute of my time you can spend the night with us/

/Godawfulgodawfulgodawful, the things I know/

/Name and comm-code, please …/

And that was it really.

But something told me I should talk with him. I wanted to hear about this list. Mayhap he *did* know something. Mayhap he could help me find the kid, because at that point I'd run aground. He had just disappeared. Or someone had disappeared him. Still, what can you do? I continued to search for a needle in a haystack.

BIT CALLED

WALKING THE BAD LAND

/Where is my babba?/ spoken with cracked voice.

/Well … you gave her away/

/Didn't. Didn't mean to/

/But you did. We're looking after her. We're treating her eczema and feeding her properly. The child seems happy/ Jeri unfolded her arms and sighed. /You've been gone two days/

/Know that/

/Where were you?/

The kid could not look Jeri in the eye. He stood in the rain, on the threshold of the container, looking beyond the other into the dim interior.

/Please. She's mine/

/She *was* yours. But when you give something away it is hard sometimes to get it back. And this is a child we're talking about. A special child/

He did not know where to turn or what to say.

/Where have ye been?/

/At the statue each day. I feel something great is happening here. I feel there is something special here. And your girl is …/ Jeri's smile was near-deranged. /But don't get me wrong. We're not abandoning you, or punishing you. That wouldn't be Christian. We just don't feel you're ready to father this special child/

/Does everyone know?/

/Yes/

/What can I do?/

/Come back tomorrow. I'll set up a palaver with Father D. Find out what has to happen/

△

For those two nights, he had run.

Down into a deep valley, away from the camp, as wild as any place he'd seen in life or on the TeleVisio. Fern and bulrush had risen from the pennywort, and ferns ten, fifteen feet in height, with branches that spread out in long, droopy awnings. Rainwater came in through leafy gullies only. He had pulled down the hood from his skins to take it all in. Reckless, wild with psychic pain, he gasped at the serious sounds of water.

The following morning he'd found he could make out in the undergrowth the traces of old country walls, and soon came to a cracked, pebble-dashed bungalow, all broken windows with grasses sprouting out of them. Out of the place where the roof had been stood a giant fern, thirty, forty feet high, and any garden or driveway there had been was long gone now too, swamped by nature.

On he went, sheltered from the rains by the overgrowth. Not knowing where he was going or what he would do. A couple of times, grebes and redshanks swung across his pathway, diving for the cotton grass and stands of dwarf birches. He had abandoned the child, he admitted to T. His first clear thoughts were that it was for the best. But they didn't last long.

He found other houses, all mired in ferns and rushes and giant water lettuces and other plants he could not name.

/Tommib/ he said. /Tommib and France gave the world to plants/

He remembered that first evening Sweeney had taken him up to the fish farms for some casual work. They went up there in Sweeney's old punt and it was fair quiet was what it was.

/You listen close, moc, and you'll hear the ghosts up here/ Sweeney said to him as they docked.

Now, a long time later, after he had lost T and given away their child, he thought the run of the water against his boots was a ghost, and the fat leaves slapping on his head, and he realised that he himself was a ghost, a haunted ruin of a boy, and that she was all he had left.

Δ

/Jeri says you're good with songs and lines from old things?/ said the sailor-priest.

His container was empty bar the duffel bag on which he sat, and an old door which he had laid over two breeze blocks to make a table of. On the table he had two lit candles and a tattered paper bible.

/Give me something. An example/

/In the floods of life, in the storm of work, in ebb and flow, in warp and weft, cradle and grave—/

/—an eternal sea .../ the sailor-priest continued, scratching his beard. /A changing patchwork, a glowing life. At the whirring loom of Time I weave the living clothes of the Deity... Good. You been saving that one for me, kid?/

/Jeri said you'd like it/

/Sit down there/

As he was told, the kid sat cross-legged on the floor, the other side of the table. The other produced his notebook from the folds of his two shirts and scribbled in it.

/What is it you are always writing in that book?/ the kid asked.

/Only notes/

/From where?/

The sailor-priest looked at him like he was daft. /My head/

He began to chew on a baby fingernail, his fingertips wrinkled nubs, like they'd been worn out over the years. /Now. If you're to have any chance of a kind hearing you must first be honest with me about everything. That clear?/

/Yes/

/You ever been to confession?/

/No/

/Okay, say after me/ The sailor-priest bowed his head so that it shadowed the flickering of the candle and darkened the container.

/Bless me Father, for I have sinned/

/Bless me Father, for I have sinned/

/Is your first confession then?/

/Yes/

/Tell me what you've done wrong/

The kid hesitated. /Have given away my babba and shouldn't have/

/Is the babba your child?/

/... Yes/

/Your daughter?/

/Yes/

/Why did you abandon your daughter?/

/I panicked. Thought I wasn't able to mind her/

/How old are you?/

/Thirteen, I think/

/How old is the child's mother?/

/Is dead/

/How old *was* she?/

/Fifteen/

/How did she die?/

/In childbirth. Was pregnant twelve months. Impossible to survive they said/

/You know this for sure?/

/No. Was not let near her during her pregnant months/

/Why not?/

/Her father did not allow it.../

/What was her name?/

/T/

/T is only an abbreviation. What was her full name?/

/I... don't know. She didn't ever say. Only knew her as T/

/Did you love her?/

/Yes/

/Then how could you not know her name?/

/.../

/Can you guess her real name?/

260

/No/

/Theresa?/

/Mayhap/

/Tabitha? Tina? Tracy?/

/Don't know! Mayhap she didn't know the full name herself/

/What was her father's name?/

/The Earlie King is the only name I know for him/

The sailor-priest stopped to flick back and forth across a few pages of his notebook. Then he settled and faced the kid with the glimmer of the candle spasmodic in his black eyes.

/Now, the next question is most important. I will know if you are lying and will not forgive you or your predicament if you do lie. Understand?/

/Yes/

In fact, it felt good to dwell on it, to sit in the darkness of truth and let it flow out.

/Before the babba was born, how many times did you make love to T?/

/Make love?/

/Penetrate. Do the juicy/

The kid paused. His heart gave out a gentle pounding.

/You told Jeri ye never did it, even once. That you didn't know how she got with child/

His eyes searched the floor of the container. He was hoarse when he tried to say, /Don't/

/How many times?/

/We were drunk. I don't remember/

/You told Jeri never/

/I lied/

/I don't believe you. I believe God made that baby/

/Was only me and no one else. The child is mine. Look in her face and you see me. Look in her eyes, you see me/

The sailor-priest smiled wide and clapped hands once.

/God is good/ he said, showing the kid his palms. /You've confessed at least. Are young, naïve .../

261

He pulled a stone from beneath his leg and threw it at the container door, and a moment later the door began to open from the outside. Light began to nose its way in and seek out the objects of the darkness.

/Will set up the séance/ the sailor-priest said to the boy, /And your T will decide who keeps the child/

Sssshhhhh. Have a look at this now. He starts in the men's toilets of the government agency office, in his maintenance gear, standing on the toilet rim first, and then on the cistern. Stretching, pulling himself onto the partition and arching up to lift a ceiling tile free. The tile resists at first, probably not touched since installation, but is then easily released, inciting a cosmic swirl of dust particles and vortices of fluff. Balancing calmly, he pulls himself up into the hidden space of the dropped ceiling. You wouldn't think of an old fellow like him as that strong, but who's there giving him a boost—only our very own, one and only, Mister Violence! All dressed for the occasion in black serpent tie. Slitherysmooth buckaroo is Mister Violence. Knows how to dress the part when the occasion demands. His eyes are Hubble TeleV: he follows Vinny Depaul up into the empty plenum, to a land of lint, cable, light fixture, dead air, exoskeleton.

Soldier-style goes VDP, bent arms pulling his trunk, trouser legs akimbo.

/Go on the bad penny!/ calls Mister Violence to egg him on.

/Vanish in flames, salamander/ whispers Saint Vincent Depaul. For fire is the purifier of the world.

He crawls. Slow. Careful. A flat networked plain of lint, of cable, of gloom; ceiling tiles that just about take his weight. There, above smoke detectors, above the grilles of fluorescent light, he lays and watches through thin cracks the work of an office, a contingent world. There is a supervisor perhaps, she who always asks people to do what they do not want to do, stood over a blond employee. He might be taking dictation, but neither

VDP nor Mister Violence cares. Vincent knows what to do with information, with power. *They* entrust it to the machine; *he* burns it.

/Dopey, malignant creatures/ he whispers. /I'll free them all/

/Oh, that's the poetry!/ squeals Mister Violence, his black eye seen through a crack, ill-slept and full up to the whites with gorgeous yellowy trauma.

Someone carries a biscuit in her left hand, holds it protectively between finger and thumb; she is smiling at somebody or something else. Here comes a dripping courier with sheaves of forms in plastic. It's a journey in death, yes, but a journey in life too.

/The whiteness of their throats!/ exclaims Mister Violence, there above the flithering of the air-conditioning.

The feeling builds and builds in Depaul's chest. Below him: technocratic, clerical, collective consciousness. Like a hive. To work, to work, to work. And *him*? Well, he is in the process again of waking up to what he is *again* capable of doing. He is the *seachange*.

Everything has been set, yet he likes sparking it the old-fashioned way. In the office, they begin to smell it. They know something is happening. They are waking up too, in their own way. Into doubt, and fear. Into panic. Smoke-stained paper curls and forms a crust. Smoke begins to fill that empty plenum. He crawls along, undetected, only just faster than the smoke. Not even the fire alarms know the full extent of what he has done. And he eludes everyone, bar good old horny Mister Violence, his eyes—two shattered headlamps—filled with smoky tears.

BIT CALLED

A STONE TRIP

Jeri told him that a room in a certain B&B had been secured. That they had to be careful in such a religious context. He was to eat nothing for the day. Which he hadn't been eating well anyway, on account of not having the babba. He missed her big dark eyes. He missed the weight of her in his arms, heavy as a bagful of shopping, all chubby skin and love. He missed the gurgles and the coos, and that mysterious way she shot her hand into the air. She loved him. He knew by the way she looked for him when she tried to stand and fell. They belonged to each other forever— and all this he had caused by his own weakness and anger and fear.

Six in the evening, empty stomach, alone.

/There will be four or five others/ Jeri had said. /Myself and Father D will be there. Relax, it'll be fine. All you're doing is asking questions; someone else will be answering them. Time to man up a bit, kid. Sulking will get you two things: nothing and nowhere/

He crept across narrow streets, paused to inspect doorways when others passed, in case he'd be noticed by the locals. Fat rain fell down on this street he walked, crashing and spilling over the tarmac. His skins streamed rainwater, writing a thousand nautical trajectories. His mind was blank, bent forward to the purpose of the evening. His mental trajectory was straight and sharp and fixed: get there.

And if he had awoken from his purpose, what would he have been thinking of? What would he have remembered? His mother?

Her who had worn the yellow skins first and told him all stories, and given him lines she remembered from youth. Her? Would he have been thinking of her religion? Of the Fadinhead—how she became addicted to dying? The disappearance he could do nothing about? His brother? The alleyways? The cycling tours of the city, collecting and delivering? Would echoes of other mundane phrases call across his mind? /Would be a grand country if we could put a roof on it... She's not the day you'd ask for.../ Or did he see his life and his words spoken and heard and every deed done as the delivery of one long garbled message? Mayhap delivered to the intercom and spoken through that fuzz and lost? His lines of poetry and ancient prose, his job, his babba... Was he only the words of a rambling intercom in some city he couldn't see?

No, none of that. None of that as he stole across a narrow lane of squat terrace houses and knocked on a red door. Only: get there.

He clenched his hands together beneath his skins as he waited. Deep in his hood, his eyebrows were furrowed, falling in over his eyes. In the other houses on this street, what? TeleVisio. Dinners eaten. Gaming. What people did in normal homes. Sleep. Argument. Love being exalted: sweaty bellies, hard knuckles, cold feet, beating hearts. Swearing. Boredom.

And in here, beyond the red door, the channel of darkness.

And yet as the door opened he was met by a big smiling grey-haired clucking chicken of a woman.

/Hello, gasúr! Are you here for the prayer session?/

/...Am/

The sounds from beyond her were from some TeleVisio talk show: /You kin sit an dope dream of de past, but ah don bee-leeve dat—in dis day-nayge—dat anybody really tinks dat so-sightee's about information. Is about bur'yin psy-chic paayne. Loss. Trummin and aur—/

/Skins on the hook first. Then is just above our heads. First floor. Room three/

This docile animal led him breathlessly up carpeted stairs, her hips touching the wall and banister as she half-staggered. The carpet she cherished, and she explained as she went its depictions of farmyard animals. He thought of Honest John.

Δ

The sailor-priest and Jeri sat by the window, looking out, and welcomed him to the room with brief smiles. Cloudlight made their faces grey and tired. Deep barrels of laughter rolled by from the street outside.

Two others—a man and a woman—sat at the table dealing to each other from their own decks of the tarot. The man was gaunt. He looked up when the kid entered, and sniffed at a head cold, but seemed to take no real notice, continuing to deal to the girl, who had straight blonde hair and chubby cheeks and dressed all in black, who smiled and said hello. The kid recognised them from the Wandering Question Mark but neither had ever stood out.

/This is India and Luke/ Jeri said, standing at last to leave the sailor-priest alone by the window. /Our two best links/

India and Luke began to pack away their cards and to set up the table. From a rucksack India pulled four fat candles, each a different colour. She lit the candles and placed them in the centre of the round table, which was a deep and strange green colour, the paint of it moving in swirls. The kid still stood by the door: he was suddenly starving. Luke pulled two bottles—one of red wine, one of what looked like absinthe—and put them on the table also. His mouth hung open as he did his jobs—heavy lower lip—and it made him seem stupid, or doped.

/First we have a short mass/ Jeri said, approaching the table to help. /And then we get into it. I'll be the medium, so if we find T she'll speak through me. You know, kid, when sailors first heard whales in the sea they thought they were ghosts/

/Okay/ the kid replied. He watched Luke pour the absinthe into the cups.

/What I mean is that ghosts or spirits are just another part of our world, but from a part of it that we don't know so well. We don't need to fear them/

/Okay/ the kid said, fists unknowingly clenched by his side.

/Come/ Jeri said. /Sit/

The four of them sat, the kid between Jeri and India, facing Luke, who was lost in the rim of his cup. He heard still the Tele-Visio voices coming from another chamber, and rain outside. Only when they were all seated did the sailor-priest join them wearily, pulling his trousers up at the thighs as he bent to take his place between India and Luke.

/A short mass/ he sighed.

/First/ Jeri corrected, /We drink/

The kid could never figure out which of the two of them was in charge.

/We will drink three cups of absinthe this night, in order to open our gates fully to the darkness of the spirit world/

Jeri raised her cup, as did they all, and drank the first.

A burning moved down through the kid's chest, that same burning from the first night on the ferry. He refused to cough it up though. He took deep breaths. It hurt, but to him it was T returning, the love and pain of T. It settled in his sternum and burned, a fire on the inside.

/A mass/ the sailor-priest said, and he began, outstretched palms raised to the ceiling.

Δ

Mass was said. He was all deep breaths. The burning filled his insides, ate his pain and his hunger. Head tilted to the ceiling he saw farmyard animals in a cornice that ran round the top of the wall. All of them were there. But was that two cherubim over the window, arms folded, watching with interest, smiling as he observed them? Or was it just a couple of pigs in a pen?

/... this kind of experience/ the sailor-priest said. /There was a great mind once, ages ago, the mind of a mathematician and phil-osopher called Pascale. One of Europe's great minds, ever reliable, ever seeking out knowledge. A man of science. But after he died his housekeeper was sorting through his effects and checking the pockets of an old winter waistcoat, when she found a strange lump in one of those pockets. And when she tried to pull it out she found she couldn't. She realised that, whatever it was, it was sown into the lining of the waistcoat. Well, she eventually cut it out and found that it was a piece of parchment, and on it was written, *On 23rd November last, from half past eight in the evening until half past midnight: fire. God of Abraham, Isaac and Jacob, not God of the philosophers or the scholars. Fire to walk with me. Fire to consume me. Forgetfulness of the world and everything outside of God. The world has not known you, God, but I have known you. Joy. Joy. Joy. Tears of joy. Fire. Fire. Fire. Pure fire of pure joy…*

/And it seems to me that these personal experiences of the mystics—of Pascale, or Saint Teresa of Avalon—these experiences are the microcosms of the macrocosms. Why can't every atom of the universe have its own night of fire then? Why not? … So, when we walk out into the darkness this is what we seek, this microcosm of experience that is the macrocosm. That shows us God, whether fire or not. Joy of God. Pure joy of pure God. And so we pray …/

And they began to chant prayer again, prayers his mother had known by heart. He was drunk, yes, but beyond drunk, beyond silliness. In some trancelike state he felt. Outside of silliness, outside of time. The fire was in him.

/We drink again/ Jeri said. /To end the mass/

The kid witnessed his hand raising a second cup and could see the dark swirls of wine mixed in with the luminous green absinthe and it brought him an image of MacDowd's skull in the Pup&Pendant, glowing on the mantel.

They all chanted: /I tell you they have not died …/

And the kid knew it and joined in:

/Their hands clasp yours and mine
/They are now glorified
/They have become divine …

/I tell you they have not died
/They live and breathe without you
/They walk now—here at your side
/They tell you things that are true/

Δ

Each lit candle on the table was a different colour. He began to cry and then stopped.

/They give the spirits warmth and light/ Jeri said to the kid. Mayhap she was talking about the candles. /And the food offers them nourishment they'll remember from their time on this plain/

Where *had* the soup and the bread come from?

/T liked candy floss/ the kid chuckled.

/We have no candy floss/

/Did not want to be flootered for this/

/You are not drunk. You are between two worlds. It is disorientating, like being drunk/

/What is the contraption on the rad?/

/We try to record what we experience. We look for disturbances in the Unified Field/

The green of the round table was swirling, forming and re-forming: seas, fields, rain-soaked mountainsides. Burning of the third cup. Each lit candle on the table was a different colour.

/Each candle is a different colour/ he informed them.

The lights went out, the curtains closed. Footsteps rapped at the pavement far beyond the window. Rain tap-tap-tapped at the window pane.

/Our beloved T/ the sailor-priest's voice said reasonably to the candlelight. /We bring you gifts from life into death. Commune with us. Come across the darkness and move amongst us ... We send this message out into the void/

Let me in, the rain said, as if it had a story to tell, or an answer. Let me in. Let me in. Tap tap tap. LET [tap] ME [tap] IN [tap].

/Into darkness we cast our lines. Here on the bestial floor we wait... We send this message out into the void/

What was that smell? He knew it. Knew it from somewhere. Was it the rusted metal of the merries? Someone was gripping his left hand; someone else hung limp from his right.

A whisper: /Keep the circle unbroken/

Jeri held the right hand. She seemed asleep.

/Breathe in unison. Move into a welcoming state. Think of a time you wanted something or wanted to see someone so much/

The babba, her black eyes.

/Keep the circle unbroken ... We send this message out into the darkness/

A bell began to tinkle at the centre of the table and the candle flames swooned.

/Is someone there?/

/Hello?/ Jeri said in a weak, childish voice. /He-e-llo?/

The table began to rattle in the dark. The rain rap-rap-rapped at the window.

/Hello?/ Jeri said again, from a place of fear and blindness.

/Is the girl speaking/ the sailor-priest whispered.

/T?/ the kid asked. /You mean T?/

/Aim-ee? My love?/

/T? Where are you, T?/

/I ... I don't know. In darkness. Am lost, I think. Where are you?/

/Am here, T. Still here/

/Where?/

/In ... In Ireland/ The kid then whispered in the direction of the sailor-priest: /How do I know is her?/

/How is our girl?/ Jeri said.

/Our girl?/

/Our babba. I miss her inside me/

/She is okay. Is healthy. I love you, T/

/She is? What does she look like?/

/Has blonde hair, and big dark eyes. Sleeps a lot and smiles a lot. Rarely cries. Is actually a bit chubby, you know! Likes to go wandering/

/She walks?/

/Crawls/

/.../

/T, are you okay?/

/Am snake-bitten/

/I miss you/

/Hear voices sometimes, like from interference or something. They don't make sense/

/What happened you, T?/

/I woke up in darkness, hearing these voices, like echoes/

/T?/ said the sailor-priest. /Am Father D, and I have some questions to ask you/

/Have heard this voice before/ said Jeri. /This voice wanders the darkness, asking questions/

/Is me/ the sailor-priest acknowledged. /Have some questions for you/

/Aim-ee, am afraid. Should I answer him?/

/Answer/ the kid said, full of regret.

/Who is the Earlie King?/ Father D asked.

/Is my father. I fear I will meet him wandering the darkness too/

/Did he give you the child you bore?/

/No! But feared he'd take it. Aim-ee promised me he wouldn't let that happen/

/Did you dream of sun while you were with child?/

/The sun, yes!/

The hand that was not Jeri's gripped the kid's hand so tight, pressing the knuckles together 'til it seemed they would crack or burst. He began to sober up.

/Are you White Bead Girl?/ Father D asked.

/Am snake-bitten/

/What was your sun dream?/

/That the babba came from the heat of the sun. Heat was the seed. But the kid in yellow is her father. The yellow was his sign/

/Yet he has given her away. Aim-ee has let the child down/

/Have not!/

274

/Aim-ee?/

/Did not!/

/Lies weaken the signal, Aim-ee! We can care for her. Believe she is special. We are a yellow people, an Easter people, an *alleluia* people. Believe she is the beginning of something new/

/You gave her away, Aim-ee?/

/Only for a moment. Was afraid, T/

/We have cured her eczema. We feed her properly. Is happy/

/Aim-ee? How is my girl?/

/I … I love her, T. She is the only thing I have left in my shitty life/ He could taste his own tears, more now than the absinthe. /Don't know why I did what I did. Please don't take her away from me, T/

/Has she a better chance with them?/

/She understands lies/ Father D whispered again.

/Don't know/ the kid sobbed. /T, I love you. I love her. Ye are all I have/

/Let her stay with them, Aim-ee. Is best for her. She is best with them. You stay with them too. You love her too … But we need them. *She* needs them. You cannot do it alone. Are afraid. Am snake-bitten. I do not know where to go/

/Don't do this, T. Please. I can be her father/

/We can help you to move on, T/ the sailor-priest said.

/How?/

/Look up/

/T!/ the kid moaned.

/Look up/ the sailor-priest said. /Accept the snakebite. Think of the sun as a cure/

/A cure?/

/Yes. See the sun/

/See sun/

/Let yourself rise now/

/See sun!/

The kid looked at Jeri. Her eyes flickered. She was smiling T's smile.

/Please, T!/ the kid moaned. /I won't fail. Let me be the father/

/Go up/ the sailor-priest said.

/Are all I have in my shitty fukken life. First you, then her. All I have/

/Go up/

/Am going up/

/Where is she going? T? Please, T!/

The candles suddenly flickered out. A floorboard creaked. He came back to the room and felt the presence of something else. Or the absence of something gone.

/What did she say?/ Jeri asked the darkness, returned to her normal voice. /I remember nothing of the transaction/

But Jeri's hand went lax. Something thumped hard on the table.

/What?/ Luke asked. Then he began to gurgle.

In the dark, India breathed hard, as if she was having an asthma attack. The kid wondered if all of this was normal. Then there was another bang on the table, as if someone had dropped a large block of wood on it. The kid jumped up and fell over his chair on the way to opening the curtains.

There, in the gloom, he saw Jeri looking towards him, or the light, holding a neck black with wine. The hand at her throat was covered in wine, her mouth open wide. She seemed shocked at her throat, feeling for something that was gone. Then her face sagged from its bones.

The sailor-priest was asleep on the table, where spilt wine spread out and the candles had been knocked. Luke had fallen back in his chair, exhausted, arms spread out in acceptance. India had collapsed to the floor, where yet more wine had spilled. Over them, breathing hard, was Bart—the Bard, the Crooner—folding his knife and putting it back into his chest pocket.

/What is this strangeness you are engaged in?/ he asked the kid, who screamed.

Δ

Dublin at that time was a city full of unhinged people, walking around talking to themselves. It was as if that rambling intercom was contagious, as if the nonsensical stream of data that flowed out into the rainy streets and dirty markets had infected the minds of its inhabitants. Slumkids prattled on to themselves as they filtered out of the rubbish what could be used or sold to the factories; administrators shuffled home from work through empty parks, muttering conversations and confrontations they wished they'd had at the office; mothers and fathers admonished long–run-away children, pleaded with lost lovers. Countless messages were sent back and forth between devices. Returning to his chambers, the reporter rehearsed informing the kid in yellow that his brother had been murdered:

/Am sorry to be the bearer of bad news, but your brother has been killed in the last month … At home, at the hand of the Earlie Boys. I know Crooner Bart was involved, and Mike the Hat, and the Eel. Have reason to believe that a runner named Clem was present also … All of whom you no doubt know well … Yes, was quick … The guillotine … I do not know the precise reason, but can guess … / And he would begin the count to eleven.

By way of diversion, he let his feet wander the cobblestones of the Old Temple Bar, the red-light district, and crossed the river at the Ha'Penny Bridge.

/Am sorry to bear bad news but your brother has been taken from us … Am a friend … Am a local reporter … Try to let people know what they need to know … What do *you* need to know? It was quick; he would have suffered only briefly. I can provide further detail but only if and when you are ready … Am so sorry for your loss … /

His conversational perambulations took him to his doorstep, whereupon he was shocked into awareness by the sound of loud cheering from inside the Pup&Pendant. It was them—the Earlie Boys—and they were roaring and cheering like the rain had stopped. He cursed his feet for letting him meander, and burst up the stairs to eavesdrop on the news. It was there that he learned, through a hoover's hose, and through the roars and smashings and hollerings of the gang, that Bart had found the kid.

Δ

It turned out not all of them were dead. Luke stirred, then Jeri groaned, so Bart drew out his blade again and finished them off with the ease of a man signing his name to a few documents.

The kid remained frozen, on the floor by the window. Not sober, he did not understand what was going on, and the world seemed transparent, filmic, dreamlike, these bodies unreal.

/Are you going to kill me now?/ he asked Bart.

The Bard ceased going through the pockets of the dead to look at him. /I wish! Can't kill you, no. Can only take you to the King. Who will ... well, you owe a debt to him/

/The King is alive?/

/Of course he is. Why? Thought you could kill him?/

The kid found himself sitting on the floor, by the window. Bart was counting out change, then smelling the absinthe bottle and wincing, then poking with a delicate tongue the inner of the long bottle neck. The hammering rain at the window begged to be let in.

/Is the most amazing thing, you know/ Bart said to him. /I came to the statue to pray for the King, and to pray I'd find you one day, and the child. And look, here you are! My prayers were answered! Now, what does that tell you about whose side God is on?/

/How long you been here?/

/In Dingel? Been watching you for days/

/Is a bad dream/

/For you maybe!/

The Bard came and stood over the kid. His hands jingled in grey trouser pockets, the toes of his boots pointed different directions.

/Where is the child?/

∆

The kid knew the container where O' Leary slept, and they waited 'til late. They took the babba quietly, and O' Leary died quietly.

While the Bard did the killing, the kid stood back and looked away, like a child embarrassed by his parents. He was soaked and shivering, his skins left back at the B&B, and waiting only for the chance to take his girl. He gulped, but did not cry. He couldn't think straight enough to reck what was best for the girl, so he did what he was told. Bart would kill him, he knew; Bart would kill anything.

When it was done, the kid grabbed the babba's things and pulled her into her skins, and they slipped out the groaning container door, and out the front gate of the merries yard. But the babba cried in Bart's rough hold—more a grip than an embrace—and when she would not stop he handed her back to the kid.

/You quiet her/ he demanded. /Can't strike the child of the King, can I/

∆

On a dark, wind-ruffled back road the kid tried to flee through a ditch with the babba.

But tearing through the dark, he felt a sharp hot punch in the back of his right shoulder, and he fell to his knees, nearly spilling the girl.

Jungle leaves flapping sounded like great birds' wings.

Panting, the Bard pulled the kid to his feet and, as he did so, he pushed his thumb into the simple knife wound he'd made near the kid's shoulder blade.

/Very lovely games I'll play with you if you don't keep straight/ he spat in the kid's ear. /Only have to get you back alive. Doesn't have to be in one piece … And listen. Think on this. If you try to run again, or do anything stupid, mayhap I'll just do you in. Mayhap I'll do the child in front of you first, and tell the King that you killed the child, then I did for you in a rage/

/He'd kill you for the mistake/

/Mayhap not. He'd be disappointed yes, but mayhap it would be the end of the story, so would be easier for him to get over it. Either way, you're dead and your child's dead/

He pulled his thumb out of the wound and used the same hand to rub the crying babba's tufty head.

/Like your brother/ he said.

/Stop/ the kid said.

/Oh/ Bart said. /I'll never stop. We guillotined your brother at that shithole flat. Job was done in five simple minutes/

And he began to sing as the kid followed him back through the ditch and down to the wetlands where his boat was moored.

BIT FROM THE PLAY—

The Pup&Pendant lounge, with SISSY and KER at their
usual stools, their elbows pressed on the counter.
They are, as always, mid-conversation. Throughout the
scene, CORCORAN appears and disappears, lumbering
thoughtfully on various errands. The skull on the
mantelpiece glows behind them.

KER.	Here's another one. All sums considered, what would you say is the value of a single human life?
SISSY.	A fine question.
KER.	Humour me.
SISSY.	Depends.
KER.	On what?
SISSY.	Your belief system ... The category of the answer you seek ... For example, I think in economic terms. In fact, would go as far as to say that I think that if our former notions of natural pride in our country had instead manifested themselves into a pride for economy we might not have collapsed the way we did. See, we never faced up to the fact that we were no longer citizens but consumers—
KER.	[interrupting] —So then, in economic terms, what's the value of a human life?
SISSY.	Well, would go back to supply and demand—a key principle. Are so many billion lives on earth, so the huge amount of them lessens the value of each one.

KER looks at him with a bewildered frown.

SISSY.   [sighing] Think of raindrops. So many
                raindrops fall each day in Ireland.
                Trillions. And rain in Ireland is of
                no value. But imagine if you took
                that rain and shed it over a land
                in drought. Each drop would be near
                priceless ... Hear me?

KER.   Comprende. And I like that idea. Each
                drop of rain as its own thing. The rain
                as a multitude of drops.

SISSY.   Yes. But from a human point of view is
                quite depressing, no? Kind of reverse
                engineering. If everybody has a life,
                and are all supposedly equal, then
                the value of each one is diminished,
                neither less nor more than the person
                next to us on the ferry, and therefore
                little at all ... So doesn't it only show
                you how worthless and replaceable and
                unoriginal we are? A drop is worth
                nothing if there are a trillion others.

KER.   [throwing up his hands at the
                pessimism] But maybe that's the wrong
                way round. Maybe what you're actually
                proving is how big we are. I am not the
                issue. I am no longer the question. We
                are rain, a whole thing. And maybe my
                value—if I am part of that rain—is
                equal to the value of the whole thing?
                If each one disappears, is no rain.
                [bangs the counter in victory] There!

SISSY.   But, going back to your question about
                value. Would say one part of a whole—
                the smaller the part and the bigger

```
                        the whole——is of little value. Almost
                        nothing in fact. Think about all the
                        competition in the world now, for the
                        sun's energy, for space on the ground.
                        Are simply too many people, fighting
                        over what's left. Don't you think that
                        lessens the worth of each separate
                        human?
KER.                    Stop! Your words are drenching the
                        place.
SISSY.                  Was your question!
```

For a moment the two men sigh and shake their heads,
then lapse to silence, and consideration of their
pints.

```
KER.                    Is awful quiet.
SISSY.                  By god and it is.
KER.                    Where are they all?
SISSY.                  Dunno. Something must be brewing.
```

...

BIT CALLED

DAYS BLEEDING

He looked aft to vague, misty hillsides, where stilted motorway and leafy valley resisted each other. He wished it all away and gone. The babba crawled up his body, playing, a smile on her face now that he was back with her. That she had been glad to see him warmed his heart, even with all the trouble. But again and again the lights of distant boats in the drizzlemist brought it back, everything that had happened. Every blurred light and far-off bird cry reminded him that he was in a world of bad memories, in hell.

/I tell you they have not died .../

/Ah, shut up/ the Bard said. /No one likes poets. People like singers, like me/

They came up through marshes, moving slowly. Skinless, the kid sat with the babba under a bow tarp. Bart sat astern in his skins and steered, talking to himself or the kid the whole time. He had stuffed the kid's wound with glue and laughed when he told the kid it looked infected.

/You realise that whole séance thing was a crock of shit?/ Bart said. /A trick so they'd have no trouble from you about the child. They were taking her from you just like that/

/Then how did they know my real name?/

/How does anybody know anything? HubbleBank you dunce!/

Δ

The babba was often lulled to sleep by the motion of the boat.

/What will happen to me?/ the kid asked the length of the vessel.

The Bard shrugged. /Have been asking the same question myself. I know he'll kill you, but mayhap he'll hurt you for a while first. Mayhap for a long while—is hard to say/

/And the babba?/

/Oh, he loves the child. Will be grand again once we get her home. Things will go back to normal/

/.../

/Here, look, see the stone I got in Dingel? Got it in that overgrown estate you found/

Δ

He couldn't sleep—the pain was too much. When he did sleep, there were nightmares. As time passed, pins and needles spread down his right arm, so he fed, lifted and cradled the child with his left. He mixed her formula with river water now, because he had no clean or hot source. He waited for her to get sick after her bottle, but she didn't. She slept in his lap, cooing and dribbling. Despite the sores and the rash, the pallor and the greasy hair, she was to him more lovely than ever.

They moved north and then east, tacking across great lakes, creeping through marshlands. Bart said that once they came to the olden motorway it would be more or less plain sailing. He talked constantly, mostly about himself.

/Am lonely/ he complained. /Is a long time since I was so long on my own/

The kid could no longer bring himself to speak to the other, his mind aflame with hopeless plans, worries, pain.

/You think you count?/ the Bard said, bailing rainwater from the boat. /You don't. Are dead to me, kid. As good as a ghost… Probably four hundred miles now have been on my own. One-twenty to the Shannon Barrier. One-thirty then to Dingel. Then traipsing around Dingel once I found you. Imagine: I prayed to a statue that I would find you and within twenty-five hours I found you. In the exact spot, more or less, that I was praying. That *is* a miracle, isn't it? Am fukken blessed/

His eyes were magnified by thick-lensed glasses held together by tape.

/Me own ma dropped me when I was a babba myself. Is hard to see but I have a dent in the right hand of my forehead now. You see it? She was afraid to let go of me after that... Don't mind living with her. Don't have to cook; she doesn't get worried ... You ever drop the girl? Wouldn't admit it, would you? Probably right. But the King will know—oh, he'll know! Me? I think whatever doesn't kill you makes you stronger/

Dead and rusting turbines rose into the cloudbruised sky. Bart pulled his glasses down to wipe them, exposing red eyes. His face above the dripping grey goatee was ravaged.

/Will tell you/ he said. /When I was drinking one of the evenings on the way down here, waiting out that big storm, I met two scientists. This was nearly outside Limerick now. Two river scientists looking for electric fish. These are fish, you understand, that use electricity to communicate with one another, not even to eat each other. Is that not wild?/

The kid was reminded of the old salmon that Sweeney told him about so many times. It seemed long ago now.

/Those two scientists though. Were drunks. Had been in Limerick two years doing the same thing. Looking for a few fish that they never found yet. And I found you in four days! Imagine!/

Δ

One day bled into the next. His wound festered; his whole back felt aflame. The Bard pulled him forward by the hair, one morning when it was plooping down bombs of rainwater on the river. The violent act frightened the babba to tears.

/Ooooohh ... is looking bad/ he said. /Will only get worse/

/Help then/ the kid said.

Bart gave him a blank stare. /But you're dead to me/

And yet he fed them cold beans each morning, from a batch of cans he had. He gave them no cutlery, so the babba ate from the kid's good hand. Bart laughed at that and the babba laughed too.

She was slowly warming to the Earlie Boy, though he wouldn't go near her.

/Couldn't forgive myself if something happened/ he admitted.

Then, at some point in the journey, he glanced over his shoulder suddenly, and said to the kid: /You think anyone is following us? I swear I hear a motor. Distant, to the southwest maybe/

And the kid began to hope then.

He didn't care who it might be: the Heavies, or the blonde woman from the ferry. The whole of the Wandering Question Mark mayhap, leaderless now, looking for different answers now.

/You know, could have sworn I saw a croc on my way down here/ the Bard said, distracted from the idea of pursuit already. /A fukken big one too. Just this side of the barrier, when I came down off the motorway. Lying low in reeds, in the dip of a bank. Caught it from the corner of my eye I did, rolling like a log and gone. You see anything like that on your way down?/

Δ

/I can give her a better life than the King. Can give her a *good* life/

/What in the fukk would you know about a good life? Imagine: she can be raised by the King, live with money and protection. What can you give her? Nothing. What is a good life with you? For fukk's sake. His daughter is dead over you. The depths of your stupidity not even the longest rain could reach/

Δ

On the water, when he wasn't yapping, the Bard sang. All the classics: 'Return of Mac', 'Young Bucks', 'Would I?', 'Moving Heart', 'Hey Polly'. The babba sat and stared when he did, so amazed at the deep sounds, the dulcet folds and turns of his voice, shooting her hands to the air now and then. He loved the attention. /You've a great ear/ he told her, /like your grandfather/

Between each verse the kid listened for the sounds of a motor.

They passed through wildness and dereliction, great swaths of jungle river, and abandoned farmhouses and factories, and islands man-made from broken tarmac and satellites and solar panels and roof slates and traffic lights.

/Am homesick, yes/ the Bard said, yet again. /You know people are starving out here? Actually starving and dying. That doesn't happen in the city/

The babba scooted along the floor of the punt on her bottom, squealing as she went.

/Don't let her get wet/ the kid croaked, doubled over with the pain of his right side.

/Ah! The ghost speaks!/

Λ

Wildness and dereliction. Bart investigated his stone while the kid watched rats searching the long grasses at the water's edge. Sometimes in the distance he thought he saw riverbuses, like memories in the deep of the rain. Beams of red and white sought him out through the Shiv'ring, but he could not tell where they came from, or whether they were even real. He wanted so badly for the world to be transparent, so that he could see what he had to do. But it was not. He could not.

They went by remote wave stations, great engineered snake-machines gathering energy from the flow of water. Two or three times boy racers in speedboats hurtled past them, whooping and hollering, not even vaguely keen to his cries for help.

/No one is going to save you/ Bart said, disappointed at the kid's lack of dignity.

Δ

The cream for treating the sores on the back of the babba's legs had run out and there was nothing else in the bag. She began to look burned. He dabbed at her bare skin with a cool, damp cloth. She scratched at the blotches and, one-armed, he tried to get her to stop. She pushed at his hand sternly.

/Don't/ he pleaded.

The formula mix was running out now too. Soon they would be solely reliant on the Bard's store of cold beans.

/I wonder/ Bart said. /Would we ever again see a wild salmon in a place like this/

/.../

/Would love a drink, to be honest. But is not to be ... Yet/

And the Bard sang on, his voice rolling out across the lakelands.

Bit from
WORD OF WARD—

Nights I lay awake next to Joolie as she slept. I remember always that beneath the night's ticks and whirs and shufflings and twitches there seemed to be this low, pulsing engine noise from beyond the walls. It didn't come from somewhere; it came from everywhere. Like an urge, or a flow. But it was just the city, you see? All the sounds added up.

And I lay awake in the dry bedroom, living it, breathing it, afraid to move in case I'd wake herself, watching an empty windowsill in the dark. I was aware that as I lay in the apartment a kid and a baby were out there somewhere, and O' Casey was out there somewhere, carrying out his own investigations, and Sweeney, and the Earlie Boys too. All of them were out there, beyond that sill, in the sound, and I wanted to make the good ones safe and the bad ones answer for their crimes. For the first time in my life I wanted this, and I don't know even now what triggered it.

The Bard was off-register. The fact that he was gone meant any of three things: one, he was lying low after the beheading and our surveillance; two, he was at the King's side, if the King was even alive; or three, he was gone to find the kid. There were ways he could have done that: hacked Hubble drones; device trackers. The Earlie Boys were well able to source information when they wanted to. For all I knew, a crooked officer at my own HQ was running the same searches as me on their behalf. And maybe he had more information than me, or was simply better at it.

Mornings then I found it difficult to stir.

'Are grown lazy,' Joolie would joke. We never had a single argument, you know, me and Joolie, until after all this.

And, sleepless as I was, I began to doze during surveillance. And Roe, he didn't know we were now looking for something, so saw no need to wake me.

'Did I miss anything?' I would ask.

'Not unless you're counting raindrops and mad cunts,' he'd say, yawning himself.

No results. Drowsiness and guilt and plenty of wonderings were all I found. Mayhap it was too late to start caring now, I told myself. I was a poor officer of the law, stumbling around blindly, too long avoiding work to find it again.

And so I turned to O' Casey, the mystery drunkard, and for a few nights I followed him as he too stumbled blindly, from one chronic drinking session to another. He had his own routine. Either he watched the Earlie Boys, or he crossed one of the city's thousand bridges and off he went, his feet finding the cafés and pubs and restaurants of the Old South Side—sometimes the Financial District—and there he drank until he couldn't walk. On his way into the binge he was always stopping at lantern posts to peel away the many stuck flyers of the city's brassers and call services, throwing them into the gutters and rivers. Then on his way out of the place he was always grabbing hold of the same lantern posts to steady himself, shouting to himself the whole time.

I'd see him into a place and watch from the vehicle, tapping into the venue's Hub inflow through my device. He'd order a bottle, finish it, order another; try to get someone to share a third bottle with; sit with them, often insult them, and more often than not be on his own again before he ordered the fourth bottle. That fourth bottle usually went unfinished, was bundled into the pocket of his trenchcoat or knocked blindly to the floor. One particular night, after the purchase of his second bottle, I said fukkit and went in there after him.

I ordered a beer, sat out of his eyeline and tried to listen to anything he said, to himself or anyone else. But, as usual, I was terrible at it. I was distracted so easily. I found myself eavesdropping on a closer, more interesting conversation, about a cheating boyfriend, then watching a girl who sat alone. She had brown hair, matted in clumps, hair like choppy water, and her legs were crossed underneath her. She wore pink socks and was reading not from a device but from an actual paper book. Making notes in an actual paper notebook, scratching her leg with soft white hands, unmarked by tattoos or jewellery. Smiling at babies that were carried past, sipping her drink now and then, tucking her hair behind small shell-like ears. I wanted to know this girl. To read the notes she'd written. She was a rare thing. Do you see that? In a city of drones and intercoms and devices and violence and ugliness she was an artefact. And I forgot all about the reporter, and when I stirred from my boyish fantasies he was gone, and I had messed up yet again.

Then, a moment later, a shadow darkened my table.

Wagging a bottle of wine over me, here was the man himself, trenchcoat slung over the arm that did not wield the wine bottle.

'What happened to all the writers?' he asked me. 'The filmmakers? The intellectuals?'

I didn't know what to say, but he continued regardless.

'Will tell you what. Swept away by disease they were. Hunger. Poverty. The need for an easy life. All the other stuff.'

He dropped his bottle square on the table.

'See you admiring the intellectual,' he said. 'May I join you and bring a bottle of good cheer into the bargain?'

I invited him to sit, still not able to find words for myself. I had imagined interviewing him, and yet now that he was here not a single question came to mind.

'Yes,' he said. 'The intellectuals are a rare breed now.'

We were at a corner table, with a view of the whole café and the street beyond the front window. We watched the girl, who was oblivious to us of course.

Finally, I asked him if *he* was an intellectual.

He shrugged. 'I dabble.'

'Ah.'

'Chief! Chief! Another glass please!' He near-swung out of the waiter, trying to get his attention. 'Is ignoring me, the blaggard. You get him there.'

I tried to catch the waiter's eye and it is true that he ignored the reporter, who elbowed me, hissing: 'Go on! Is only so we can share!'

I went to the counter and got a glass myself. He filled it to the brim, then refilled his own to the brim.

'Yes. I dabble. Am a reporter.'

I asked him what kind of stuff he wrote.

'Human stories. All kinds. I am the mirror, telling the city the story of itself. Very small mirror of course.'

I suggested that lots of crazy things happened in the city.

'Aye.'

Lots of crime.

'More than you know.'

'More crime than before?'

'The Heavies have given up. The government, this administration... administration after administration. Given up.'

'Mayhap you are right.'

'The whole system is corrupt.'

But things had always been bad, I ventured. For every generation.

He waved a hand out there, over the table. 'Never this bad. People have stopped hoping.'

'The baddies have won?' I suggested.

He shrugged.

'What about Saint Vincent Depaul? He serves the poor?'

'He of the "incorrupt heart"? Don't get me started on him.'

Only later, when we'd nearly finished the bottle—or at least he had—did he come back to that point and correct me.

'The baddies *are* winning, yes, but they haven't won yet.'

'Oh.' I supped on this, waited on elaboration.

'Am working on something... Of the utmost importance.'

'A story?'

'A list.'

'A list?'

'A ledger.'

'A ledger?'

'Names of the disappeared. Names, dates, circumstances, suspects, reasons, motives.'

'Names of who?'

'Cannot tell. Is a work-in-progress. Highly confidential.'

I seized the chance. 'How long have you been following the Earlie Boys?'

He snorted. 'Following? Following! Not I.' He laughed. 'Listening. Hearing. Noting... Many listen but few hear.'

I understood little. Dim fragments wouldn't connect up for me.

'I am a guard,' I said, without irony or triumph. 'Maybe I can help you.'

Reaching out for the wine he snorted again.

'Cut the music!' he suddenly cried. 'Stray dogs make better music!'

He wiped his nose with the back of a hand and failed to open his eyes to inspect the consequences. Eyes yet closed, he sniffed, cleared his throat and mumbled away. I could make no sense of him any more.

'Where is the Bard—Crooner Bart—gone?' I helped his hand towards the glass.

'Praying,' he said. 'Gone praying in Dingel.' Then a fit of coughing. Then, reasonably, he continued. 'Found the boy, would you believe.'

'The kid?'

'The very buachaill.'

'Jesus. Is the kid alive?'

'He's alive—believe it or believe it not. Ready for the ledger though. No doubt about that.'

'Where will they take him?'

'A place I don't know.'

'What is that place? Maybe I know it.'

'They call it the Death Bag, or sometimes they call it the Dark Chamber.'

'Where is it?'

'Docklands somewhere, I think.'

'Where?'

'Don't know, do I. Cut the fukken music! The deaf childer of the Croke Park Flats could do better!'

And I got no more sense out of him that night. I doubted whether he would even remember the conversation.

BIT CALLED

PEON

The kid's whole back shuddered with pain when anything touched it, so he sat up straight all day. He changed the babba's nappy one-armed and burped her over his knee. When he tried to sleep he slumped forward on his stomach, often crying out in pain.

Then they came to a place that had once been a train yard. Swampies peered out of the double doors of old carriages to see what the sound of an engine had brought them. Their dogs barked furiously, and splashed with their paws at the pink and yellow of the sundew on the shoreline.

Soon enough a speedboat with a single peon at the helm was following Bart's vessel, catching up surely though not in pursuit. Bart killed the engine and waited. To the kid he said: /These out post cowboys can be dangerous/

When the peon came alongside and calmed his own engine, the Bard slapped the outside of his starboard quarter and called: /You see the sign?/

The kid leaned out and saw the eye of the King sprayed there.

/See the sign/ the peon responded. /No harm, no threat meaning. Come to see what you need/

The peon was not much older than the kid. A long bone piercing cut through his nose and he had metal skulls implanted in each broad cheek.

/Will need a hand pulling the boat up to the old road/ Bart said. /Kid here is lame/

The peon nodded, pulled at a flesh tunnel in the lobe of his ear. /Fifty/

/No problemo/ Bart said. /How far is it to that more gentle slope? Thirty miles?/

The peon thought about it, then shrugged. /Meet you there in two hours or so. Else you need? Wanna sell the nene?/

/No thanks/ Bart said. /Important child that/

/Medicine/ the kid croaked. /Meds and rash cream. And nappies/

The peon considered the kid, and then considered Bart, who, while he thought, smoothed out the legs of his grey pantalones with wide palms.

/Yes to all/ he finally said. Probably he did not realise that the pills were for the kid.

As their vessel rolled in the waves of the peon's wake, Bart grinned at the babba.

/The kindness of country people, aye?/

Δ

/You really kill my brother?/ the kid asked.

Bart smiled kindly. /Oh yes I did. He screamed and kicked and we gave him the guillotine. Right on the kitchen table. I slammed it down on him and off came his head! Pop! Fell to the floor with a right thump!/ He pounded the floor of the boat for emphasis. /He was suffering, lad. His whole dead face was suffering. We told him too was your fault. He knew why alright…

/And we did for your pony too. We found him in that field. Well … he was brave enough. I kept the hooves, if you'd want them? Is supposed to be bad luck to get rid of them. Hah! Oh, I am excited to get back to Dublin, aren't you?/

Rain was coming down wigwam style. At the dockside by the entrance to the park we sat in silence, watching three slumkids go through a set of bins. The pathways of the park shimmered and the Croke Park Flats loomed. Along the wharf the cranes had stopped for the evening. Boats tinkled across the dark water; we rocked gently at our mooring, waiting for the runner to make the usual pick-up.

'Roe,' I said. 'If he comes to make the pick-up I'm going to take him in. I've had enough. I want to know what got that poor lad beheaded. And I want to find this missing kid.'

And I left it at that.

In fairness to the man, Roe didn't flinch. He rubbed his thumb at the vessel's window, cleaning some smudge or other. The idea settled.

'Could be the start of something bad,' he sighed.

'I know.'

Δ

Beacons flashed over the city, always. Time passed slowly on surveillance, as ever. Seconds hauled themselves over and over.

Then a streak of silver wobbled into view, coming down a path in our direction.

Roe confirmed with the zoom function of his device: 'Silver skins, same bike. Is him.'

The runner fell onto the bench and threw his boots up on his cycle. Began to roll some herbal.

'How are we going to do this?' Roe asked me.

'Don't know,' I said. The kid's skins were so shiny bright, like foil. 'Let's just get down there and see what happens.'

Up out of the boat and onto the warped paving slabs of the dock. We were stood over him before he ever noticed us, so enthralled was he in the building of his spliff.

'Clem,' I said. 'Do you know who we are?'

The runner looked up at us and a broad smile became a fit of laughter.

'Hello!' he said.

'You won't be so amused when you figure it out,' Roe warned him.

'Heavies?' he giggled. 'Two big fat Heavies!' And he burst out laughing again, his legs coming up off the bike and the bike clattering to the ground.

Roe grabbed the kid by the hood and began to drag him back towards the boat. I went after them, leaving the bike behind, then running back for it.

By the time I got to them, Roe must have belted the kid four or five times. At one point they were so close to the water I thought they'd fall in.

'Calm down!' I was shouting, wheeling the bicycle along.

But it was still all hilarious to the stoned runner, and I was still wrestling the bicycle into the back of the boat when Roe had him on deck and cuffed to the rail, and was slapping him repeatedly in the face, saying, 'Laugh. Laugh. Laugh. Laugh it up.'

In fairness to the kid, he did what he was told.

I let the bicycle down and turned to watch in confusion—and then horror—as Roe brought out a syringe and jammed it hard into the kid's thigh.

The kid gasped and stared at his leg with big wide eyes.

'Jesus, Roe!' was all I could say.

'What the fukk?' the runner gasped, squirming, suddenly aware that both hands were cuffed, that he was trapped.

'Not so fukken funny now, is it?' Roe said.

'What the fukk was that?'

304

'Was what we call truth serum,' Roe said. 'Means your mind is ours and is the end of you, my young buckeen. Now… let's find a place to sink you.'

And I remember Roe's face as he turned. He was smiling. I couldn't believe it.

In the cabin I was shaking him by the shoulders before I knew what I was doing.

'What the fukk are you at? What's in the needle?'

'Relax,' he said calmly. 'Is only a little Fadinhead.'

'Jesus-fukk!'

'A small enough dose. Will be fine.' He started the engine. 'But he's going to tell us everything *before* he's fine.'

I went out to take the ropes in; the kid was still trying to escape the cuffs, contorting his body furiously but making no progress.

'What's he done to me?' he asked.

I just shook my head at him and turned away.

Δ

We tore south along the bay.

'Where are we headed?' I asked.

'Needs a little while for the bad vibes to kick in,' Roe said. 'Will take him somewhere spooky.'

I asked him where he got the F.

His eyes stayed on the water. 'A mistake in some paperwork.'

'Fukken hell.'

At Dun Leery we cut inland along a tributary. I watched the kid through the back window of the cabin. His face, his whole body soon morphed from pure wonder to pure terror.

'Know an inlet down near Dahl Quay with some caves,' Roe said.

'You realise we could be killed for this?'

'I know,' he said. 'Told you it would be the start of something, didn't I?'

I wanted to explain that I didn't know he'd abduct the runner and fill him with drugs. But I stopped. There was no point talking about it. It was done. And we had an opportunity now: mayhap we could do good from it.

We came to a deep crevice in headland, a quiet inlet where waves chopped, collapsed upon each other amidst jagged black rock, thrashing before being sucked under and born again. The pier was an ancient stone-cut monolith at the bottom of a string of steep steps that had been cut out of the cliff. The vessel rocked savagely in circles, like a merries ride, even once we'd moored.

Roe cut the engine. 'I lead,' he said. 'You follow.'

I nodded.

'Find out whatever it is you want to know but have been keeping from me.'

We were finally partners, I suppose.

The kid was pale and soaking out on the deck. The hood of his skins had been blown back and his head was drenched. He gasped for breath, and coughed in gulps. He was a rake of a lad, spindled out over the boat. Roe knelt over him and I stood back.

'Now,' Roe said. 'Am sorry to say that you are going to die tonight. Am the one that's going to do it'—he turned to me—'not him…And am not changing my mind. Is a simple fact, your death. Sorry it had to be such a shock to you.'

The kid's mouth formed a *why*.

'Why? Because you have lived a bad life, a life of crime. Now you pay the price.'

'What's in my leg?'

Roe knelt back straight, considered it. 'What's in your leg won't kill you. Is truth serum. Alters your mind so that you can't lie. I am the one that is going to kill you. I'll decide if you suffer…' He was so matter-of-fact. 'Are you scared?'

The kid squeezed his eyes so that tears escaped. He nodded.

'See?' Roe smiled. 'Serum's already working.'

'Your breath smells of meat,' the kid said.

'Good! Now, think of this conversation as confession before you go. A chance to clean the slate. My partner here needs information, and you can help him.'

The kid looked at me and said, 'An angel.'

I said: 'We're trying to find someone. I only need a few words.'

'What are words?' he asked.

'Sounds,' Roe interrupted, sarcastically, 'that come out of people's mouths.'

'Birds don't have them. But sounds come out of *their* mouths. Dogs don't have them.' The boy named Clem looked at me, searching my face for something. 'Only people have words, and look at the shite they talk.'

'Just answer the questions,' Roe said.

'Oh shut up, *meat mouth*!'

Roe gave him a sudden hard slap that set him to whimpering again.

'Am gonna die,' he moaned. 'Am gonna die this night, oh God.'

'The kid in yellow,' I said. 'I want to help him.'

You could see the recognition. The sudden focus.

'I want to help him, and the baby he has with him. You can help me do that.'

I saw Roe out of the corner of my eye, watching me with great seriousness.

'I know Bart is bringing him back to the Dark Chamber,' I said. 'Or is it the Death Bag? But I don't know where this place is—'

'—Aim-ee I let down most of all,' the runner said. 'With T and the babba and all that…'

'Aim-ee?'

'Is his name. A girl's name he was always embarrassed about. Short for Amerlin, or something like that… Remember one time we took out a postal drone with billy guns. We were delighted! But you know what we got? Fukken knickers is all we got. A box of frilly knickers, and the two of us skitting as we hopped around the alley with them on our heads! You know, we would've been pals forever. Would've been at each other's funerals when we were old.'

'Where is the Death Bag? Where is the Dark Chamber?'

'Bart is bringing him back to the King.'

'The King is alive?'

'Of course.'

'But where are they? Where is he taking Aim-ee?'

'What he done was stupid. How could he be so stupid?'

I pulled out a laminate map of the Docklands. 'That's not important now. What's important is that if we get him before the rest of the Earlie Boys mayhap we can save him.'

'You believe in love? Like fukken *true* love?'

'I think Aim-ee's life is worth saving, and his daughter's life. But we can't figure it out ourselves.'

Clem fell back and let the rain onto his face. 'Was there when they killed his brother. Helped hold him down. The brother just accepted it...'

'Who killed the brother?'

'Was as if he ... crumpled. His body, his spirit, everything ... He actually stretched his own neck out. Like he was welcoming it.... They say there's an underground river...'

'Who dropped the guillotine?'

'Oh god, am *dying*... Can feel it in me. Am actually fukken dying!'

'Who dropped the guillotine?'

'Bart of course. He always wants to drop it.'

'And the same man now has your pal and his baby?'

'Yes.' Realisation came into his face. 'Jesus.'

'Where are they?'

'You won't find them. He takes the backwaters, old roads and lost rivers. Are due in tomorrow I heard. Evening probably. Show me the map.'

'Where is this place on the docks exactly? We can't find it without your help.'

'Am not sure exactly. Have never been ... But I can show you the sector. You think you can stop them?'

Δ

We got rid of him before the F brought him to the brink, let him off near a petrol stop in Dahl Quay. Told him he did the right thing, that he'd be okay.

Later, I uploaded the recording of his testimony to the case file on the system. Carefully edited Roe's 'truth serum' out of it. I completed the paperwork, gave my electronic signature to it all.

You know, there comes a point where you begin to reason, in your own mind, about the value of your life. Or your life versus another's. And it's ironic how long I've lived since. Life can be so long to hold … and so many things happen, and there is so much to know, and to carry, and to accept. And holding on to these … things … these memories …

I told Roe everything I knew on the way back, and apologised to him.

No problem, he told me. He wanted to help.

'A bit of action at last,' was what he said.

BIT CALLED

OLD DUBLIN ROAD

The peon waited on a firm part of the shore, by a long sloping grass hillside that rose up to the old motorway where they would straighten their trajectory to Dublin.

/Hail fellow!/ Bart called to him, who, arms folded, watched the child quietly.

He had a plastic bag, which he gave to Bart, who dropped it at the feet of the kid, who went straight for the pills, fishing them out with his good arm. Popping one from the foil, he washed it down with a scoop of muddy water from the shallows of the lagoon.

The Bard blessed himself, hiked up his pantalones, and gained land right foot first.

The kid wrapped his good arm round his babba in her skins, and, dizzy and wobbling, stood in the rocking boat. More and more, she was becoming all that was left in the world. Water receded. Rain blurred. Land fell away.

With her in his arm, he stood out from under the tarp and into the spraying rain.

The shuddering and the dizziness passed after a moment, but hot waves of pain rolled down the right-hand side of his body. She squirmed and whinged to be put down, and as the kid tried to get out the boat wobbled and his left boot struck shallow water instead of land.

Pain jolted through him, and cold. Screaming, he did all he could to fall forward and not back, and to let his girl down gently onto the wet grass and not hurt her. And the pain of impact was too much. As he retched he could hear Bart's howls and cackles above him.

When he wiped his mouth and lifted his head, he saw his girl with one hand on a curious slug, and she watching the slug with a frown.

/No/ he croaked. /No/

She was all he had left, and he was losing her, losing the strength to protect her.

After he pulled her back from the slug, he took the plastic bag out from the boat and popped two more pills. The babba pointed in the direction of the departed beast and moaned for her new friend, while the kid started to wash her hands with lagoon water.

/Will be okay/ he croaked. /Will be okay/

Δ

The Bard did not seem in a hurry to get up to the motorway with the boat, so the kid rested on the slope, his sweat cooling in the rain and the wet grass, until he was shivering again. His girl roved about on her knees, pulling at clumps of grass. The Bard and the peon talked about some kelpie called El Familiar, who was known to come and abduct the swampies. Bart said the factories and fish farms of the city had the same thing, but in the city he was called Mister Violence.

The Bard climbed the slope then to check that the water was deep enough on the road.

/Please/ the kid said to the peon. /Take us with you. Kill him. Anything. Have money. You can take the boat. Is good. You can have everything, just let me and the babba go. I have to save her. Please/

The peon looked up the slope, then turned back to the kid.

/Have to save her/ the kid repeated.

But the peon shook his head, and went back to his own vessel to bail out rainwater.

Δ

They got Bart's vessel up the slope without too much trouble. The Bard pulled it by a rope and called directions while the peon pushed.

The kid struggled to follow them the whole way up, lifting the babba a few feet at a time. She resisted and whimpered all the way, slapping at his hands because she wanted the water.

Bart called from above for them to hurry up.

/Suerte/ the peon said as he passed them on his way back down.

/Fukk you/ the kid replied in his wake. /Are killing us/

He stopped and sat to watch the outpost dweller—his last hope—leave in a speedboat, a few coins the richer. /FUKK YOU, YOU FUKKEN CUNT!/ The words drowned out by the roar of the engine, the words to his bawling self as much as to the peon.

/Come on ta fukk/ Bart called lightheartedly.

When he came panting to the top of the slope, the greygreen rainmisty land spread out before them. Vast tracts of marsh and lagoon thrashed in the wind, and rain shivered across everything. Nature swarmed upon the motorway's curve.

/Will get some real speed up now/ Bart recked, hands on his hips.

On the other side of the flooded road, the kid's eyes fell on a faded sign for Dublin that flapped in the wind.

We knocked on every door on Sweeney's floor, just so it wouldn't seem to anyone watching us that we were looking for him specifically. At his door it felt liked we'd knocked for hours before he answered. There was no small talk: I showed him a photo, asked him to report any sightings of the missing kid, handed him the note and hoped he'd come.

We went for O' Casey next. Stood on the threshold of his chamber above the Pup&Pendant, I asked if he remembered me.

He cocked one eye in the doorway. 'Vaguely,' he said.

I handed him an exact copy of the note I'd given Sweeney. I told him it was about the kid in yellow. That it was very urgent business.

Δ

'Think they will meet us?' Roe asked on the way back to the city barracks.

'O' Casey will,' I said. 'Out of sheer curiosity. Sweeney... I don't know. He's a strange fish.'

'Can we do it without them?'

I thought so at the time, but the more you knew the better you could plan. Sweeney and O' Casey had information we'd probably been ignoring all along. The more we found out, the more chance we had of saving the two children.

'Do you think we could actually catch him though?' I asked Roe. 'The King?'

'Is possible,' he shrugged. 'But what'd happen to him d'you think?'

317

'He'd walk.'

'Exactly. Is all sorts of corruption above our heads.' He yawned. 'You know the story of the cuckoo?'

'What cuckoo?'

'The cuckoo chances upon another bird's nest. Lays an egg, leaves. That egg hatches and as the cuckoo chick grows with its stepsisters it is fed by a stepmother. Then it starts pushing the other stepchicks out of the nest, until there's only the cuckoo chick getting all the food for himself, food brought back by this bird who's had all her babies killed. But she keeps feeding the little cuckoo anyway, because she doesn't know what else to do. She was built for motherhood. She follows her instinct. Keeps feeding it until it is a big strong cuckoo itself and can fly off and make young and do the exact same thing to another nest. Is not wrong or right. These animals just do what they know to do. Is nature. We arrest the King; he walks because our superiors know nothing other than corruption. We kill the King; another takes his place. Nature is not good or evil, it just... *is* ... '

'And what are we, in that story?'

'Dunno ... Mayhap the chicks that get pushed out.'

'So, it doesn't matter whether we catch him, kill him, or not?'

'Like I said, maybe we're just the chicks that get pushed out of the nest.'

'Did a cuckoo chick ever get pushed out by the other chicks?'

'Not in any version that I heard.'

We considered all of this over the length of a canal. Traffic was appalling.

'Is weird though, isn't it,' Roe said. 'Thinking about death. Thinking about maybe it's your last day or two on earth.'

I remember a seagull breaking the skin of the water's surface, after some half-sunken chunk of waste.

'You believe in life after death?' he asked.

'Not really,' I said. 'Only maybe in the way that you live on in people's memories. Or in stories about you. Like a footprint you leave maybe.'

'Then what does it matter?' he said. 'If you're gone, you won't know about people's memories or your footprint.'

I shrugged. 'I suppose.'

'Is absurd, isn't it?'

'It is.'

You put so much effort into life, he said. Your heart pumps blood around your vessel for years, decades. And you spend so much money and so much energy just keeping it going. And then one day, poof. Gonzos. He said the way we went about pretending it wouldn't happen was absurd. All the years he worked the barracks back home. Keeping the peace. Building a legacy. Resolving petty disputes. Counting crimes. Counting hours. Counting stock and checking lists. Lists the length of a country fukken road. It was bananas, he said, birth and death and all the counting and listing in between.

He didn't have to do any of this, I told him. I wasn't dragging him into it; I could do it alone.

'They shat on me,' he told me.

I thought I'd misheard.

'The Earlie Boys,' he said again. 'They shat on me. One night.'

'Fukken hell, Roe.'

'I never told anyone this. Was when I first came down from the country. After the barracks. I walked everywhere then—to get the lay of the land you see, to scope out the city. Then one evening I got grabbed up by about four of them. They must've been following me. Still in my work skins, walking back streets alone is what I was. Naive is what I was. Two of them took a turn each. Laughed it up.'

'Jesus. Do you know which of them it was?'

'No. Either I've blocked it out or the drink took it. Laughing their heads off they were. Is what I remember.'

I told him what Sweeney had told me about it, as if it was a consolation.

'Could smell it for weeks after, no matter how much I washed,' he said, looking out to water.

BIT FROM THE PLAY——

Curtain up on woodland: a deep, dark circular pool
surrounded by hazel trees. Sound of dripping, from
hazel leaves into the deep pool. A gentle drizzle falls
throughout the scene; the action happens through
its veil. An engine's roar grows in the distance,
and soon enters the scene. In the boat are BART, the
KID IN YELLOW——who is, at this stage, without his
yellow skins, and therefore is just a skinny, soaking
kid——and the BABBA. BART sits aft and attentive,
controlling the motor and looking all around him. The
KID is slumped over under a colourless tarp at the
other end of the boat. The BABBA is mostly unseen,
though often heard, and now and then sticks her head
up over the boat's side to peer into the water and at
the audience.

BART.   Fukken lost. Knew it. Fukken lagoons!

The KID is clearly suffering, shivering and wiping
his wet hair out of his face.

BART.   Don't understand how we get on a
               motorway, and somehow end up on a
               river getting narrower and narrower.
               How in the fukk does that even happen?
               [scratches his head].
BABBA.   Nahh.
BART.   Shut up, you. Are no help. [looking to
               the KID] What does the ghost think?
               Where did we go wrong?

The KID knows he is being spoken to but doesn't
answer.

BART.	Like I thought. Is just what he is.
	[half-stands to look around]
BABBA.	Fa! Fa!
BART.	Is right, girl. Reck we got a bit
	muddled way back down on that sunken
	interchange. Fukken deep pool this.

The BARD starts to work on his device, singing away
to himself as he figures out locations and directions.

THE KID.	[stirring a little, taking the BABBA's
	hand with his good hand] See this
	place, my love. Is a special place. Is
	the most special place in Ireland.

The BABBA looks up into his voice. Not overly curious
but simply reacting to the sound of it.

BART.	Is yea.
THE KID.	[to the BABBA] Is where the salmon of
	knowledge is said to live. Is called
	Linn Feic.
BABBA.	Fa! Dhn.
THE KID.	And what happened was a man looking
	for knowledge came here, a'cos here
	he knew he'd find the salmon of
	knowledge. Once you ate that fish you
	knew everything; you saw everything
	about the whole world. Knew what life
	was, and why we had life, and what was
	beyond us. He'd read about the place
	in books, you see, this man, and knew
	that the pool of Linn Feic was guarded
	by a ring of hazel trees, like these
	ones here, see? [he points at the trees
	and the BABBA looks at his hand]. And

well one day this old man——his name
was Finny Gus——finally found this
place, and started fishing for that
big old salmon of knowledge. Once he
had that fish he'd have the whole world
recked for himself, and no one could
take it away. So Finny Gus fished and
fished and one day didn't he snag
that salmon of knowledge. This was
a time when salmons were free, and
mysterious, and made great journeys,
not like the fish farms now you know.

At this point, BART has stopped investigating his
device, and is listening to the KID's story, though
not letting on that he is listening.

THE KID.   And well so Finny Gus hauled the big
                  old fish——as old as himself and s'pose
                  a lot older really——out of the pool
                  we're in now, and the fish finally gave
                  in to him. The deal was you had to eat
                  the fish to gain the knowledge, and
                  so Finny turns to this kid who's been
                  helping him and he says to the kid,
                  Take this fish and cook it up on a big
                  fire so's I can eat it. Don't you do
                  anything else with that fish now but
                  cook it. So the kid goes and starts
                  a big fire, and when the fire is good
                  and blazing he gets the fish on the
                  spit over it, and he's cooking away
                  into the sunset. And when he thinks
                  is nearly done, he puts a thumb on
                  the fish to test if is cooked or not,
                  and doesn't he go and burn the thumb!

	[the KID here mimes the testing of the fish on the girl's arm, and makes a big hoo-hoo-hah-hah of burning of the thumb] Ooh! Aah! [the child is made giddy and laughs, so he does it again and again. BART becomes increasingly keen, in his face and posture, to hear the end of the story] And so the kid shoves his thumb in his mouth to ease the burn [the KID acts this out, and the BABBA copies] and what happens, you reck? He tastes only a tiny bit of the fish and gets all the knowledge in the world! This little kid knows it all in the end, and old Finny Gus, who's been looking so long, gets none of the knowledge!
BABBA.	Dhn. Dhn. Fa!
THE KID.	You want to see a fish? Let's look! Let's look for a fish!

The KID begins to peer with the child into the water, pointing out to their reflections.

THE KID.	And even if you don't see the salmon of knowledge, they say that if you see your own reflection in the pool of Linn Feic then you'll always know yourself. You'll know yourself full well.
BART.	What I tell you afore? No one likes these bullshit stories. Singers and songs are what people like. Fish of knowledge. Such horseshit.

The KID ignores the provocation and continues to enjoy playing with his girl.

BART.   Well, it so happens that I know where
                     we really are, and where we're going,
                     and am going to get us out of here now.
                     [begins to gently reverse the vessel
                     back, coming closer to the bank, then
                     kills the engine] But mayhap will just
                     get me a nice stone from this nice
                     little place, for a keepsake.

BART stands and leans towards the bank to fetch a
stone. But as he is doing so he is also trying to look
into the water to see his reflection. As quick as a
flash, the kid unfurls. BART is caught by his own
reflection, looking for the fish, or seeking knowledge
of himself. One hand on a bank that the boat is
drifting from. The KID rises. Rushes. Pushes BART
from the boat into the deep pool of Linn Feic. BART
disappears under the water. The KID grabs the motor
and tries to start it. But it does not start first time.
The boat wobbles and crashes against the bank.

BART.   [rising to the surface, splashing
                     around, sinking and rising] Fukk!
                     Fukken cunt! Am gonna fukken kill
                     you. Kill you!

The G# note of the clarinet suddenly blares. The KID
tries to start the motor again, and it fires, and the
boat crashes against the bank again. BART starts to
swim, scrambling for the boat, screaming. The BABBA
is toppled by the commotion and falls onto the floor
of the boat. The KID rams the boat against the bank
twice more, scraping against the bank, and BART is
flailing for the wood of the vessel now. But the KID
straightens it, and accelerates out of the lagoon and
to stage right.

Now, the stage backdrop needs to suddenly run across
a panorama of flickering images. The boat's engine
roars, the clarinet's high G# pierces, the myriad
country scenes on some kind of rolling backdrop give
the impression of a landscape passing by. The KID
is intent the whole time. The BABBA watches out of
the side of the boat all these places passing her by.
Eventually lights dim, as if to curtain, and as lights
dim things slow down, the G# dissipates; the rolling
backdrop slows to a halt, but the lights fall too earlie
for the audience to be able to see where they are.
But no curtain. Only darkness. Total darkness. And
silence.

THE KID.   [out of darkness] Come here. Are free
                    now. All the bad men are gone now. Come
                    here to me, my lovely girl.
BABBA.   [to be heard squirming and whinging]
                    Agaa!
THE KID.   Come here and will tell you a story.
                    About the man who can't find his key.
                    Comes home one evening in the dark and
                    the key's not there. Dark like this now.
                    Where we don't have to be afraid...

Beat.

THE KID.   No, let's change the story. A kid and
                    his babba have no keys. And are out in
                    the darkness looking for a key. And in
                    the distance they see the light of the
                    city. But they know what's there. They
                    know the badness and the goodness of
                    it. So they won't go there. They'll go
                    out into the dark looking for the right
                    key. [the BABBA quietens increasingly

as the story is drawn out] They don't
need to search the light they know.
They have the darkness, and they like
it. Off they go out into the dark,
looking for the key to the next thing.
And out there in the dark is her
mother, his love, and she is going to
help them find that key, the perfect
key, to the perfect house, in the
perfect place. They only have to go
out a ways into the dark to look for it.
To not be afraid. Are not running any
more. Are searching the darkness for
the key, and all is going to be okay.

Beat.

Beat.

Beat.

CURTAIN.

BIT CALLED

WANTING TO KNOW THE WHY

/HEY!/ Bart yelled. /Curtains up!/

The kid stirred. Sounds of waves against the boat, and rain on the tarp, and on the water, and wind buffeting the tarp and ruffling the water, and distant unseen engines.

/Pull up them curtains on your eyes! We're nearly there. And you're nearly dead!/

As if she understood, the babba started to cry. The kid struggled to her as his heart sank.

Δ

Forests of hornwort swirled beneath the surface. Bart was always there when the kid awoke, always giving him that hateful grin.

The kid told his babba the story of the man in the dark and his lost key.

/I did wonder why you needed so much F/ Bart mused, shortly after he had made a visio of the two captives to send to the King. /Wondered were you going into business, or were you going to top yourself. Funnily enough, the plan was to catch up with you after you'd paid for it and take it back off you. But you're a slippery fish. Will give you that much!/

/.../

/But why *did* you do it? Why try to kill the unkillable?/

/.../

/Did he not give you a life? Did you feel no gratitude for what he or I done for you?/

/.../

331

/Between you and me, am surprised you got as close to him as you did/

The babba shot up her hands in the air.

/Why/ Bart asked. /Why the child? Why would one child want another? God knows how many chicklets I've sired out there, young scuts roving about, and I want nothing to do with any of them. Have my family—the Earlie Boys, my ma, the King—what else could a man want?/

The kid focused on the soaking untied laces of the other. Said: /When that wicked King was slain, not even the dogs licked his blood/

And he looked off into the Shiv'ring, the feel only of his daughter's body keeping him in touch with that horror world. Bart laughed away bitterly.

Bit from
WORD OF WARD—

These memories don't fade: they grow, grow, grow.

It was the same café at which I'd drank with the reporter previously. Ferry Dreamz it was called: a huge cavern of a grey stone place that used to be a bank. Tables spread across a wide floor and all over the walls up to the high-vaulted ceiling there were old paintings of ferries. All ports, all kinds of weather, hung crooked, hung frameless; they gave the place the feel of some old sailor's memories. The waitresses and waiters were faded glamour-types in onesies, all in lipstick and rouge. A chanteuse sang quietly, eyes closed, in the corner: I didn't recognise the language.

I chose the same table at which O' Casey and I had sat, in the back corner. If I get out of this, I told myself, I'll buy an old paper book, and read it, in a place like this. I thought about Joolie, who had no clue any of this was happening. I might never see her again, I thought. I was low then. Why do we do the things we do?

While I waited, I scrolled through the details of the case on my device. On the severed head we had only gaming data. Aged eighteen according to two registrations. In one game profile he had registered over four thousand kills, uncovered over forty secret levels and earned enough coin to go anywhere and do anything in the world of the game. What I'm saying is that in his second life, this kid had been a god-warrior, but in his real life he hadn't a name, a registered genome, a con'flux, nothing. His comm-code was an illegal one, with no birth linked to it. He'd lived, a ghost of no consequence, in a vast system. It seemed strange to even register him as dead.

Δ

O' Casey was bang on time. Shifty, bolt upright, pulling his trenchcoat around him. We shook hands and I ordered a bottle of wine.

'We met here last week?' he asked.

'We did.'

'Talked about the Earlie Boys? The kid?'

'Sort of.'

He didn't appear convinced.

'What do you want to know from me?' he asked.

I said we needed to wait. We were still expecting at least one more.

It had begun to rain hammers outside—you could hear it over the music of the chanteuse—and yet beyond the window you could still see above the cityscape soft bulbs of cloudlight in places, passing over.

'You and I,' I assured him after a while, 'are on the same team.'

'Are a Heavy,' he said to me. 'You only have one team: is not mine.'

I poured myself a glass of wine.

'This ledger?' I asked. 'You could give it to me. It could be of use.'

He poured steadily from the bottle. 'Ledger? What d'you mean?'

'The list. Of the murdered and disappeared?'

He said: 'I know of no such list.'

'Right,' I said.

Only a good few years later would I hear from him again about that ledger, and the work that followed it.

Δ

Roe arrived not long after, taking an age to hang his skins at the door. He watched the streets, as if he was looking for someone. When he sat, he sighed and showed me the message on his device: WARRANT DENIED—INSUFFICIENT EVIDENCE.

I introduced him to O' Casey, and we were about to start into it when Sweeney came bursting through the door in his patchwork skins, the dregs of a spliff flung out to the street behind him.

'Hail, hail!' he cried as he approached. 'The gang's all here!'

'How is your slug?' I asked him.

'Can we move this candle?' he said, taking the liquor bottle rippled in wax to the next table. 'The flame is...distracting.'

I poured him a glass.

O' Casey had a look of horror on his face.

'I recognise you!' he said to Sweeney.

'And I you,' Sweeney replied, supping his wine. 'They call you Mister Deth.'

'Mister Deth?' O' Casey whinged, distracted. 'Who does?'

'They all. The mothers. The Earlie Boys...'

'The Earlie Boys know me?'

'Aye, moc!' Sweeney laughed. 'Course they do. You been pretending not to follow them for years now. Skulking the same bar counters and corridors as meself.'

O' Casey flung a hand in the air. 'Why Mister Deth?'

Sweeney smiled, genuinely amused. 'Because you follow Mister Violence around.'

'But if they know me, why haven't they killed me? If they know...'

'Because you're making the myth for them.'

The reporter sank into his chair. 'And what about *your* myth? I *recognise* you!'

'Comrades,' I interrupted. 'I believe we have a common interest, and I want to see whether you can help me this one time. I'm asking this not as an officer of the law but just as a man in this city. Roe here is the same.'

'You want to kill the King?' Sweeney guessed.

'I don't know about that,' I said. 'But I want to save the boy.'

I told them everything I knew, all the fragments we had

pieced together to make a story that we had to try and put a good ending to. The story that I've told you. Both Sweeney and O' Casey stopped me at different times, to correct me, to fill in a blank spot here and there. The kid had had a mother once: problems with addiction; she'd either died or run off with a cult. His housemate—the Head—had been his elder brother, by a different father. The mother had been a good person, Sweeney said. 'A strange woman, unable to cope with the many burdens of the place.' The kid had begun running for the Earlie Boys almost straight out of primary school, about the time she disappeared. He'd been earmarked as a kid with potential.

'And you want to know where this place is?' Sweeney guessed again when I finished my story with the question of the Death Bag or the Dark Chamber.

'Correct. We've narrowed it down to a block, to a sector, but we don't know exactly which building. Time won't be our friend here so we need a precise location if we're to have any chance.'

O' Casey shook his head. 'Have heard it mentioned many times. But don't know where it is exactly. I believe it to be an underground chamber. But that is a big sector. A vast network of underground chambers and pipe formations and storage areas and everything else.'

'They say there are underground rivers,' Sweeney chanted.

I agreed with O' Casey. 'It's too large to try and cover ourselves, in one night.'

'Have you manpower?' Sweeney asked, chewing the tip of a thumb.

'No,' I said. 'We have just this hour been denied an arrest warrant.'

'Crooked.'

'It is just the two of us, and two new guns.'

Of course, neither of our informants put their hand up to join us on our mission.

'So you'll do what?' O' Casey said.

'Try to rescue the boy and the child that is with him.'

'No plan?'

'That's the whole plan.'

'You do not inspire confidence.'

'Are not confident,' Roe admitted.

'Then why go?'

I shrugged. 'Because it's right.'

Sweeney laughed. Helped himself to a top-up of wine and toasted us. 'A woman one floor down from me,' he said. 'A while back. She had two dogs, both setters, one red, one black. The red one old and the black one young. The red one was dying since I knew her.

'Cared about nothing but her dogs this one. Gave steak and fish to them. Let them drink milk while she drank water. Mayhap she loved that they were dogs not humans. Not many had them then, you see? But I remember this: every evening she would go down to the steps that led up to the Flats' entrance and she would lay down plastic and on top of it a woollen blanket. Then she would carry the old red setter down in her arms—with the black setter at heel—and lay her on the blanket so that they could watch the sky turning. This was when the city's orange glow was the strongest. Rains came down into it and disappeared as if they'd dried up in mid-air. All three would yawn out the day in a state of pure wonderment. She'd hold an old curtain over the three of them and never once heard the abuse the kids called over. Her and her two dogs. I never remember that old red setter moving of her own strength, and yet I never remember her dying.

'But I do remember the black setter running away. Disappearing into the city one evening as the three of them watched the light die. He just bolted, as if to a call. As if the temptation grew suddenly out of his ribs. Grew too much. That black setter just had to know what was out there.

'That woman's wails that night were heard through the Flats. How much she pleaded with God and the city for her dog back ... But he never came back. He'd made some choice not one of us—nor her—could ever know. Only he knew what he was thinking.'

'Why'd you tell that?' Roe said when it was clear that Sweeney was finished. 'Is a few people telling us meaningless stories lately.'

'*All* stories are meaningless,' Sweeney said. 'Only you yourself put meaning on them. The whole lot of life is meaningless. You just try to put your meaning to it day by day.'

Roe fell back in the chair, the cut of pure frustration. 'Fukken herbal,' he said.

'Sometimes they call it the Death Bag,' Sweeney said. 'And sometimes they call it the Dark Chamber. It is an old electrical plant chamber, near a petroleum store, which might be very big. But I never knew which sector until you just told me. Get out your map there.'

And between us we narrowed it down to two locations, and then Sweeney stood.

'Can't tell ye more and won't go with ye, but I do wish ye luck. Let all things be done with charity...'

And he left then, with O' Casey staring at him like he was a ghost.

'What shall I tell your wives?' O' Casey asked, as I fished for money to pay the table.

'I've no one,' Roe replied. 'Frees you of a trip.'

I shrugged. 'Tell her what you know.'

See how astoundingly easy it is to gain entry to Dublin Port and the surrounding docklands. And how astoundingly leaky they are! And yet it is as if they turn a blind eye to the crooked dealings there. As if the place doesn't exist. They say there are underground rivers, well they are drenched in centuries-old petrol, and oil, and every other happy flammable juice. These are fuels that came out of the ground, put there by the energy of the sun. Ancient energy, the essential root, even when that old sun hasn't been seen for decades upon decades upon decades.

So *He* leaves behind the riverbuses, the fountains, the drones, the moths and pylons ... the disembodied rambling of that intercom. With a vendetta on his mind, he leaves behind the calls of the squawkers and hawkers, the streaming lights and the filthy canals. He transcends the city, and who carries the tails of his black skins—only Mister Violence!

Mister Violence has spent years riding the trains and riverbuses. He has ordered coffee from the street vendors and burned his tongue on the first sip. He has seen countless acts committed of course, but all the time he hoped for someone like this. Someone transcendent, with *real* commitment to the cause. Someone whose clothes stink of the purified stuff. Someone whose head swirls with intent.

Tracking the place down is now a matter of good old-fashioned detective work from this ... force of nature, this man of Ireland who is by now Mister Violence's *absolute* favourite. Ruling out buildings one by one, going door to door on each warehouse in that rotting sector. It takes neither more nor less time to find than it should, and turns out to be next door to the old Shell petroleum facility, the largest in the country. The facility is unremarkable of course: square, looming, featureless, derelict, it carries no logo. You wouldn't be sure whether the walls hold up the fire escapes or vice versa. Mister Violence hums with the pleasure of what is about to happen. He purrrrrrrrs.

/Yes, moc/ the vigilante says to himself. /This is it/

/Yes, YES, moc!/ Mister Violence cries. /ABSOLUTELY!/

And does this wonderful individual, this *noble*, know about the old underground tunnels, and slick pathways, and the leakage from flammable pipe networks? Probably not, but no matter! For who breathes fire into these equations and makes something for us to describe?

None other than good old Mister Violence!

Hail! Hail! HAIL!

BIT CALLED

DREAM OF SUNLIGHT

The Bard sang:

/ What days of madness and disorder!
Everybody kills to boot
And nobody obeys an order!/

The kid shivered.

The child moaned in sleep.

/The King of the Ten Peers is coming for you!/ the Bard giggled, rubbing the chubby ringed fingers of his hands together.

The babba whimpered and the kid drew his rattling arms around her warm body.

/Love you/ he said. /Will be okay/

The sky was huge over his head, heaving, rolling, metalblue, crashing over them. If only I could see the other side of it, he thought, and understand. If a great hand would only come down through it and rescue us, he thought.

Δ

They came in from the river along a wide canal, down through basins to the feral yards of the Docklands. Throughout, derelict warehouses and lonely boom crawlers and masts and processing plants and stacks of ancient containers hung in the Shiv'ring. The orange orb of the city light was both within the rain and without.

No boat passed them. He heard only the sound of their motor, and the odd drone above. The dark tops of cyclopic traffic lights stood out of the water, watching them as they passed. He saw reflected the loom and cut of their dark vessel across the water's rippled membrane.

/Am so excited!/ the Bard sang. /Will drink fifteen pints this night! Once the business is done of course!/

He cut the engine and set out the oars and began to pull. /Row me ashore, oh Lord/ he continued, down to a whisper. /Row me ashore/

Corrugate warehouses turned their backs so they couldn't see. Forests of old defunct aerials looked away so they wouldn't witness. Floodlights on solitary masts closed their eyes to all that happened in these bad yards. Voltage boxes sat low in the water. Abandoned train carriages faced the other way. Stacks of concrete sleepers played dead. A whole skyline of relinquished cranes and masts and pylons and dark high-rises were too far away to claim to have seen anything. Fire escapes leaned drunkenly. Then the road rose out of the water like a slipway and they came upon land.

/You been here before?/ Bart asked as he climbed out to pull the vessel aground.

The kid did not answer. He tried to stand, then lurched forward out of the boat and splashed into the shallows with the babba, who stirred and stretched her young muscles. The Shiv'ring engulfed the kid, whose thin body shook, clung to by a drenched cotton shirt and pantalones that hung heavy at the waist. Only his child's body held him some way warm. He looked only at her now.

I could spare you this life, were his loving thoughts.

I could run into the water now and hold you down. Is deep enough. Bart will be too late.

This is what it came to.

He looked to the Bard, who had pulled the babba's bag from the boat and looked at it with confusion.

He wouldn't need more than a foot of water and a few seconds.

He felt that same water cold against his shins, lapping, saying, /Come on in/

It will welcome her, he thought. She'll be comforted. Waves could take away all suffering.

He bent to it. This was what it came to in the end.

But of course he could not.

Not a single cell in his body would obey the thought.

He rose again, the babba cooing.

Bart had tethered the boat to a half-collapsed hoarding, and said now: /Come on! Time to go down/

/No!/ the kid cried. /No!/

He began to back away, into the tide, looking around at the dark warehouses and factories for some other escape.

/Is nowhere to go/ Bart said calmly, as a father might. He held the babba's bag out from him. /Come with me and I'll let you take the child all the way. Will let you hand the child over to the King yourself. That way you've some time with her now. See?/

And that worked. Bart suddenly, tenderly, wiped the kid's cheek with his sleeve, as if to clean it, and the kid followed like a dog where the Earlie Boy led.

/In we go/ Bart said to his quarry.

Δ

They came up through a graveyard of electrical transformers, flooded, rusted, abandoned for a century. A square building of grey concrete slab sat at the top of the avenue. Mike the Hat leaned against a door at the side of the building, watching them come, and when they came he stood aside and pushed open the door for them.

/Welcome back, kiddo/ was all he said.

The dark chamber was beneath the facility; the generators of the old substation had once been stored underground. The air cooled as the two Earlie Boys and their prisoners descended the staircase through a veil of drunken flies, their song, as if inherited from the place, a sort of electrical hum.

At the bottom of the stairs, a series of doorless chambers marked the walls of the dark corridor. There were six on each side and each empty chamber—their generators long ago stripped and stolen—was the size of a closet, lit by a single naked bulb. The bulbs twitched and faltered. The whitewash walls of the chambers bled the rust of old embedded brackets, and petrol and kerosene smell seeped into the mineral smell that crept through the earth and the Docklands. The kid counted them off as he followed the two Earlie Boys up that dark, damp corridor, his curious daughter in his good arm, watching pipes that ran along the walls and the ceiling overhead, pipes that dripped with drenched cobwebs and ragged insulation, fulfilling their own pathways and networks. Wet earth clung to the wall in places. Everything was stagnant, mouldy, alive and sad. Everything sad but the babba, who smiled up at him now for some reason. No, not smiling: she was chewing her gums, and making a great effort in doing so.

/Hush/ he said, as she began to whimper, breaking away from his arms in these last moments, wordlessly pleading as if she herself wanted to go with the King. */Tommib* and shush and calm and hush/

But then he realised that he did not need words either—what good were they? He needed only his eyes and his hands and his smile, which he now gave to his daughter, and she—grumpy, curled bottom lip, soft dark cheeks, wet eyes—did not return his smile, but neither did she need to. He did not smile to see her smile back. She only needed to know that his smile was there, and that it was for her alone, and would always be there for her, even if it was only a distant memory, or the echo of a half-remembered dream. I am alive, the kid was telling himself. Even now I am alive. I am alive in you. And T is alive in you. As long as you are alive, we're with you—in you—and we're all together. See?

The babba whined, pushing and pulling at his wet clothes.

At the end of the corridor, a single bulb held in its dim yellow glare a double doorway. With a fist Bart pressed against it and they entered the Death Bag. They were alive, even now, the kid, T, and their daughter—alive within each other—and they would always have one another.

Δ

The Death Bag was a large empty room with only an old administrator's desk on the wall opposite the doorway. In front of the desk was the Earlie King—sat in a wheelchair, the kid realised—and he was flanked either side by a half-circle of his peers: the Eel, Barrett, Freddi, Francis, Rice, Holloway, Chan and the Spanyard. Mike the Hat and Bart went to join them. Clem skulked too, in a corner of the room, shoulders hunched, hands in pockets, head hung low. And all of them seemed nervous. It dawned on the kid that in their Kandinskees they looked ridiculous. They *were* ridiculous. They were dumb animals that did not understand anything outside of survival, and violence.

At the end of leashes, three cormorants fidgeted, strained, squealed at each other. The Eel handed the leashes to Mike the Hat when he found his place in the line. The birds flapped and snapped at the strain of the tethers, quivering with fear, or rage, as though they knew already the torment to come. The kid watched the babba, who watched the birds with fascination. She did not seem to be aware of the other men in the room. She wanted to get down to the floor now, so the kid sat in the centre of the room with her in his lap, waving at the cormorants.

And now, as the kid sat with his girl, the King stirred into an awareness of his presence.

/And here he comes/ he announced, as if out of a reverie. /I dreamed of you. Did you dream of me?/

The kid did not answer.

/I do not remember what we said .../ The King was calm, but not so strong in voice as before. /But I know that we spoke, and that we understood each other. I was one thing, you were another. We clapped hands on it.../

He moved little. Had advanced, it seemed, in years.

/Do you know what it is for two people to understand each other?/ he continued. / It is everything. Two people is all it takes to end the world ... Did you dream of me?/

The kid wouldn't answer. He looked into the eyes of his girl as she looked back at him, a question in her face. When he presented his two forefingers she wrapped a hand around each one, then shook them as if something would come from them. Everything seemed to wait... The bare bulb for darkness... The Earlie Boys for orders...

But the King only continued to talk:

/I dreamed too of sunlight. Constant sunlight. Every night I went to sleep and my dream was pure blazing sunlight. Joy was on me. The whole world.../

He twisted in his seat, uncomfortably, and then slowly stood and pointed.

/You took my daughter from me. And this beautiful child... Now, where, I ask, is the call of your soul?/

The cormorants watched the babba, as something they didn't understand, or something they could eat, but the kid knew he would protect her. His eyes said to her, his hands said to her: I will protect you as long as I'm here. He pulled his arms around her, there, on the floor, on their knees, and a room of bad men stood over them.

/Your time has come now/ the King said. /But sunlight is coming. Sunlight will—/

And as he stood there, as if by some prayer or spell incanted, the room did fill with sunlight.

From the floor, the kid looked up at the King, whose head had become the sun, the sun bursting out of his head, blazing so brightly.

But it was not sunlight.

Δ

/Fire!/ the kid whispered.

Flower of the world, fire spread before his eyes, and before the eyes of the child. It came from above—he did not know how. It filled the ceiling and fell down in floral blooms.

And the King's head was not sunlight, but was aflame. And his hands rose to this crown of fire, as if to understand it. And his face seemed to drag right, as the kid watched, full of wonder, and his beard rolled up and his black skull began to press out.

And the head of each Earlie Boy was aflame, and they danced around in their bones, their skulls flashing and grinning at him as they screamed.

Did he hear bells amongst their plaints and laments? Did someone, somewhere, make a sound like /TOHUBOHU!/?

Blobs of wet flame feasted on the walls—walls that wept.

He watched as the men in the room became fire monsters, and then ghosts. He watched Crooner Bart's ghost tear the glasses from his face.

A peace presided. He held the babba close. The blaze accordioned above them, fierce clouds of it, its wingspan immense. Heat pressed down. Ah, Clem, he thought, seeing the heap burning in the corner. Look at you.

Shimmering, glimmering, petal and stamen. Fire that bloomed. *Tommib* and fire. Heat filled him. He sat on hot earth. He shivered no more. Smoke brought tears to his eyes. A figure moved freely, in a black cloak, with a white grinning face—Mister Violence himself.

/See the phosphorescent gleam?/ the figure said. /Is the spirit set free! Little wings!/

Moths on fire skittered back and forth. The babba buried herself in him.

One burning cormorant folded its wings and tucked its head away; one burning cormorant attacked the charring body of Mike the Hat; one burning cormorant broke free and took flight out of the room.

The conflagration calmed the kid. He thought of T's room and the sunlight there.

The sunlight chanted. The fire chanted. Fractals of fire, dancing out the patterns.

Waltzing.

Waves of fire flooding the room, rippling, unfurling in him.

Holy fire. Petal and stamen.

Then the feel of a heavy black blanket, pulled over them by some shadowy figure.

Together, kid and babba were shrouded in darkness.

/A spark/ said an unseen voice, the inferno's mayhap, /and annihilation/

Kid and babba were pulled back together then, pulled further into darkness.

Where a boat moved across still water. A key was lost; they looked for it in the dark.

Bit from
WORD OF WARD—

We knew it was the place by the boats hidden all round. *Their* boats. Outside, a calm came over me that I hadn't felt since I could remember.

I remember too as we went through the door and descended the staircase a broken length of strip lighting over our heads, the plastic even stripped from it, and soggy wooden boards under our feet, with who knew how many centuries of grime ground into them. The air was earthy, musty; it filled the throat.

Neither Roe nor I said a word. He stepped into an empty generator chamber on the left while I stepped into one on the right. Our weapons were drawn.

Even then we had no plan. I'd no idea what we'd do when it started. Yet stillness I felt.

Bulb-lit pools of liquid in the floor I saw, as we crept along the corridor, chamber by chamber. The pools had mystic petroleum swirls in them. Under the light of the bulbs, hundreds of exoskeletons of insects I saw, tiny unnamed things, upturned in the dirt, or stuck to the whitewash brickwork, their tiny legs folded in. Under the bare bulb these insect corpses were almost translucent. There were worlds that were beyond me, I thought, whole worlds beneath our world. These are matters of size and volume I'm talking about, not of spirits or gods. And all of them were stagnating in this dank place. Sinking into earth and mineral and human waste. The place, I realised, was drenched in a heavy metallic smell.

I became aware that someone was talking. But as I listened to that voice I heard rainfall. Thunderfall even, so hard and sudden and rumbling it was. I witnessed in Roe's face, in the chamber across from me, a look of pure wonder, and I stepped out to see what he saw.

Fire was the rainfall I heard. Blazing fire. A whole ceiling of it. Consuming the whole place. I'm talking about flames unleashed. Raging. Each flame fixed to its rage. Each flame for the whole, hellbent on its purpose.

More raging than this there wasn't. More pure than this there wasn't. I saw the King's sign sprayed on a door, and both sign and door were being eaten by flame.

We dropped at the same time. Thick black smoke pushed down hard. Roe crawled back the way of the door but I went on for the kid.

Through my tears I saw only smoke. The ghosts of feet pointing different ways. No kid could I find, no babba.

Eventually, I had to give up. Flame and smoke forced me back.

The chambers along the corridor were filled with the light of the blaze, like burning columns, and the bulbs were bright teardrops until they began to explode. Purer than this fire there wasn't.

When I got to where the stairs had been, they were collapsed, the blaze eating them without mercy. But Roe lay on the floor of the threshold above, face covered with the cloth of his underclothes, arms stretched down to pull me up.

I looked back. Smoke and fire was all I saw. No kid. No infant.

Smoke streamed out over Roe. Screaming at me he was.

I turned again, to see was anyone coming.

But there was no one, only fire. The whole place was melting, transforming into something else.

I tell you: no one else was coming out of that place alive.

Roe whacked me on the head. I turned and raised my arms and he began to pull me up, when suddenly some flaming bird went blazing out over us into the sky.

Above, outside, in tides of smoke, we hurried away from the burning substation. But the same fire poured from every building

I could see, as if from trumpets blown, rising up from beneath, raging against the night. The steel frames and corrugated roofs of warehouses, storage tanks and hangars were lit. Processing plants, truck yards, substations: this fire exhausted them all, and dark smoke filled the rain, and the world began to fall away from my eyes, into inferno and smoke.

/The vessel!/ Roe was calling as we coughed and spluttered.

Soon it was as if the sky itself was aflame, the whole world burning. I heard the wings of thousands of birds fleeing out to sea. Thousands upon thousands between fire and rain and the steam they made together.

Δ

Empty sandbags bobbed by the side of the vessel, and we bounced off levees until we found our way out to dark sea. The shrieks of gulls filled the sky. From time to time I looked back to see the rim of blazing skyline above the port. Already, burning cranes drew flame patterns upon that skyline, and later they would bend and buckle from the ankles, down into the pyre. Fire clouds stretched up like antennae, formed hands and reached. Grew wings and moved on the wind from one darkened waterside shape to the next. Fire blooms reflected in black water. Even the breaking waves of the tide burned.

I saw tankers and trawlers explode, one by one, as the prison ships fled to sea. Port streetlights exploded like stars, as the conflagration moved inland. I saw the first smoke rising from amidst the Croke Park Flats, and the first tiny portholes of fire in the easternmost block. Later, I would see canals blazing in ferocious channels, shadows fleeing as roofs collapsed. My city in flames; not even the rain could stop it. And in places the pavement did melt away, drawing people down into burning sewers, into hell. That night, and after, the city felt suddenly like it was in the centre of a vast typhoon, and beyond its swirl was only the blaze. It was all like a dream, in flames.

Alerts came over the device: Vincent Depaul had struck again.

Struck big this time. But then the servers began to burn and the networks crashed. We lost everything, just like that.

Trees of smoke would rise over Dublin for weeks. Old pipe networks and a riddled history of leaked petroleum stores would spread the beast throughout the northeast of the city. It spreads afore my eyes in flowers. I see the sea black, like oil, and steam over it like a great fog, and a dark cityscape aflame. Half the city was evacuated. Fire swells in the TeleVisio screen. Its purity, its heat under the rain. It was clean, and true, and ate up every human-made thing it crossed.

We'll never know for sure what the vigilante intended, but either way some mark was found, and from there the fire spread to everything else. Paper burned; petroleum and oil burned; the country's server stores burned; the streets and canals burned; schools, banks, shopping centres, factories. It spreads afore my eyes even now. The Great Port Fire took the data on citizens: financials, con'fluxes, health records, everything. Took buildings, took lives. The Earlie King and his boys burned, and of course many more. I see it now as the start of everything being lost, except for the few bits of paper and memories I have still. I see this island blazing as it sinks, like a ship going down in the night.

And did the kid and his child burn?

I don't know.

From that dark sea, I watched fire and smoke drift through the grim dome of the city. Flames flowed out from the silhouettes of buildings until they were lost in smoke. We waited for news—anything—but of course all the networks had collapsed. And that, as I've said, was only the beginning.

And in the darkness on the boat, and for years after, I waited for news of the kid. And even today I wonder whether he did transcend that night of fire—a fist of bright yellow himself—or whether father and child vanished in flames. They say there are underground rivers; mayhap they escaped by those. Mayhap they escaped from Bart somewhere along the way, and never even made it to the Dark Chamber. Roe and me, we shook our heads when the time came to summarise what had occurred. And later I went to old Sweeney like a pilgrim—he was the last man to have known that boy.

/The salmon/ Sweeney told me, /made unreal journeys, by instinct alone, river and ocean and all the obstacles. Why couldn't the kid be out there with his beloved girl, on the water, across the water, doing same?/

And it was Sweeney who told me about the kid's sign—the T in the yellow heart—and when for years after I saw it emblazoned in different places—on walls, on train carriages and boat hulls, on trees and even on the bodies of believers—it gave me hope. Mayhap the signs were old, or others made them, having heard the story. But maybe he is out there, a new sort of king, one of love, and maybe he is grown old, like me, and maybe that babba is getting old herself. Maybe that sign is sprayed in Singapore, or Argentina, or Eritrea. In memory of T. Maybe you'll find it, out there, making unreal journeys, by instinct alone.

ACKNOWLEDGMENTS

The author could not have discovered, compiled, honed and presented this manuscript without the care, generosity, wisdom, and belief of the following sages:

JP O' Malley

Ciarán Dowd

Cate Huguelet

Dan Toner

Mike McCormack

Max Porter

Lucy Luck

To each, thank you so much.

To Christine Lo, Stephen Guise, Lindsay Nash and Lamorna Elmer, bravo, and thank you for making this thing *real*.

To Max and Lucy, I am indebted, and eternally grateful.

To Rachel, *guapa*, I owe everything.